The Shattered Man

by

Tom Towslee

The Shattered Man - Copyright © 2022 Tom Towslee
ISBN 978-1-940224-26-8
Cover design by Chris Holmes
Published by Taylor and Seale Publishing, LLC
Daytona Beach Shores, FL 32118

All rights reserved. No part of this book may be reproduced, distributed or transmitted in any form or by any means, electronic or mechanical, including photocopying, recording or by any information storage or retrieval system, without permission, in writing, by the author or publisher. This book was printed in the United States of America. For information, contact Taylor and Seale Publishing, LLC.

Publisher's Note: This is a work of fiction. Names, characters, places, and incidents are a product of the author's imagination or used fictitiously. Locales and public names are sometimes used fictitiously for atmospheric purposes. With the exception of public figures or specific historical references, any resemblance to actual people, living or dead, or to businesses, companies, events, institutions, or locales is completely coincidental. Any historical personages or actual events depicted are completely fictionalized and used only for inspiration. Any opinions expressed are completely those of fictionalized characters and not a reflection of the views of public figures, author, or publisher.

To Len
(1945-2022)

Acknowledgements

Thanks to editor Veronica Helen Hart, to fellow author and friend John Anthony Miller, and, of course, to my great love Dinah Adkins.

The Shattered Man

Chapter 1

The room felt like a sauna and smelled of sweat and take-out Thai food. Guys in cargo shorts and Pink Floyd T-shirts stood behind television cameras at the back of the room. In front of them two dozen indignant reporters shouted angry questions, usually two or three at a time. Half of them worked for legitimate news organizations. The rest had websites, Twitter accounts, or referred to themselves as "Influencers." Sitting cross-legged on the floor were a half-dozen still photographers, their SLRs aimed like sniper rifles at the discouraged, disgruntled, and disheveled figure of District Attorney Miller Devlin.

With his loose tie and wrinkled shirt, he looked every bit like what he was—under siege by heat and humiliation, capable of doing little more than repeat shop-worn talking points over the din of protesters outside the building chanting, "Hey, hey Miller. Find the killer."

The questions came like grenades.

"How many more women do you think will be killed before you catch The Meat Man?"

"Do you think the killer is making fools out of the police?"

"Let's be honest, you don't have the slightest idea who this killer is, do you?"

"The investigation is continuing," Devlin said. "I have every confidence that we are close to an arrest."

The answer landed flat. The quote so familiar no one even bothered to write it down.

In the last two weeks, seven women had been killed in brutal and identical ways. With no suspects and no leads, all Devlin could do was wince at the shouted questions, try to ignore the protestors outside, and point to a white board behind him with a hastily scrawled website address, an 800-number, and a Twitter address.

"Anyone with information that could help us find the killer is encouraged to contact us," Devlin said. It was another cringe-worthy answer.

"These guys couldn't find shit in a bird cage," one camera operator muttered to another.

Dr. Alex Windsor squeezed further into the shadows of a corner near a door with an exit sign over it. The scene of reporters sensing blood and the DA looking like cornered prey was hard to look at. Windsor had done what he could to help Devlin, which took some doing. The DA was an over-confident, inexperienced lawyer six years out of a second-rate law school who was elected the county's chief prosecutor because no one else worthy of the job wanted it. Windsor only agreed to help him out of a sense of civic duty and a career-long fascination with serial killers. Together, they came up with a plan that left Windsor feeling uneasy with the realization that lawyers don't work well with others, except other lawyers.

After the third murder and confident an arrest was imminent, Devlin naively and eagerly assumed the role of the investigation's point man. Eventually, everybody else—chief of police, county sheriff, state police superintendent, and the mayor—took one step backward. Even the state and U.S. flags seemed to have retreated to the corner of the room to cower out of camera view. Now, he was alone to issue more empty vows to find the killer dubbed "The Meat Man."

Each victim—and those yet to come—were etched on Devlin's once-youthful face as if by the same butcher knife used on the victims. His promising career battered and bloodied. No future run for attorney general, governor or senator. All hopes dashed thanks to a brutal and elusive killer who had drawn the temporary attention of the entire nation.

And the killer wasn't done. Windsor knew it. So did Devlin. So did the reporters.

The murders had put the entire City of Portland on edge. Gun sales soared. Women's groups marching in the streets demanding justice for the dead and protection for the living. More cable news reporters and online bloggers arrived each day.

The City of Roses had become the City of Corpses.

"Is it true that the killer leaves pages of the Bible behind?" a female reporter asked. "One page for each murder?"

The DA looked stunned for a second. Windsor knew it was not a question he wanted asked and certainly not one he wanted to answer. Certain facts had to be held back to weed out the killer wannabes that haunted all murder investigations. With enough homeless in the city, it was only a matter of time before one of them copped to a murder or two in exchange for three hots and a cot in the county jail. After that it was back on the street, living in a tent, and peeing on the side of buildings.

When Devlin answered "I can't comment on that" it only generated more questions. "No comment" was an answer that died an ugly death years before by those trying to hide something. It was the ultimate sin committed by people who didn't know better. No way could Devlin get away with resurrecting it.

Despite the no comment, Devlin knew the answer. So did Windsor. The killer had carefully cut out pages from the Bible, neatly folding each of them in half and slipping them into a zip-lock bag before placing them inside the bodies of his victims. The passages from the *New American Standard Bible* were carefully underlined in ink.

Victim 1, Pages 1 and 2: "In the beginning …"

Victim 2, Pages 3 and 4: "The Lord saw that the wickedness of man was great on the earth."

Victim 3, Pages 5 and 6: "… the earth was filled with violence."

Victim 4, Pages 7 and 8: "Let us make a name for ourselves."

Victim 5, Pages 9 and 10: "I will make your descendants as the dust of the earth."

Victim 6, Pages 11 and 12: "And the fear of you and the terror of you shall be on every beast on the earth."

Victim 7, Page 13 and 14: "Come, let us make bricks and burn them thoroughly."

The Bible had something for everybody—even deranged killers.

Despite some of the citations being taken out of context, it all added up to a religious fanatic hell-bent on ridding the world of randomly selected women living in upscale neighborhoods.

To Windsor, the whole Bible thing didn't make sense, but what sense can anyone find in seven motiveless murders with probably more to come? All it did was raise questions about how many pages are in the Bible.

Chapter 2

It was after the fifth murder that Devlin asked for Windsor's help. He wanted Windsor, a forensic psychologist, to get inside the killer's head, provide some explanation for what he was doing, and why. In other words, help find him.

On orders from Devlin, the task force running the investigation gave Windsor unfettered access to the files on all five murders. He spent hours combing through thousands of pages of evidence, endured endless hours of gruesome crime-scene recordings, and sifted through reams of autopsy reports.

Focusing on the religious angle, he talked to theologians—Catholic, Episcopal, Protestant, Jewish, and Muslim. They offered little more than prayers for the victims and their families. At least the Episcopal priest was willing to provide a list of biblical killers starting with Abel and ending with Zechariah of Israel. Windsor researched each one hoping to gain some insights into the killer. What he learned is that some had been monsters, but nothing compared to The Meat Man. His methods defied even biblical descriptions.

In the meantime, two more women were murdered.

Windsor visited the crime scenes, watched the technicians, and talked to the investigators. With what he'd learned from them and what he already knew, a profile of the killer slowly took shape.

That's when the uneasiness set in.

The idea of writing an opinion piece had been the DA's idea. It came with one condition: Describe the killer as a sexually repressed woman hater who had been abused as a child by one or both parents and was unable to perform sexually.

"That's what I believe," Devlin had said. "I think that you'll agree once you've seen everything. Just don't mention him being a religious fanatic. Some things need to be held back."

Windsor had made no promises. Instead, making it clear that he would let the evidence paint a picture of the killer and, perhaps, his motive. If it led him somewhere other than what Devlin believed, then that's what he would write.

"This is non-negotiable," Windsor said.

The DA pissed and moaned for a while, but eventually went along with it. With bodies piling up, he had little choice.

In the end, he wasn't disappointed. Based on what Windsor learned from the files and talking to profilers from the state police and FBI, and to clerics, it was all true.

The DA was right. The killer was all those things and probably more. Much more.

Even though Windsor was confident in what he'd found, there was something unsettling, even smarmy, about putting it out there for an overwrought and hungry media to feed on. He paused at the thought of lurking bloggers, conspiracy theorists, overly caffeinated talk show hosts, and internet trolls reading between the lines and parsing sentences. There would be TV stations and cable news networks wanting an interview. He could deal with it. The question was did he want to?

In the end and despite deep reservations, he agreed to go along with the idea, rationalizing that if it helped find a killer, it seemed worth what little personal risk there was to him or his reputation. The result was a guest opinion piece published the previous day in the city's local daily newspaper and online describing what Windsor believed motivated the killer.

"There was an opinion piece published yesterday that said the killer is an impotent, sexually frustrated momma's boy," another reporter asked. "Do you agree with that assessment?"

"It will do for the time being," Devlin said, then, with a curt "thank you," got up and left.

To avoid the mob of reporters, Windsor was first out the double doors at the back of the room, determined to end his involvement in The Meat Man Murders. The rest was up to the DA and the police. He was fifty feet down the hall and on the verge of escaping when a television reporter holding a microphone ran up behind him. He'd seen her before. She had interviewed him a few years earlier for a story on teen suicide. A man in a sweat-stained T-shirt and a camera perched on his shoulder like an overgrown parrot huffed and puffed ten feet behind her.

"Tina Anthony from Channel 5, Dr. Windsor," she said. "We met a couple of years ago." She held up her hand to signal the cameraman to not start rolling yet and lowered the microphone. "I'd like to ask you some questions about your opinion piece."

She was tall, slender and a little older than the usual perky female reporters fresh out of journalism school and eager to please. Annoying would come with more experience.

"I'm sorry. I really don't have anything to add. The piece pretty much speaks for itself. Again, I'm sorry."

"It's not about what you wrote, but why you wrote it. Did the police ask you to do it to flush out the killer? You know, make him angry by calling him an impotent momma's boy?"

"I didn't use those words."

"They meant the same thing," she said, looking directly at him.

He knew where this was going. Make the best of it.

"Come with me." He glanced at the cameraman. "And leave him behind. This is going to be all off the record. You good with that? If not, then we're done here."

She took a few seconds to decide. "Okay," she said, nodding toward the disappointed cameraman.

Windsor led her across the hall into an empty room reserved for jury pools. It was filled with butt-worn vinyl chairs. Black-and-white photos of long-forgotten judges lined the dingy walls. She sat in one of the chairs, arms crossed, eyes defiant. He stood in the center aisle looking determined to make the interview as short as possible.

"What makes The Meat Man different from other serial killers?" she asked.

"Most serial killers sexually assault their victims before killing them. Sometimes after. This killer is different. I believe he doesn't assault his victims because he can't—because of some traumatic experience from his childhood. Something that possibly involved a parent, a relative, a priest, a scout master. Because he can't … perform, he channels his rage into other … things."

"You mean hanging women by their feet like a side of beef and eviscerating them as a substitute for rape?"

"Put bluntly, yes. He also doesn't take trophies. No locks of hair. No fingers. No toes. If he takes pictures, he hasn't posted them on any website we can find. I believe he's a painfully shy introvert who does everything to feed his desire to kill except seek recognition. He hates notoriety. I doubt he reads the papers or watches television news. He just does what he does and will keep on doing it until he's caught."

"Why no progress in finding him?"

"Each victim was killed in the same way. The only difference is where he hangs the bodies. Sometimes from a tree in the yard. Other times from rafters in the garage or a covered patio. What he does to those bodies never changes. That tells me he's compulsive and meticulous, probably autistic. Maybe Asperger's."

"Asperger's?"

"Aggressive behavior, repetition, depressive mood, lack of social awareness. The list goes on."

"DNA?"

"No sexual assault means no semen."

"Fingerprints?"

"Gloves."

"And the whole Bible thing?"

Windsor sighed. "That's more complicated. Sex being the original sin might further explain why he doesn't assault his victims. I'm just not sure. What I do know is there's nothing holy about men who butcher women, although I'm not sure where some so-called Christians stand on that."

"And your role in all of this?" Anthony asked. "Why the opinion piece?"

"There are only three ways to catch a killer. First, he makes a mistake. Second, the police get lucky and stumble on a clue of some kind. Third, you get into the killer's mind. The first two weren't working, so we tried the third."

"The killer's mind?"

"According to the Spanish writer Javier Cercas, it's more important to understand the butcher than the victim."

"Do you think The Meat Man will kill again?"

"I'm sure of it."

"Will you say that on camera?"

"Not a chance."

"Can I contact you again? You know, depending on what happens?"

Windsor thought for a few seconds, then wrote down a phone number of the back of his business card.

"You can call me, but don't waste my time."

Chapter 3

When Windsor left Tina Anthony behind and walked out of the Justice Center it was a little after ten o'clock. After the sticky heat of the news conference, the cool night offered welcome, if minor, relief. Despite the hour, the temperature was stuck in the sweaty doldrums of the mid-eighties. The week of hot weather had local meteorologists as excited as the crime reporters. For the weather folks, hundred-degree days in Oregon were the equivalent of a Category 4 hurricane in the Gulf. Something to be fawned over and compared to records from past years no one could remember.

Even though Windsor didn't mind the heat, he still felt odd. Maybe because he hadn't eaten since lunch, or the ten cups of coffee needed to keep moving. Maybe it was the strain of trying to get inside the mind of a killer, of trying to find something that would help the police end the murders. Whatever it was, having watched Miller Devlin squirm in front of the cameras wasn't helping.

The string of murders seemed to be fate's idea of piling on. With a summer of protests, Portland's government buildings had been covered with graffiti and surrounded by temporary barricades. Plywood coverings on store windows in the heart of downtown were there to hide what damage had already been done or hopefully prevent more. Adding to the chaos of demonstrations and counter demonstrations were myriad homeless camps dotting the city like open sores. With little opposition, the city had taken on the tarnished veneer of a dystopian wonderland of abandoned grocery carts, piles of bicycle parts, colorful nylon tents, and mountains of trash left to rot by a constipated and overwhelmed local government. COVID, nightly shootings, and The Meat Man had added to the chaos and the body count.

Seemingly overnight, Portland had gone from delightfully weird to dangerously incomprehensible.

Windsor had thought about moving, maybe to some cozy, tree-lined suburb where the worst thing that ever happened was a broken corkscrew. Instead, he decided to stick it out, hoping that someday things would get better. As he drove by more homeless camps, he was beginning to question his commitment.

Windsor had left Portland when he was fifteen years old. He returned thirteen years later with a Ph.D. in forensic psychology. After two years on the staff of a local HMO, he went out on his own, renting office space in Portland's trendy Pearl District and setting up his own practice. That was seven years ago. His doctoral thesis had been on the relationship between wealth and rebellion. Fortunately, Portland had plenty of both. As a result, most of his clients were well-to-do parents tired of bailing their rebellious children out of jail or seeing them expelled from one expensive private school only to try getting them into another. Desperate defense lawyers looking to get their clients certified as insane by anyone who called themselves "doctor" made up the rest. Most of the time, he'd been no help.

With the lucrative private practice augmented by a part-time position teaching at a local private college, he was content to stay above the fray. That suited him fine. His life had found a comfortable rhythm. What few ghosts haunted him were banished. He slept better. A regimen of exercise had brought his creeping waistline under control. He'd even added some muscle to what had been an atrophying frame that was stocky and a shade under six feet. His wire-rimmed glasses sat atop an aquiline nose and covered pale green eyes that had regained their glimmer. All of it added up to a look of a successful psychologist, minus the Harris Tweed and meerschaum pipe.

He'd even found time for the novel he always wanted to write. His first attempt was an angst-ridden tale of baby boomers coming to grips with the ambiguities of a new millennium. Its modest success earned him a two-book contract with a small advance from an East Coast publisher. The book had the added advantage of making him the go-to contact for reporters trying to understand what was behind Portland's persistent riots and what motivated the angry young men behind them. He didn't have much to offer other than citing a cartoon of a crowd shouting "What do we want? Nothing. When do we want it? Now."

That blossomed into appearances on local TV's morning happy talk shows, panel discussions at the City Club, and visits to editorial boards. By the time The Meat Man committed his sixth murder, Windsor had shelved the second novel in favor of trying his hand at true crime. What better place to start than with a homicidal maniac loose in the latte-and-tear-gas-fueled world of Portland, Oregon. The DA's plea for help made him even more sure.

Now, a two-day growth of dark stubble made his face itch. The Oxford shirt felt sticky. The khaki pants long ago surrendered their crease. Shoes made his feet feel like steamed sausages. All he wanted was a shower and a cold drink.

Windsor thought about stopping at The Ridge, his favorite dive bar, for a beer, but decided instead to go straight home. It was hot. He was tired. There was plenty of cold beer at home.

Windsor knew his wife had plans for them to get up early the next day to first hit a Starbucks, then, after that, wander around the farmers' market on the South Park Blocks downtown. Lunch would be street tacos at her favorite food cart near Reed College.

It all sounded good. His job was done. He'd put in the work. Gave the reasons behind the murders his best shot. Time to put it behind him, get back to his private practice of counseling angst-ridden teenagers and their over-indulgent parents.

There would be more killings, but not because he stayed on the sidelines.

He drove south on SW Broadway, then east toward the river and south again on SW Macadam past John's Landing for another three miles before turning off onto a narrow street that snaked into the hills above the Willamette River. Five minutes later, he pulled into the driveway and turned off the car's headlights, so his wife wouldn't know he was home yet.

He wanted to sit in the stillness for a few minutes, rid his mind of what had occupied it almost constantly for most of the last week. He also wanted to shield Jennifer as much as possible from the fear that had become a daily part of life in the city. He didn't want to walk into the house stained with the emotional blood of seven women. Only that was impossible. For the time being, there was no way to escape the death, destruction, and protests. It filled the evening news, covered the front page of the paper, and dominated social media. All he could do was try.

On the passenger seat was that day's edition of the city's only daily newspaper. The tasteless headline over the story about the seventh victim said it all: "The Meat Man Cometh ... Again." There were pictures and profiles of each of the victims, interviews with friends and family members, and more excuses from the police and the district attorney. A map used red dots to show the location of each murder. Windsor hadn't bothered to watch the television coverage but knew from experience that it was more of the same, only more frenzied. Protecting his wife from all of it was impossible.

He glanced at the house. The dim lights inside made it look like what he craved the most—a warm and friendly refuge from the sweaty darkness that defined his days. But not his wife, Jennifer. Her Spanish blood made her love the heat, giving her an erotic mix of impishness and passion. On the night he asked her to marry him, she put an arm around him, pressed her lips to his ear, and began singing the Marty Robbins song *El Paso*.

"He fell in love with a Mexican girl," she had whispered, then giggled.

It was exciting just thinking about the mood she'd be in tonight. She was so much younger, not yet thirty. Fierce and independent, she could've had any man, but she made her choice and never looked back. He could barely remember what life was like before her. He just knew that he'd never been happier.

He tossed the paper back on the seat, hit the garage door opener, and waited as the paneled door rose slowly in front of him.

It took days before he remembered everything that happened after that, but only seconds to realize why.

Chapter 4

The room felt and smelled odd. The ceiling was white, but the texture different. More like acoustic tile with little squares covered with what looked like popcorn. The bright-white sheets were heavily starched and smelling of bleach. Someone had changed the carpet. The Berber was gone, replaced with something with a plush pile and covered in empty miniature liquor bottles. Why was there a television? There had never been a television in their bedroom. And why was he still dressed?

It started coming back to him. Slowly at first, then all too fast—a sudden rush of images that made him open and close his eyes, hoping it was all a nightmare and all he needed to do was wake up. After that, he would figure out where he was and why.

He vaguely remembered checking into the boutique hotel downtown, rummaging through the mini bar, ripping off the tops of the little bottles and downing the contents one after another. Two vodkas. Three gins. One rum. After that he lost count. What he didn't lose were his last images of his wife.

He stumbled into the bathroom to wash his face and stare into the mirror. He recognized some of what looked back at him. The rest resembled a Picasso painting. The images became clearer. Standing in the driveway surrounded by police. Talking to a detective. Getting awkward glances instead of condolences. They all knew the truth: His opinion piece had summoned a killer into his own house.

There were not enough mini bars in the world to wipe that away.

Grabbing the edge of the sink, he fell to his knees, sobbing. He had helped others deal with grief. No way could he help himself. Only one reality remained—she was gone, and it was all his fault.

The only thing left in the mini bar was an over-priced bottle of white wine. He twisted off the cap, undressed, and took it to the shower. He drank half of it then poured the rest down the drain. Eventually, he called the front desk to ask that someone bring his car around. When the clerk said he didn't have a car, more of the previous night came roaring back into his head: police cars, cops in uniform, an ambulance, flashing lights, people in white hazmat suits. Him standing dumbly in his driveway answering questions while search teams combed through his house and front yard. After that it was riding away in the passenger seat of a patrol car, leaving behind a house encased in yellow police tape.

He asked the desk clerk to have an Uber pick him up. Ten minutes later he was waiting outside staring at the passing cars. On the way home he used his cellphone to check for messages. It was all the usual stuff. No condolences. That would change once the police released Jennifer's name. He wanted to wake up, shake the nightmare out his head, and reach out to pull her close. Only waking up wasn't going to happen.

When he got home, the yellow crime scene tape still circled the house. At least the police and technicians were gone, replaced by four of Jennifer's law school friends.

They stood in the driveway looking like they wanted to help, but uncertain what to do. Windsor remembered one of the women from a dinner party a few weeks earlier, but not her name.

She walked down the driveway to meet him. "This is all so terrible," she said. "Is there anything we can do?"

"I don't know. I really haven't had time to …"

"We've been talking. Why don't you let us take care of everything? You know, shutting down her practice … other arrangements."

"Thank you. Anything you can do would be great."

"By arrangements I meant the funeral," she said.

"Oh. Yeah. That would be great. Thank you."

She answered with a weak smile, more tears, and a nod.

He spent the next three days out of sight, mostly sitting in their bedroom feeling less like a psychologist and more like he needed one. He went through the seven stages of grief several times, but always stumbled on the last one: acceptance. He kept coming back to the same place. It was his fault. There was no way to rationalize it. No one else to blame. No way to accept it, no matter how many times he tried.

On the third night, he drove downtown to visit the bars and restaurants where he and Jennifer would go on date nights. At The Ringside, he got through two martinis, but passed on the onion rings. From there he visited other bars or stood outside restaurants watching people laughing and eating. He didn't remember driving home. Only waking up sitting in the car in the driveway, the window down, the motor running. All he could see out the windshield was the garage door. No way he was opening that again.

Then he remembered what day it was.

Chapter 5

At ten in the morning, the sun hung in the east, eager to rise and drive the temperature into the nineties. A Catholic priest Windsor didn't know uttered a liturgy Windsor didn't hear. All he could do was stare at Jennifer's coffin and blame himself once again for why she was there. It made him want to crawl into the hole with her silver casket and wait for everyone to just go away while the dirt piled up around him.

Hung over at this wife's funeral. Can't get much lower than that.

Jennifer's family huddled together on the other side of the grave. Her mother, father, and two younger sisters had taken anguish to a level even Windsor couldn't comprehend. Her father, Enrico DeGarza, wailed as he watched his daughter's casket being lowered into the ground. Jennifer's mother made useless efforts to console him while the two girls clung to their mother's dress looking more frightened by their father's muffled sobs than by watching their big sister disappear into a dark hole. Her father called Jennifer his "estrella," his star. His dream was that she would be the family's salvation. He'd even given her an anglicized first name so her Hispanic heritage wouldn't hold her back. Now, a lifetime of hopes and dreams had vanished.

Windsor stared at the old man, hoping that feeling sorry for a father who buries a child would make him feel less sorry for himself. It worked for about five seconds.

Enrico DeGarza had sorrow and loss to cope with, but at least he wasn't responsible for what happened.

The other faces standing around the grave were a mixture of those he recognized and those he didn't. He spotted Patrick Callahan, the rotund, rumpled CPA with offices in the same building as his. Best he could tell, Callahan had two clients: a trust-fund baby living in Mexico and a third-round draft choice of the Portland Trail Blazers. Standing next to him was Windsor's part time secretary. Next to her were a handful of Jennifer's friends from law school. Red-eyed and stone-faced, they could only stare dumbly at the ground. The woman who made the funeral arrangements looked up long enough to give him a sorrowful smile. He nodded as a weak way of saying thanks. In the back were a handful of middle-aged men with baseball caps and scruffy beards. At first, he thought that they were some guys who drifted over from some near-by homeless camp, then he realized they were probably some of Jennifer's clients—the ones who didn't get jail time. In front of them all was a line of familiar faces that included some friends of his parents, a couple of fellow psychologists, and one of the accountants from the San Francisco firm that handled Windsor's finances.

He looked around for Cassie Terrace, a newly minted homicide detective and an old girlfriend who Windsor stayed in touch with. He didn't see her. That didn't make sense. It wasn't like her.

The only representative from the law firm founded by his late father was Chandler Stockdale. Despite not having seen him in years, Windsor remembered Stockdale as an immaculately dressed and groomed litigator who charmed juries and, if the stories were true, married women with the same high rate of success. With the founding members of the firm either retired or close to it, Stockdale has assumed the role of managing partner. For some reason, he looked uncomfortable, straightening his tie, and repeatedly checking his watch. As the priest droned on, Stockdale nervously shifted his weight from one tasseled loafer to the other.

Next to him stood the older, stooped figure of Dorothy Evelyn Hawkins, a circuit court judge and his late mother's closest friend. Windsor had known her his entire life. Lately, they had neither seen nor talked. Hawkins, now in her early seventies, reached under her veil to dab her eyes with a lace handkerchief. Her judicial reputation was mixed. Prosecutors loved her. Defense attorneys bombarded her court with change of venue motions. In the final analysis, only her size and shape would cause anyone to confuse her with Ruth Bader Ginsburg.

Stockdale looked at his watch, then leaned over to whisper in Hawkins' ear. She nodded, glanced at Windsor, then looked away.

Standing at the edge of the crowd looking nervous and out of place were Bud and Moon Schwartz, two refugees from efforts to stop wars and save whales. They owned The Ridge, the tavern where Windsor spent most of his time before marrying Jennifer and some after. Bud wore khakis with a plaid shirt and a Jerry Garcia tie. The rotund Moon was dressed in sandals and a muted muumuu.

Windsor had few friends, but Bud and Moon were two of them.

Windsor wondered if somewhere in the crowd—unnoticed and easily forgettable—was the killer. Would he be brazen enough to stand innocently among the other mourners? Windsor doubted it, but he scanned the crowd one more time. Of the few faces he didn't recognize, anyone of them could be the killer. Or none of them. At that point he really didn't care. All he wanted was out of there. But where?

A possible answer stood alone in the shade of a flowering Japanese plum tree a few yards away from the other mourners. All the man seemed capable of doing was hanging his head and endlessly fingering the brim of his cowboy hat. Sam Westlake was barrel-chested and straight-backed with a shock of steel-gray hair. The old man's eyes were circles of pink. The thumbs up he'd given Windsor during the service at the mortuary was a well-intentioned but weak sign of encouragement.

The three of them had met four years earlier when Jennifer, looking for a romantic getaway to celebrate their anniversary, rented a cabin on Westlake's ranch in Central Oregon. They'd returned four or five times since, and Westlake would have dinner at their house on his infrequent trips to Portland. It was an unlikely friendship, but one in which Windsor, who had no family of his own, found a certain serenity.

The first call Windsor made after finding Jennifer's body was to 911. The second was to Westlake. He was there in less than the three hours it normally takes to drive from Central Oregon. He stayed for three days helping Jennifer's friends with funeral arrangements and dealing with the details that Windsor couldn't face. He also invited Windsor to live at the ranch for a few months while he got his life back together.

"It's God's country, son," Sam had said. "It's just what you need."

It was a tempting offer. Sam's ranch with its trout stream and wide meadow would be a mountain sanctuary away from Portland, The Meat Man, cops, prosecutors, and reporters. In Sam Westlake's world, BLM stood for Bureau of Land Management. The idea of getting away from the constant threat of pointless riots and pointless hand wringing about the homeless only made the offer all that more welcome. Still, Windsor had been non-committal. The time since Jennifer's death had been a blur. He could barely cope with the present. Why bother with the future?

As Jennifer's casket disappeared below the edge of the grave, it was replaced by Enrico DeGarza's muffled wails. Watching the grief-stricken old man, Windsor thought again about Sam's offer. He glanced over at the old man standing by himself under the tree looking the way Windsor felt. In an instant, he made up his mind. Maybe Sam had the right idea. He would spend a few weeks licking his wounds in God's country, as Sam called it. After that he'd decide what to do ... or not.

When the service ended, Windsor planned to get to the funeral home limousine as fast as possible. It didn't happen. Reporters who'd kept a respectful distance during the ceremony, rushed him as soon as it was over with questions even they seemed embarrassed to ask. A reporter Windsor didn't recognize worked up the nerve to ask if he felt responsible for his wife's death. Rather than say yes, Windsor muttered his apologies, put his head down, and walked quickly to the line of waiting cars. A few more yards and he would be out of there. It became another plan that didn't work out.

"You killed my daughter! You killed my beautiful Jennifer!" Enrico DeGarza had come up behind him, his family in tow. Tears streamed down the old man's cheeks, his face twisted by hate and grief. Before his wife and daughters could pull him away, Enrico beat on Windsor's chest with callused hands. Within seconds, they were surrounded by television cameras eager to capture the moment. His wife pulled him back at the same time Windsor retreated a few steps.

"She should've stayed with her own people," the old man said between sobs, "but you made her go with you and now she's dead. You did this! What you wrote killed her!" He spat in Windsor's face.

Windsor stood frozen in place, feeling embarrassed for himself and for the old man's all-to-public display of grief. Unsure what to do or say, he could only watch as DeGarza's anguished screams disintegrated into wracking sobs until he dropped to his knees. He cried and yelled in Spanish. Windsor didn't understand most of it, but it didn't matter. The old man's claims were just another reminder of what had happened and why.

Windsor was not trained for this. All those years of studying, learning, writing papers, and taking tests were useless. As a forensic psychologist he was supposed to understand people's emotions and motives, to find some way to help those who committed crimes and those traumatized by them. While a student, he had angered his professors by dismissing the Rorschach inkblot test and disorders such as repressed memory and multiple personalities as old-school fads. Despite his betrayal of orthodoxy, he graduated Summa Cum Laude. He left college well versed in the meaning of psychopathy. He just never thought he would come face to face with it in such a personal way. Physician, heal thyself. How does that work?

With the cameras focused on the sobbing Enrico DeGarza, Windsor backed out of the crowd and made his way across the parking lot to his limo. Two men in dark suits and cowboy boots were waiting for him.

"Dr. Windsor? I'm Detective Arnett, Oregon State Police. We have some information about your wife's death. I apologize. I know this is a bad time, but it is important." He looked past Windsor's shoulder as the DeGarza family walked toward the other limo, Jennifer's mother doing her best to console her inconsolable husband. "I saw what happened. I'm sorry. What he said. He's wrong."

Most of the detectives Windsor knew were overweight, out of shape and looked as likely to commit a crime as solve one. Arnett was different. He was all hair gel and Brooks Brothers: middle-aged, muscular with a buzz cut, a thick black mustache and a no-nonsense, military demeanor. Even in the mid-morning heat he wasn't sweating and didn't seem the slightest bit uncomfortable.

"Thanks for that," Windsor said, pointing at the dark blue limousine. "Ride with me. There's plenty of room."

Windsor had ridden alone to the cemetery. The DeGarza family wanted nothing to do with him, demanding that they ride in a separate funeral home limo and that it be the first car behind the hearse carrying Jennifer's body. Windsor didn't argue. He just paid the bill and never said a word about it to Enrico.

After nodding to his partner, Arnett got in the limo for the twenty-minute ride back to the funeral home.

"Is there something I can do for you, detective?" Windsor asked as if just realizing Arnett was sitting next to him.

"No, Dr. Windsor. I came to tell you that two days ago your wife's killer turned himself in. He's confessed everything. All eight murders. We've been interrogating him ever since. We searched his parents' house and found the murder weapon—a butcher knife. It all checks out. He's our man. Everything has been arranged. He'll plead guilty later today and be immediately sentenced to life in prison. That's the deal the DA made with his lawyer. It's over, sir. We thought you should know."

The blunt delivery took Windsor's breath away. Hatred and revenge were what he expected to feel when Jennifer's killer was caught. Now, he just couldn't do it. Finding her killer wasn't going to change anything. All he could do was look out the car window as they drove past her grave and out of the cemetery.

"You said he turned himself in," Windsor said.

"Yes, sir. He walked into the Justice Center with his father."

"You're sure?"

"In cases like this we always get oddballs who come in confessing to crimes they didn't commit. That's why we hold back certain information from the press and the public, information that only the killer would know. He's had all the answers."

In another time and place Windsor would've probed, questioned, and demanded answers. Are you sure? Why did he do it? Could it be a copycat? Not anymore. It was over. That's all he wanted or needed to know. At least Arnett had the courtesy to tell him face to face.

"Thank you, sergeant, I appreciate you telling me in person," Windsor said, then pointed toward the satellite vans and cars with TV and radio station logos still in the parking lot behind them. "This must not be public knowledge yet or those reporters wouldn't still be here."

"We've managed to keep it quiet for two days. It won't last much longer. It's a miracle we kept the lid on this long. In one hour, the DA is going to announce that he'll be having a news conference this afternoon. He'll lay it all out for them then. He … we … wanted to wait until after the funeral. Give you a chance to be there if you'd like."

Windsor never heard the invitation. "Does he have a name? The killer."

"Yes, sir," Arnett said, pulling a small notebook out his jacket pocket. "William Charles Broadnax. His father calls him Billy."

"Tell me more."

Chapter 6

The cabin sat nestled in a vast stand of towering ponderosa pines overlooking a large meadow burned straw-colored by a relentless summer heat. The massive, red-barked trees provided the only shade from an August sun that hung in a cloudless, cobalt-blue sky. Large, orange stone flies buzzed around the trees like miniature helicopters. Higher up, two crows angrily dive-bombed a Red Tail hawk that had encroached on their unmarked territory. Chipmunks on secret missions darted back and forth across the dirt track in front of the cabin.

Firewood filled most of the cabin's wrap-around porch. Broken down tables and chairs, a rusty pair of cross-country skis, and a couple of snow shovels filled what little space was left. A black, dust-covered BMW sat lost and lonely on a patch of gravel at the end of the porch. Beyond that was more firewood stacked neatly between two trees and partially covered with a rotting blue tarp.

The man standing on the cabin steps was young and gangly with jet-black hair parted down the middle and tucked behind each ear. His chalky face was in the post-acne years. The usual dress code for guys like him involved frayed sport coats, plaid shirts, wrinkled pants, and Converse sneakers. Instead, in an apparent nod to his surroundings, he wore a save-the-whales T-shirt, baggy OD green cargo shorts, wool socks, hiking boots, and a baseball cap turned backward on his head.

The disguise wasn't working. From halfway across the meadow Alex Windsor knew who he was and why he was there. He wanted none of it. As soon as he got to the cabin, he would let his visitor know it.

Windsor reeled in the fly he'd been fishing with and hooked it to his fly rod. He waded out of the water and up to the well-worn path along the bank. Slowly, he walked along the river, then across the meadow to the cabin. The heat of the day quickly replaced the cool relief of the icy water. The ten-minute walk from the river to the cabin gave him time to think about the fastest way to get rid of his visitor. There were several options, starting with shooting him and ending with ignoring him until he went away. He decided on something in between.

"You must be Alex Windsor. I'm Arnie Stetson from the …"

Windsor pushed by him and up the stairs to the porch. "I know where you're from and why you're here. So, save it. Leave. Now."

Windsor carefully hung the fly rod between two hooks over the cabin's front windows. He shrugged off his vest and hung it on a hook next to the rod. He sat on a rickety wooden bench to pull off his boots and chest waders. Stripped down to T-shirt and sweatpants, he hung the waders on a hook next to the heavy wooden door and disappeared inside.

Stetson stayed on the porch, looking like he was unsure what to do. "It took me three days to find you then a three-hour drive from Portland—all to deliver a message. Am I ever going to get the chance?"

If Windsor heard him, he didn't act like it. He returned to the cabin door a few minutes later wearing jeans and a faded T-shirt from Carlos and Charlies. He had a beer in one hand and several more in the refrigerator that he had no intention of sharing.

"Why are you still here?" he said.

"I need to talk to you," Stetson said, eyeing the beer.

"You're wasting your time. Go back and tell your editors that I am not interested in talking about it. I know it's been a year. I know how much you all love doing anniversary stories. Count me out. Again, count me out! Go back and tell them I'm crazy as a shithouse rat. Tell them I'm up in the mountains eating roots and grubs and howling at the moon. Tell them anything you want. Just leave."

Windsor drank the last of the beer then went back inside for another.

"They didn't send me," Stetson said, still standing on the porch, looking unsure if he should go inside. "I'm here on my own,"

"That makes it even easier," Windsor said over his shoulder. "You can drive back, go to work Monday, and no one will ever know that you wasted a perfectly nice summer day driving to Central Oregon and back for no reason."

Windsor watched as Stetson took one brave step inside the door to lean against the jamb. Past Stetson's left shoulder was the scene Windsor had been looking at every day for nearly a year. At least on those days when whiskey, drugs, and the occasional snowstorm didn't turn everything into a hazy, impenetrable fog.

Even now, with the alders leafed out and shimmering in the breeze, he could still see Sam Westlake's low-slung ranch house on the other side of the meadow, sitting on the small rise a couple of hundred yards away. It was hard not to marvel at how it seemed to melt into the background. Its log siding matching the Ponderosas looming in the background. The slate roof miraculously fading into the green canopy. Plate glass windows and massive deck offering an unobstructed view of the meadow, the river, and the snow-capped peaks in the distance.

"You don't understand," Stetson said. "I'm not here about a story. I need to tell you something."

"No," Windsor snapped, "*you* don't understand! I have no intention of helping you or any other newspaper, TV station or radio station rehash those murders. If you took the time to find me then I don't have to tell you why. There were seven other victims. Go bother their families. I tried to catch a killer. It didn't work out the way I wanted. End of story. Now, I just want to be left alone."

The cabin where Windsor had spent the last year was one room divided in half by a low wall. Books on fly fishing with a liberal smattering of hardback classics and cheap paperbacks filled the shelves on one side of the wall. On the other, a neatly made king-size bed and a cheap four-drawer dresser. Hanging in the door-less closet were two pairs of jeans, a couple of long-sleeved shirts and wool pullovers.

The other half of the room came with a well-used leather couch and two matching chairs that surrounded a square, hand-made wooden coffee table. All were arranged to look at a well-used, ash-filled brick fireplace. Cheap paintings of men fishing, pen-and-ink drawings of Rainbow and Brook trout, and shadow boxes of ornate flies with exotic names like Royal Coachman, Gray Ghost, and Yellow Humpy covered the knotty-pine walls. In addition to the small beer-filled refrigerator, the kitchen built into an alcove toward the back contained a microwave, a two-burner stove, and a small sink. The kitchen counter was lined with bottles of Bushmills—some full, most empty. The medicine cabinet in the cramped bathroom was stocked with several different kinds of painkillers, all fatal taken in certain amounts or combinations.

The inexpensive stereo system encased in a cheap glass-front cabinet looked lost and out of place amid the rustic décor. Speakers sat on either side of the fireplace next to a dozen pieces of seasoned firewood. Tapes and CDs piled on top of the cabinet were an odd collection of blues and rock 'n roll, including a live concert by The Grateful Dead and the complete works of Pink Floyd. A picture of Windsor and Jennifer sat on the mantle above the fireplace.

Stetson moved his gaze from the photo to Windsor, who was leaning against the kitchen counter, arms crossed. Best cut to the chase, he thought.

"I don't think Billy Broadnax killed your wife," Stetson said. "That means you're not responsible for what happened to her. Someone else is."

Chapter 7

Windsor hadn't heard Billy Broadnax's name since the previous winter when he woke up alone in the middle of a sub-zero night screaming it while kicking at sweat-stained sheets. His yells echoed off the cabin walls and rattled the empty liquor bottles on the kitchen counter. Hearing it again brought back demons he'd spent a year trying to banish.

But did he really want to? Windsor had come to grips with what he'd done but could never bring himself to be at peace with it. Jennifer would never be just a sad memory, one he resurrected during late nights in front of the fire, the whiskey bottle sitting at his feet. She deserved better than that. Maybe someday he'd feel the same way.

Now, all he could do was stare at Stetson, letting his emotions change from anger to resentment then, finally, to curiosity. He had never for one moment thought that anyone other than Billy Broadnax killed Jennifer or that he wasn't responsible.

Now Stetson shows up with a different story.

Looking out the window, Windsor could see Sam Westlake walking across the lawn fronting his house on the other side of the meadow. The old man's gait strong and unaffected by a lifetime of work that would have bent or broken lesser men. Seeing him always had an odd, calming effect on Windsor. It seemed that just knowing the old man was nearby made Windsor feel less like wanting to silence Stetson with a single bullet. Lucky for Stetson, Sam wasn't on one of his frequent trips to Bend, Portland, or Salem.

Windsor took a deep breath, focused, and thought maybe he could listen to the message rather than shoot the messenger "What's your name again?" he asked.

"Stetson. Arnie Stetson. I work for the …"

"I don't care who you work for. Just tell me why you're here."

Windsor watched as Stetson took a deep breath. "Everyone thinks Billy Broadnax killed your wife because of what you wrote about him."

"I already know that."

"That might not be true."

"Might?"

"I'm not sure and I can't prove anything," Stetson said. "At least not yet. If it checks out, I'll write about it. There's no reason to involve you other than …"

"Yeah. Yeah. I know. The grieving husband."

"Something like that."

Windsor moved from the refrigerator to plop down on the worn leather couch. He wanted to think, to rest legs tired from standing all morning in the river's cold, spring-fed waters. He also wanted to get away from the gun on the shelf over the refrigerator and any thoughts of just shooting Stetson and dumping his body in the woods to let the coyotes gnaw on his bones.

"What have you got?" he said finally, still unsure he wanted to know.

"There's a private investigator in Portland named Harold Gilroy," Stetson said. "Most people call him Squid."

"I know him. Small guy. Ponytail. Always wears a three-piece white suit and really nice shoes. Hangs out occasionally at a bar called The Ridge."

"He's been making the rounds of all the news organizations in Portland saying he's talked to Billy and that Broadnax told him he killed seven women, not eight."

"And the one he didn't kill was Jennifer?"

"That's Billy's story, according to Gilroy," Stetson said, stepping carefully inside the cabin. He sat down at a small, scratched-topped table, its surface littered with feathers, thread, yarn, and fishhooks. Attached to the table was a vise that looked like something from a dentist's office. Clamped in the vise's small needle-nose was a colorful imitation of an insect.

"And you believe him?"

"I'm not sure yet," Stetson said, sounding a little embarrassed by the thin story.

"You took the trouble to find me and you're not sure?" When Stetson didn't answer, Windsor pressed him further. "If Billy didn't kill my wife, then who did?"

"Gilroy either doesn't know or won't say. He wants money."

"Have you talked to him—to Broadnax?" Windsor found it hard to even say the name.

"No," Stetson said. "My editors want nothing to do with it. The world has found new monsters, Dr. Windsor. Billy Broadnax is yesterday's news. None of my bosses seems eager to remind people of what happened."

"Unless Gilroy is right?"

"That would be news," he said, fiddling with a spool of neon yarn on the table. "Look, doctor, the way you were blamed for your wife's death. It left a bad taste in everyone's mouth. I know what happened at the cemetery. I wasn't there, but I heard about it. This could change all that."

Out the window, Windsor could see Sam creeping across the meadow toward the river. He had on his leaky waders, tattered fishing vest, and battered straw hat. In his hand was the ancient bamboo fly rod that had caught a lifetime's worth of fish from 10-inch trout to 26-inch Dolly Vardens. Running out in front of him was Maggie, Sam's eight-year-old golden retriever whose job it was to bark and snap at any fish Sam hooked and landed. It was a job she took seriously.

"Why did Gilroy come to you?"

"The editors at the paper wanted nothing to do with him. He started asking around. Tracked me down at The Ridge."

"What's he selling?"

"Access. He claims to be able to arrange an interview with Billy, guaranteeing that he will cop to the first seven murders, but not the eighth. The thing that makes it appealing is that no one has ever interviewed him. He hasn't said a word publicly since being sentenced. Anyone who tries gets blocked by his lawyers or officials at the prison. Everyone wants Billy Broadnax and what he did to be forgotten."

"And if you don't pay?"

"Gilroy says he'll take his business elsewhere. Probably another newspaper, a television station or one of those cable cop shows. He's all about money."

Still looking out the window, Windsor watched as Sam stopped about thirty feet back from the river's edge. He stood still watching the slow-moving water below a log bridge. If a fish rose, he'd watch to see what kind of insect it was eating, find a pattern in his fly box to match it, and tie it on the end of his line. It was more ritual than necessity. Sam caught almost all his fish on the same fly—a size 14 Parachute Adams.

Windsor could see the old man glance expectantly up at the cabin. The two had fished the late afternoon and evening hatch together every day for the last two weeks with great success. Sam enjoyed the companionship, but what he really liked was patiently showing the novice Windsor everything from how to tie a fly on a line to the techniques and strategies needed to catch hook-shy trout. Sam's favorite was letting the fly float slowly on the current, keeping enough slack in the line so the fly looks natural with no drag. He called it a dead drift.

Windsor embraced the technique, more as a metaphor for what his life had become than a way of catching fish in gin-clear water.

"Did Gilroy give you a deadline?" Windsor said without taking his eyes off the river and Sam.

"Sort of. He said Tuesday morning, but he just wants the best offer. Something tells me he's flexible."

"How did you find me?"

"Your realtor," Stetson said, as something of an apology. "I expressed an interest in buying your house. I met her there and walked through it. Nice place, by the way. Anyway, when she went outside to take a call, I looked in her briefcase. The listing agreement said Pine Mountain Ranch, Deschutes County."

Windsor passed on expressing his admiration. "It's a big county."

"I got some help from the Forest Service office in Sisters."

Windsor held back a smile. Maybe he had underestimated Stetson. "How long have you been a reporter?"

"Three years, but I didn't start work in Portland until after Broadnax was sent to prison."

"So, you weren't there while Billy was ... active?"

Stetson shook his head. "First I heard of it was on the car radio in the middle of Kansas on my way out here."

In the distance, Sam waded into the river, false casting over the water with an effortless motion Windsor envied but could never replicate.

"Well, now you've told me," Windsor said, getting off the couch. "Have a nice drive back."

Chapter 8

He left Stetson sitting at the table to go outside to pull on his waders and vest again, grab the fly rod from over the window, and walk down to the river to join Sam. Halfway between the river and the cabin, he turned to see Stetson walking back into the woods toward the road and the locked gate where he'd probably parked.

When Maggie spotted Windsor, she stood up, barked, and wagged her tail hard enough to beat down the tall grass on either side of her. He patted her head, and she escorted him the rest of the way as if he couldn't find Sam or the river without her.

Windsor had never had a dog, but if he did it would be Maggie. She started showing up at his cabin shortly after he arrived. She came and went depending on whether Sam was home or who had the best handouts. On nights when Windsor drank himself to sleep, she'd plop down in front of the fireplace, watching him disapprovingly while the howls of coyotes filled the night. In the morning she'd lick his face. Satisfied that he was still among the living, she'd paw the doorknob until it opened.

When Windsor reached the river, Sam was standing in his usual place behind a large boulder, the waist-deep water eddying around his waders. He flipped the fly rod over his right shoulder, letting the line trail out behind him. With the same smooth, effortless motion, he powered the rod forward. The line reversed course, shooting out over the boulder into a patch of smooth, shiny water forty feet away. The tiny fly landed delicately, clinging to the surface film. It was a ballet that lasted only a few seconds then repeated again and again, each time exactly the same way.

"Not much happening," Sam said without taking his eyes off the water. "I think we're a little early."

"The hatch won't happen for another hour yet."

The two men smiled at each other. A year ago, Windsor thought a hatch was something chickens did. Now he knew the differences between a stonefly, a mayfly, a midge, and a caddis. He'd learned about dry flies and nymphs along with the techniques necessary to fish both.

He'd also learned a lot more about Sam Westlake.

Sam called himself a logger, but he owned countless acres of range and timber land with rights to graze and log on thousands more. His sons ran the business that included logging and sawmill operations, while Sam puttered around the ranch taking care of his prize Herefords, fishing, and getting richer every day. He'd lost interest in the timber business when his wife died ten years earlier. That's when he sold their house overlooking the City of Redmond. A month later he took up permanent residence at the ranch.

"I see you had some company," Sam said, eyes still riveted on the water. "Everything alright?"

"Reporter. It's been a year. Hard to believe, isn't it?" Windsor didn't feel like sharing the real reason for Stetson's visit.

"What did you tell him?"

"Thanks for stopping by. Now leave."

"Good. That much more time to fish." Sam cast again at the still water behind a rock near the opposite bank. "Maybe you ought to try working on that second novel again."

"I'm thinking true crime. It's something I know about."

"Let it go, Alex. Fiction is more fun and less work."

Windsor credited Sam with saving his life. Numb and despondent, he'd shown up at Westlake's ranch a day after Jennifer's funeral. By December and surrounded by three feet of snow, he'd lost twenty pounds. His pale green eyes had turned harsh and watery thanks to the Bushmills that Sam dropped off on a regular basis. Then there were the pain pills that seemed to magically appear in the bathroom. As a result, he'd pretty much abandoned anything that resembled personal hygiene. More than once, he'd taken the pistol down from the kitchen shelf, sat on the couch, and stared at it. Each time he put it back, but never forgot it was there.

Since Windsor seldom left the cabin, Sam would stop in periodically to drink with him and play cribbage. He'd sip at a straight shot or two while Windsor inhaled everything but the label. Sam even patiently endured Windsor's off-beat taste in music, complaining little when the drunken Windsor would crank up Pink Floyd's *Dark Side of the Moon* and pass out by the last track.

By February, Windsor had become bored with self-pity. It was time to clean up a bit. He gave himself a passable haircut, but kept the beard, which now surrounded a face that by mid-August was deeply tanned from endless hours on the river. Ten of the twenty pounds he'd lost had found their way back, thanks to more frequent trips to the store for food that was actually ... food ... and not Bushmills or three-minute ramen.

Even though there was some gray in his hair, he still felt and looked as good as he ever expected to, which wasn't much.

Sam introduced Windsor to fly fishing as soon as he moved into the cabin. "Never too soon to start," he'd said. "The winter hatch is great. You'll pick it up in no time."

Although it took a while to get up the energy, he knew from the first moment he stepped into the icy stream, felt the pressure of the water squeeze the waders around his legs, and saw a fish rise to the surface that the simple and gentle sport could help drive from his mind and heart all that haunted him. Six hours on the river and months of bad thoughts disappeared ... temporarily, at least.

Until now.

Windsor couldn't stop thinking about what Stetson had told him. If Gilroy was right about what Broadnax had said, then the reason he was hiding out in the woods no longer made sense.

Chapter 9

Windsor's house sat back from the street, barely noticeable at the end of the quiet cul-de-sac with only two other houses set a discreet distance away. Tudor style, off-white with deep green trim and leaded windows. Thanks to the yard service his accountants paid each month, the place looked good for not having been lived in for a year. The grass mowed. The flower beds filled with azaleas. Laurel hedges neatly trimmed. The phalanx of arborvitae guarding the back fence a foot higher than he remembered.

An old, perfectly shaped oak tree dominated the front yard. Its twin in the back of the house peeked over the steep roof line with its stately, ivy-covered chimney. A path of red brick wound through the yard to a broad porch with wrought iron railing leading to ornate double doors with brass handles and matching knocker.

He'd paid cash for the house ten years earlier, ignoring the accountants babbling about home-interest deductions and other tax advantages of a mortgage. He didn't care. The price tag barely made a dent in the millions he'd inherited when his parents died. Sometimes he wondered how much money was left. Jennifer called it "Windsor's Castle" and joked about how the neighbors refused to talk politics and never wore white after Labor Day. The thought made him smile.

It was after mid-afternoon when he pulled into the driveway. The three-hour drive from Sam's ranch left plenty of time to think about what Arnie Stetson had said. Slowly, he realized that he wanted him to be right. If it was a snipe hunt, so what? It couldn't be any worse. All he wanted was absolution.

He got out of the car, making a mental note to have the realty sign stuck in the front lawn taken down. He was never sure about selling the place. The best solution was to set the selling price a half-million too high, then refuse to come down to meet the two offers that came in. After a while, the frustrated agent stopped showing the place. Problem solved.

He walked up the driveway, put the key in the kitchen door, and slowly went inside, feeling like a thief breaking into a closed-up museum. The house smelled stale and stuffy, like an old trunk. Dust motes floated in the darkness behind closed curtains. Sheet-covered furniture hunkered down like ghosts waiting to be summoned. More dust covered the kitchen counters and the small table in the nook where they had breakfast each morning. Maybe if he stood there long enough, she would magically appear, sitting at the table drinking coffee, and absorbed in her laptop or cell phone.

Instead, he was greeted by a jumbled mess of conflicting memories. Jennifer dressing up as a witch for Halloween with a pointy hat and green makeup. Jennifer sitting in the middle of the front room on Christmas morning wearing Santa Claus pajamas and surrounded by packages, ribbons, and torn wrapping paper. Jennifer waking him up on the morning of Cinco de Mayo wearing only a serape and waving a Mexican flag.

Jennifer hanging naked from the rafters in the garage, the floor covered in her blood.

After living for a year in a one-room cabin, the house's rooms felt cold and cavernous, the ceilings towering over his head, the doorways tall, wide, and imposing. Walking from room to room brought back memories of intimate dinner parties, joyous holidays, nights together watching *Game of Thrones* or a Humphrey Bogart movie. Now, everything was strange and alien—the good times erased in the aftermath of horror.

Did ugly always trump beauty or was it just him?

Upstairs, the king-size bed in the master bedroom had been stripped. More sheets covered the dresser and the table where each morning Jennifer put on her makeup while excitedly talking about the cases she was working on and the clients she would see. He smiled, remembering how stressed she was the day of her first court appearance and how excited that night about how well it went.

Windsor laid down on the bed, staring up at the ceiling trying to remember what it had been like to live there with her, to sleep in that bed with her next to him. To make love with her. Her playfulness. Her passion. Does the faint aroma of her perfume still hang in the air or was it just his imagination?

Jennifer was Catholic. He wasn't. They compromised on a civil ceremony that only her mother agreed to attend. For the first six weeks they were married she would disappear for fifteen or twenty minutes before bed each night. When he asked if everything was alright, she always said yes. One day he found that she had created a small chapel in the walk-in closet of a seldom-used spare bedroom. Candles, crosses, and a miniature painting of Jesus Christ. He never asked her again if things were all right. He knew they were.

Windsor went back to the car to bring in what little luggage he had. Most of his clothes were still hanging in the bedroom closet. Reaching into a leather bag, he pulled out a half-empty bottle of Bushmills and set it on the counter. He got a crystal tumbler out of a kitchen cabinet, poured, and sat on the living room couch staring at the French doors that opened on to the patio. He remembered the police explaining that Jennifer's killer came through the patio doors, dragged her through the kitchen, and out to the garage.

Not long after that, the rest of the Bushmills was gone, and he was dreaming of conversations with his dead wife.

~*~

Jennifer is wearing one of his dress shirts. She's sitting in the leather, wing-backed chair in their front room, her bare legs stretched out, feet resting on a hassock. Her dark hair wet. Her face pale gray. Eyes sunken. Her fingers long and spidery. Looking at her from the couch, she seemed out of focus, like looking through a camera with a dirty lens. The chair's wings resemble stubby arms slowly trying to wrap around her, pull her further into the shadows.

"I thought you'd never come back," she says in a voice that sounds hollow and distant.

"But ..." he stammers.

"I know. I'm dead and you're not. I don't know how it happened. I don't remember any of it. One minute I was dancing through the house, naked, the music turned up. After that ... nothing."

"It was my fault."

She smiles as if knowing that's what he would say. "You mean that opinion piece you wrote. I never thought that was a good idea."

"You never said anything."

"We made a deal. Your business was yours. Mine was mine. Remember? Whatever happened was no one's fault. At least that's what I think."

"That's not what your father thinks."

"I know, but don't worry about it. He never liked you anyway."

"You don't know half of it."

"What do you mean? Are you going to tell me what happened? Why I'm here, wherever here is."

"It doesn't matter now. There's nothing you need to worry about. Are you alright?

"I don't know what I am. All I know is that you would never do anything to hurt me."

"How do I ... how do we ... fix this?"

"We don't. This is all there is."

"But ..."

Chapter 10

The phone started to vibrate, dancing across the night stand next to his bed. It woke him up. He answered, then quickly realized that the dreamy reunion with his dead wife had been interrupted by an offer of a free night at a Marriott resort.

It took him a few seconds to remember where he was. It was dark outside. His first thought was to make coffee, sit on the front porch waiting for the sun to come up so he could start another day of fishing. Then he realized where he was.

He got dressed, then walked downstairs, his footsteps on the hardwood floor echoing through the house. He looked at his watch. Nine p.m. It was just about the same time that Jennifer had been killed. Standing on the front porch, he was greeted by the smell of fresh bark dust and the sound of cars moving along the street at the end of the cul-de-sac. He walked across the lawn to stand under the oak tree where the police said the killer—where Billy Broadnax—hid that night, watching the house, waiting for the right moment. He remembered what the state police sergeant told him during the limo ride after the funeral. Windsor relied on his training to imagine the rest.

It was another warm night just like this one. He imagined Jennifer dancing naked through the house, a margarita in one hand, salsa music playing on the stereo. That would be like her. The heat brought out her Spanish blood. She would have moved from room to room with the uninhibited freedom that comes from thinking no one is watching. Out of the den, across the living room, through the dining room and into the kitchen. She would disappear for a few seconds then fly back through the same rooms, her spinning-and-twirling body framed against the picture windows, her perfect breasts bouncing with the sensuous beat of the Tejano music. Long, silky-black hair swirled around her head, hiding then revealing her light-brown face with cat-like eyes. Perfect white teeth peeked out from behind bright red lips.

Did Billy watch her from the shadows under the tree? Did the thin film of perspiration that must have glistened on her back, chest, and arms make him shiver? Did he close his eyes while imagining the aroma of her perfume, the taste of her sweat on his tongue, the sound of her heart pounding in his ears?

Windsor knew the effect Jennifer could have on other men, that she had on him. She was so young, so perfect, so beautiful. So alive. In

Billy's mind she would be like someone from a different place; an alien world where others as beautiful as her lived in a constant state of wanton bliss. Free spirits romping through a tranquil idyllic existence. A world where men like Billy were left to stand on the outside looking longingly in at them. Close enough to see. Too far away to touch.

After seven murders—all exactly the same—Windsor remembered his own diagnosis of Billy: compulsive, meticulous, probably autistic, maybe Asperger's. Whatever he was, Billy had worked it all out. He would have wanted every detail to be perfect and exactly like the others. That's what he was all about, what made all the time and effort worthwhile.

Windsor had never seen Billy Broadnax, didn't know what he looked like or how he acted. What he did know was that there had been other killers like Billy. Men who lusted after women who wore nice clothes, drove expensive cars, and, in Billy's case, lived in luxurious homes in the city's most affluent neighborhoods. They were women he would never know, never touch, never enjoy. Thinking about them would make him grit his teeth to keep from hating his life even more than he already did.

Windsor didn't know how Billy found his victims. Maybe he brushed past them in the aisles at New Seasons, Whole Foods or the line at a Starbucks. Would he take deep breaths to let their perfume fill his head? If he got too close, would they move away? Those that turned to look at him would probably crinkle their noses before quickly walking away. He would know that each one of them was disgusted by him and it fueled his rage while he stared dumbly at their lipsticked mouths, perfect hair, and shapely figures, all with promised pleasures he'd never enjoy.

That night, as he stood in the shadows watching her, all Billy could do was crave something he could never hope to attain. At least not the way he wanted. The festering consequences of all those rejections would be visited on Jennifer that night.

Windsor stepped out from under the tree while trying to imagine what Billy did next. He must have walked around the side of the house. The air would have been cool between the house's smooth stucco walls on his right and the towering hedge to his left. Afraid of leaving footprints in the soft grass, he could have stayed on the stone pavers marking the path to the backyard. Did he smile when he passed the silent air conditioning unit behind a manicured boxwood hedge? No AC meant the doors and windows would be open. He must have had a small daypack to carry the tools of his gruesome trade: rope, a meat hook, and a butcher knife. The pages from the Bible would be sealed inside a ziplock bag to be left inside her body.

Did he feel a need to hurry? He knew she was alone, but for how long? Did she have a husband, a boyfriend? Was he coming soon? Is that what she was doing dancing naked through the house, waiting for someone? Did Billy even care? One of the things Windsor learned from reading the files on the other seven murders was that The Meat Man was focused and determined. Nothing was going to keep him from doing what he had done so many times before. That's what the killer would have wanted. Another woman. Another body. Just like the rest.

With the air conditioning off, the French doors at the back of the house would have been open, light from the dining room spilling across the brick patio and on to the wrought-iron chairs and lounges with their colorful cushions. The music from inside the house escaped into the yard to die on the lawn and in the dense line of arborvitae along the back fence. It's privacy and seclusion were some of the reasons Windsor bought the house. Had he bought a condo downtown or a houseboat, maybe none of this would have happened.

He stood on the patio, staring into the house. Did Billy wait to see if she came out to dance naked around the backyard? How long did he stand there thinking about the smell of her sweat-laced perfume, the feel of her skin as he ran his fingers down her neck and chest?

Her shadow, illuminated by the light from inside, must have darted across the patio. He couldn't put off the inevitable any longer. If she wasn't going to come out, he would go in. If this was the right or wrong time he didn't care. He wanted her. He craved what he had to do. It was then that The Meat Man slipped into the house.

For a year Windsor had felt nothing but a seething anger for what happened to Jennifer and for the man responsible. Now, staring into the house, his rage had been tempered by confusion. Tonight, he imagined it was Billy Broadnax who stood outside, watched Jennifer through the windows, then killed her. Now, thanks to Arnie Stetson, he wasn't so sure. It was time to find out. That's why he came back. No time like the present.

His den was a converted spare bedroom with a beat-up roll top he'd found years ago in an antique store in the small town of Aurora, south of Portland. He paid too much for it. Getting it delivered set him back another few hundred dollars. He seldom used it for anything other than old bank statements, unopened letters from the accountants in San Francisco, and the occasional uncashed retainer from the parents of a teenage patient. He pulled open the bottom drawer and rummaged around until finding a dog-eared address book, a remnant of days before cell phones stored everything.

"Gilroy, Harold (Squid)" was the third name under the Gs, his business card stapled to the page. Windsor dialed, got a voicemail, and left a message.

Chapter 11

At three in the afternoon, The Ridge was empty except for a guy in overalls playing video poker and one of the regulars nodding off at the bar over a beer and a shot. Baseball and soccer games played silently on a half-dozen televisions. The handful of tables and a couple of buddy bars sat empty but at the ready waiting for five o'clock when business picked up. The smell of hamburgers and fries drifted out of the small kitchen at the end of the bar. Neon signs promoting local IPAs provided the only light.

Bud Schwartz came out of a storage area carrying a paint bucket, brush, and a step ladder. He disappeared into the men's room, then came out again a few minutes later.

"Hey, Moon," he yelled. "Come look at this, maybe I'm being too hasty."

"I'm busy," she yelled back.

If Schwartz heard her, he didn't act like it. He was staring at the man sitting at a table in the far corner of the bar. "Well, I'll be damned. Alex Windsor."

The big man practically ran across the bar, reaching the table just as Windsor stood up. "I can't believe it," Schwartz said, pumping Windsor's hand and giving him a bear hug. "How the hell you been?"

Schwartz sat down across the table, struggling to find the words to say how much he'd missed Windsor. All he could come up with was "nice beard," then got up and headed toward the bar. "Wait here," he said over his shoulder. "I gotta tell Moon." He came back minutes later with two glasses of a local Kolsch.

"Still rockin' the Haight-Ashbury thing, I see," Windsor said, pointing at Bud's faded Jerry Garcia T-shirt.

"Did you know there's a station on the internet that plays nothing but Grateful Dead music?"

"No, I didn't."

"Well, that's not important. Now, where have you been? Everyone thinks you were in Tibet doing that Dalai Lama thing."

"How did that ever get started? You know me. I'm not the boiled-turnip-shaved-head type."

"So where *have* you been?"

"Central Oregon. Learning to fly fish." He described some of the fish he'd caught and how he'd let them all go.

"Fly fishing? Is that right? And you don't keep the fish? Don't eat them?" Bud shook his head. "Gee, Alex, it sounds … ah … sustainable."

Windsor laughed. "Pretty much."

"So, how are you doing?" Bud asked. "It's been a year, but …"

"Better, Bud. Thanks."

"But it wasn't easy?"

"Far from it," Windsor said, then quickly changed the subject. "What's with the paint can and brush?"

"Oh, that. Someone wrote the entire lyrics of Bob Dylan's *Subterranean Homesick Blues* on the wall in the men's john. It starts over the sink, circles the room, and ends over the urinal. I was going to paint over it, but I'm thinking about keeping it. I hate painting, and it is one of Dylan's best. Besides, it kind of goes with the place, if you know what I mean."

Windsor started coming to The Ridge ten years earlier, right after Bud and Moon Schwartz bought the place, kicked out the bikers, and did a massive remodel. What had once been a notorious dive bar now featured local beers, burgers on brioche buns, chicken wings, and kale chips. What made The Ridge odd was that it didn't sit on a ridge. In fact, it was on the flats not far from the west bank of the Willamette River. The best anyone could tell the bar's name may have come from the original owner who was "Ridge" somebody. For the first five years, Windsor stopped in three or four times a week. Less after marrying Jennifer.

Windsor and Bud Schwartz had been friends ever since Windsor convinced the local daily paper to do a feature story about the restored bar. Within weeks, the place was attracting an entertaining and diverse crowd of carpenters, plumbers, lawyers, accountants, and reporters from the newspaper office two blocks away. It all made for lively conversations fueled by endless pitchers of beer. All that in addition to a reliable cast of regulars, including, an avid Bob Dylan fan and at least one forensic psychologist.

Windsor was more than happy to be part of an odd and eclectic group of drinkers and thinkers, most of whom never knew—or cared—that he was a multi-millionaire psychologist with a stable of rich clients with dysfunctional children. All they knew was that he was a regular guy who occasionally bought a round of drinks and liked to listen more than talk.

"So, you're back for good, right?" Bud said, brightening up. "You're going to open your practice again? Stop in for beers after work, right?" There was an eagerness in Bud's voice that made Windsor glad that he came back and made The Ridge one of his first stops.

"I'm not sure how long I'll be here. I just need to take care of a little business," Windsor said. "Then I'll probably go back to the ranch."

"To catch more fish then put them back?"

Windsor nodded.

Schwartz shook his head in disbelief. "Too bad. It's not the same around here without you. All the usual suspects drop in occasionally and ask about you. They don't stay long. Maybe a beer or two. That lady cop you used to date, Cassie something, came in a couple of times to see if I'd heard anything about where you were. She's nice, for a homicide detective, and a big fan of yours. She didn't say that. It just looked that way if you know what I mean. Anyway, I didn't know where you were, so there was nothing to tell her other than the rumor you were in Tibet."

"Anyone else ask about me?"

"A reporter from one of the television stations. Can't remember her name. Nice looking gal. Older than most in her business. She had your card. Said when she called the number you wrote down it rang here." Bud laughed and shook his finger at Windsor. "Nice trick."

Windsor smiled. He remembered Tina Anthony from the DA's press conference. That was the same night he went home and fell into the abyss.

Moon showed up with two more beers, set them on table then hugged Windsor. "It's good to have you back," she said, "but don't let this lazy old bastard corrupt you any more than he already has." She kissed him on the cheek then waddled off to tend bar and leave the two men alone.

"We never got a chance to tell you how sorry we were about Jennifer," Bud said. "I saw the TV news and heard what people were saying. Knowing you, you probably blame yourself. Well, don't. It wasn't your fault. All that talk was just that … talk."

"Thanks," Windsor said, then quickly changed the subject. "Do you know a reporter at the paper named Stetson? Skinny kid. Generation X type. Been around less than a year."

"Yeah, sure. He's been in a few times. Same with a lot of those folks from the paper. Nice kid. Does a good job, but newspapers aren't what they once were. He came in and asked about you just a few days ago."

"Can he be trusted?"

The bar owner leaned back and shrugged, his T-shirt rising to reveal a Buddha-like belly. "Hell if I know."

"He tracked me down a couple of days ago. I'm not sure what to think."

"What did he want?"

Windsor didn't want to get into it until he knew more. "Not sure. Something to do with Squid Gilroy. Has he been in?"

"Funny you should ask. Squid was in here talking to Stetson about three or four nights ago. I noticed them because Squid doesn't drink, so there's no reason for him to be here. Not sure why he comes in at all, to tell you the truth. Anyway, they sat right here at this table and talked for maybe half an hour."

"I've only seen Gilroy a couple of times. Stetson said he was some kind of private detective."

"Could be. He came in here a couple of years ago waving around a diploma from a trade school like he's just graduated from Harvard. I heard that he was working for some insurance company spying on injured workers and some divorce attorneys. It could have been just bar talk. All I know is that no one is more dangerous than a dumb shit who thinks he's smart." Bud sipped his beer and wiped the foam out of his mustache. "So, you going to tell me what's going on?"

Windsor shook his head. "I'm not sure myself, but I might find out in a few minutes."

Chapter 12

Windsor didn't exactly see Harold "Squid" Gilroy come into The Ridge. He seemed to suddenly appear out of thin air like some grotesque apparition. Either that or he figured out a way to ooze through the front door without opening it. All he knew for sure was that Gilroy was standing next to the bar, looking around, then walking toward the table where he and Bud Schwartz were sitting.

Schwartz gave him a passing glance, then disappeared into the men's room to take a second look at his new decoration. He reappeared with a satisfied smile and gathered up his paint, brush, and ladder. Dylan's words would apparently remain indelibly immortalized on the walls of The Ridge's men's room.

"You rang, master," Gilroy said, sliding into the chair that Bud had just left. "Portland's leading private investigator reporting for duty." He gave a mock salute, crossed his legs, and leaned back in the chair.

Gilroy was in his early thirties. Pale skin, thin mustache, soul patch, and a turned-up, porcine-like nose. Greasy red hair combed straight back was pulled into a ponytail tight enough to reveal a receding hairline and freckled forehead. He wore a dirt-gray shirt, no tie, and a threadbare white three-piece suit reminiscent of *Saturday Night Fever.* As always, the outfit was set off by his incongruous trademark—a highly buffed pair of expensive wine-colored Cole-Haan loafers.

Windsor had seen guys like Gilroy before, mostly behind bars. Cynical and sarcastic on the outside. Full of fear and insecurities on the inside. A defense mechanism that made them distrustful of others. Unwilling or unable to earn an honest living. Always looking for a quick buck with as little effort as possible. Quick to place blame on others. Slow to take responsibility.

"What's this about Broadnax?" Windsor said, deciding it was best to stay on the offensive.

Gilroy snorted out a laugh. "Ha. I knew that little shit Stetson couldn't be trusted. He was supposed to tell his editors. Instead, he ran right to you, didn't he? Should have guessed. No one has ethics anymore."

"Let's hear it, Squid," Windsor said.

"No way and don't call me Squid. Whatever Stetson told you is as much as you're going to hear. Broadnax is a gold mine. No one has ever interviewed him. You'd know that if you'd hung around instead of disappearing to Tibet or wherever the hell you went." Gilroy flicked a finger at some nonexistent lint on his lapel. "Well, while you were gone, I've been busy. I talked to Billy. We have a mutually beneficial arrangement. A contract you might call it. Whoever wants to talk to him must go through me. And it ain't cheap. So, if you're in the market either get in line or get out your checkbook. Billy is hot property. I'm going to see to that."

"What I hear is that no one gets to see Broadnax without going through his lawyer."

"Don't worry about that. It's taken care of. Now, you ready to pay the price of admission?"

"This isn't business," Windsor said. "This is personal. I want to know what Broadnax told you about my wife. You told Stetson that Billy may not have killed her. Is that true?"

"No, no, no." Gilroy waved an index finger back and forth. "I'd love to help, great one, but times have changed. You're not in charge anymore. You're not the big swinging dick you used to be. People around here still think you're responsible for what happened to your wife. You leaving town didn't help your image. Coming back isn't going to change that. There's a new sheriff in town. It's pay up or shut up."

"I get it, Squid. Now, move on."

Gilroy scowled. "I said don't call me that." He looked around, then leaned across the table like he was ready to reveal some deep, dark secret. It fell a little short. "Listen, this is my chance to make some money. The big casino. Hog heaven. I'm not going to waste it just because you want to find out who killed your wife and hung her from the rafters in your garage."

Windsor shook his head in disgust. "You're a class act, Squid."

Gilroy's face turned smug. "Relax, Windsor, and I'll tell you again not to call me that. The shoe is on the other foot this time. You dance to my tune. If you want to know what Billy has to say about your wife or any of the others he killed, the tab is fifty Gs and half of what any TV station or newspaper makes selling Billy's story. Since you're not either one of those, the price is twice that."

"That's it?"

"I want cash and all future rights to his story," Gilroy said. "Documentaries are hot right now. Maybe a movie. I'm a businessman and this is serious business."

"What proof do you have other than the word of a deranged killer?"

"Don't worry about that. Pay the freight and you'll get all the proof you need."

"How did you and Broadnax get to be such buddies?" he asked.

"Let's just say we share a little secret," Gilroy said. Smirk had replaced smug. "It's kind of a guy thing. Me and my buddy Bill."

Gilroy poked at the frayed carpet with the toe of one of his loafers and grimaced. He crossed one leg over the other, pulled a yellowish handkerchief from his hip pocket, and carefully buffed the entire shoe. "How can you stand this place? Can we go outside?"

Windsor ignored him. "You think news outlets in this city are going to pay that kind of money?"

Gilroy laughed. "Who cares? Somebody will. Eventually. Not those tight asses down at that paper where that new best friend of yours works. The orders from the chamber of commerce are that the less said about Billy Broadnax the better. He's bad for business. Makes the city look worse than it already does … if that's possible. Well, you and they have until tomorrow. If the newspaper or television stations around here don't bite, I think one of those TV tabloids will." Gilroy smiled at Windsor. "You in or not?"

Windsor's hands shot out, grabbing the lapels of Gilroy's suit and pulling him across the table.

"Listen, you little scumbag. If you have proof that Broadnax didn't kill my wife, I want to hear it. Now! Is that clear?"

"Hey, hey, easy on the threads," Gilroy said, pulling away and straightening his suit coat.

"I need proof you really have something. If Broadnax didn't kill her, then I want to know who did."

"How would he know?" Gilroy snorted. "Have you ever met the guy? No. Well I have. A couple of times. Take it from me, he's a religious nut who can barely string two sentences together. Dumb as a mud fence and half as handsome. All I know is that if he hadn't turned himself in, the cops would probably still be looking for him and the bodies still piling up. That's what he does, and he was good at it."

"The proof, Squid. Is it just his word?"

"Sorry, pal. This is strictly cash and carry. No sneak previews. Do I look that stupid?"

Given Gilroy's track record, Windsor had doubts about any proof the little man had. There was only one way to find out. "Here's the deal,

Squid. Half the money up front. If your proof checks out, you'll get the other half."

A smug smile walked across Gilroy's face. He put his hands behind his head and leaned back in the chair again. "Cash, right? And I retain the right to sell Billy's story to any news outlet willing to pay?"

"Meet me here tomorrow at two o'clock and bring your proof. I'll have the money."

Still smiling, Gilroy stood up, straightened his suit jacket, and strutted out the door.

Chapter 13

"This place is great," Harold Gilroy said to himself, looking around at the neon lighting on the ceiling, the comfortable chairs, walls covered in velvet paintings of Elvis and Spanish bullfighters. "A no-smoking juice bar with topless dancers. Damn, wish I'd thought of this."

The reflected light from the mirrored ball hanging over a cramped stage sent small spiders of light scurrying over the floor, walls, tables, and the half-dozen customers drinking Diet Coke, orange juice, and chai smoothies. An overweight businessman in a sweat-stained white shirt sat at the next table. He waved five-dollar bills at a bored dancer with dishwater-blonde hair, flabby thighs, and tits like knobs on a car radio. She danced a few inches away from him, whispered in his ear, then took the bill with a weary thank-you.

Gilroy heard that The Squeeze had just opened and was eager to try it out. It was a former pancake house located off a freeway exit in the middle of a row of mid-price motels that catered to hookers and salesmen looking to pad their expense accounts. Gilroy decided it was the perfect place to spend some of the money he was going to earn as Billy Broadnax's agent. Never too soon to start, he figured.

Screw the newspapers and the television stations. And screw the high-and-mighty Alex Windsor. By this time tomorrow he'll have a hundred thousand dollars of Windsor's money. What could be better than that?

Gilroy smiled to himself. He wasn't going to end up on the losing end this time. He was in the sweet spot. If Windsor comes through, great. If he backs out, Gilroy would be on the phone to every supermarket and television tabloid he could think of. How many are there? Twenty? Thirty? All it takes is one who wants a face-to-face with the notorious Meat Man.

Who knows? Maybe Billy Broadnax would get a real trial. A chance to leave prison for his day in court. How juicy would that be? Very. Book deals, a movie, the TV talk-show circuit. Cha-ching.

Gilroy smiled and ordered a second mango-strawberry smoothie from a passing waitress. Why not drop a few more bucks? He was so close to hitting it big. All he had to do was wait one more day. Plenty of time to get that file from that little green-haired bitch who worked for that shrink, and he'd be set. He could take care of that first thing in the morning. Despite everything going his way, he was still pissed that he let the original file get out of his hands in the first place. It wasn't his fault. How was he to know that Broadnax was The Meat Man?

"I was sitting on a gold mine and didn't know it," he muttered. "Well, I know it now. Things are going to change and change quick."

After leaving Windsor at The Ridge, Gilroy decided to celebrate his imminent fortune by taking his overtaxed credit cards for an afternoon spin through a couple of upscale men's stores downtown. He put a salesman through hell before walking out with a pinstripe suit, a couple of shirts, and a handful of ties. With the business look taken care of it was time to go casual. At a small boutique on the city's Park Blocks, he bought a beige Armani knockoff with loose-fitting pants and a double-breasted coat worn over a black T-shirt. He topped off the shopping spree with a new pair of Cole-Haans from Nordstrom.

"Smokin'," Squid had said when he saw his reflection in the dressing room mirror. "You've come a long way, Harold old boy, and it's only going to get better."

He was positive that Billy Broadnax was going to be his ticket to the bigs. Apartment in the Pearl District. An eager-to-please girlfriend or two with bedroom eyes and store-bought boobs. A new car. Maybe two.

Gilroy smiled thinking about the moment his luck changed. Two years earlier, after faking a back injury, he filed a workers' compensation claim and settled out of court for fifteen thousand dollars. Knowing this was the time to do something smart, he took night classes at a local trade school. Six months later, he emerged with an associate degree in "Investigative Arts. Within three weeks, he was earning fifty dollars an hour tailing horny housewives to Red Lion Hotels and filming deadbeats with neck braces chopping firewood or water skiing.

Now, he was on the verge of a big payoff.

After three more acts with three more sets of bad tits, Gilroy left The Squeeze unsure what to do next. Not ready to go home yet, he made a phone call then met his connection in the parking lot of a mini mart on SE Stark Street.

Ten minutes later he pulled into the dark parking lot of a Foursquare Church, pulled the pipe out of the glove box, and fired it up. He let the crack curl around his brain like a snake. Images of the dancers at The Squeeze faded away, replaced by a heightened sense of cars on the street and wind in the trees. He forgot about needing a burger and fries at Sonic. In its place was a craving for something even more basic than food. The best place to start was the small porno district on SE 82nd

Avenue. Before driving away, he took one more hit, let the euphoria set in, then slowly pass.

At a stoplight, he eyed the other cars on the street, looking for the make and model best suited for his soon-to-be new lifestyle. A bright-red Lexus ran a close second to the Audi A5 coupe. Luxury or performance? It was going to be a tough choice.

Maybe he could have both. He deserved it.

"What the hell," he said to himself. "A 500-series Mercedes. It's too late to be humble."

After driving south on 82nd for a mile, he turned into a cramped complex of small, clapboard houses. He parked in the gravel lot in back, away from the street and next to a dusty laurel hedge. He thought about another round or two with his pipe but decided to wait until later. He still had to drive home, and this was not the time to get pulled over.

Inside the adult store, Gilroy spent an hour watching a few videos, all the while hoping the sticky linoleum floor wasn't damaging his shoes. He decided to leave after watching a video featuring an overweight blonde and a midget in a dog collar … twice.

On his way out, he stopped to survey the sex toys in the glass case near the door. He was pretty sure what each one was for but had trouble figuring out why he would buy one and who he would give it to. The Pakistani attendant behind the counter ignored him until Gilroy offered him twenty dollars for the plaid dildo on the shelf next to an array of CDs.

"That's my thermos," the clerk said without looking up.

"Oh. Well, look me up if you want to sell it. Harold Gilroy, private eye. Here's my card." Gilroy slid his card across the glass-topped counter, then nonchalantly took another business card from a holder on top of the case. "Momma Mia's Escort Service."

"They any good?"

The attendant shrugged.

Outside, Gilroy walked toward his car debating whether to call the escort service, if for no other reason than to find out what he could get and for how much. He still hadn't made up his mind when he saw a black Taurus parked tight up next to the driver's side of his Honda Civic.

"Shit," he said, standing at the rear of the car trying to figure out how to get in without messing up his suit. The only thing he could do was squeeze along the laurel hedge and get in the passenger side. Having no choice, he did his best to slide gingerly between the mud-spattered car and dusty hedge, easing his way carefully toward the car door.

Then he saw the man standing in the shadows.

Chapter 14

A year earlier, Windsor had put his cellphone in the glove box of his BMW the day he pulled into Sam Westlake's ranch. He didn't touch it again until he left the ranch after Stetson's visit. He recharged it on the drive back to Portland but had used it sparingly. He was surprised when it started vibrating on the nightstand next to the bed. He picked it up and fumbled to answer. The voice at the other end was familiar, but it must have been a dream because the clock next to the bed said five a.m.

"Squid Gilroy's in my dumpster."

Windsor rolled onto his back and struggled to get his bearings. The ceiling looked different, textured, and painted an off-white. A brass fan directly overhead spun slowly and silently. Where did that come from? There were no open rafters or cobwebs, no towering trees outside the windows, no smell of fireplace ashes.

Gradually it came back to him. He wasn't at the cabin. He was home.

"Is that you, Bud?" he said, moving his hand to the other side of the bed. Empty. Knowing it would be didn't help.

"Squid Gilroy is in my dumpster. He's dead. You need to get down here right away."

Windsor lay there while the bar owner told him in hysterical tones that Gilroy's body had been found in the parking lot at The Ridge. "The police told me someone bashed in his brains, then tossed his body in my dumpster. Of all the dumpsters in Portland, why mine? He was in there with a weekend's worth of paper plates and half-eaten cheeseburgers. The garbage man found him about three a.m. The police called me about an hour ago. I thought someone had broken into the place. Instead, there's Squid tits up in the trash. I can't fucking believe it."

"Why would anyone kill Gilroy?"

"His shoes are missing! One of the cops said they think maybe someone killed him for his shoes. Jesus, Alex! What's wrong with people?"

Schwartz sounded stressed enough that Windsor passed on the chance to point out that Squid did wear nice shoes.

"I'm at the tavern. The cops are here. They want to interview you."

"Why?"

"I told them Gilroy was here yesterday talking to you. Sorry, buddy, but I couldn't lie. Cops make me nervous. Always have. I never know who they're going to shoot or why. Then there's that thing in Chicago in 1968. Anyway, they think we might be the last ones to see him alive. I've told them everything I know."

Windsor sat up, put his feet on the floor, the phone still to his ear. "Okay, Bud. Tell them you talked to me, and I said I would be down as soon as I can. Not that I need to be there at all. I have nothing to tell them."

"I know, but I could use some backup here. This is way out of my league. You've been around cops. You know what they're like."

Windsor took his time showering, getting dressed, and driving into town. Traffic was light at that hour, giving him time to think of any connections between his talk with Gilroy and the little man's body turning up in a dumpster. Coincidences happen, but this seemed a stretch. Factoring in Gilroy's new-found friendship with Billy Broadnax and his alleged claim that he didn't kill Windsor's wife made it even more so. One thing he was certain of, though, was that getting the cops involved wasn't going to help him find the truth.

When Windsor arrived at The Ridge the star of the show was Bud's dark green, heavily dented industrial-size dumpster. Four patrol cars surrounded it, illuminating the stained sides. The top propped open. Red and blue lights flashing against the brick wall, reflecting off the windows of the surrounding businesses. The smell of rotten garbage and urine. Uniformed cops guarding the perimeter. The rubberneckers included a couple of barefoot homeless men draped in filthy blankets mumbling something about how Jesus is coming back, and he's pissed.

Gilroy's body, or what Windsor assumed was his body, lay stretched out on the asphalt parking lot. It was tucked into a shiny plastic body bag and zipped up tight. No one seemed to be paying much attention to it, not even the cops.

Windsor identified himself to one of the uniforms as "suspect." Confused, but uninterested, the cop let him pass. Bud Schwartz intercepted him.

"Thanks, man," he said. "I owe you one."

Schwartz dragged Windsor across the parking lot toward a half dozen men standing around drinking coffee. Some were dressed in polyester suits and wing tips. Others wore blue windbreakers with POLICE stenciled on the back, as if they needed any identification. One of them was writing in a notebook with a pen. The rest were on cell phones. Light exploded from a still photographer's flash followed by a high-pitched whine as it recharged for another shot.

"I was hoping that your ex-girlfriend would be here," Bud said. "She's not. It's some guy who doesn't seem to know much about what he's doing. I'll let you be the judge. I'll be inside, and thanks again."

Bud hurried away just as a short, tense little guy in his thirties with thinning hair and a faint, blond mustache showed up. His burgundy sport coat looked too small. Gray slacks a little short. The flared bottoms a bit out of style but fit nicely over his black cowboy boots. He had the kind of arrogance that made him immediately unlikeable.

"You're Alex Windsor." It was more of an accusation than a question.

Windsor nodded.

"I'm Detective Blanchett, homicide, Portland Police Bureau."

Windsor forgot the name as soon as he said it. He'd seen cops like Blanchett before: No sense of humor and an intractable belief that anyone capable of fogging a mirror was guilty of something or would be given enough time. The kind that overcompensates for being bullied in grade school and lives with his mom.

"I understand you talked with the deceased yesterday afternoon," Blanchett said. "Care to tell me what you talked about?"

"Care to tell me who the deceased is?"

Blanchett looked flustered then licked his index finger and flipped through his notebook. "Gilroy. Harold Gilroy. I believe his nickname is Squid. Now, what did you talk about?"

"Weather. Sports. Women. Mostly weather. It's been hot lately, don't you think?"

"The two of you talk business at all?"

"No."

"Did Mr. Gilroy act nervous or concerned about anything?"

"He was a Mariners' fan, and it looks like they might make the playoffs for the first time in twenty years. He was pretty excited."

"Did he mention being concerned about his safety?"

"No."

When the detective started clicking his pen, Windsor peeked over his shoulder at the boys from the crime lab digging around in the dumpster. They pulled out a half dozen plastic garbage sacks and handed them to two other men also dressed in hazmat suits. One of them took a bag to the corner of the lot, poured out the contents, and poked at it with a pencil. You can never be too careful of what you might find in a dumpster outside a tavern.

"Can you tell me what the precipitation of your meeting was?" Blanchett asked.

Precipitation? Windsor tried not to laugh. "If you mean, why were we talking. No reason. We just ran into each other. I didn't know him that well and we really didn't talk that long."

"He wasn't here specifically to see you, then?"

"Not that I know of. I've been out of town for a while. Maybe he heard I was back. I come here a lot, or I used to."

Blanchett closed his notebook. "You're the Alex Windsor whose wife was one of the ..."

"Yes. Is there anything else I can help you with?"

"No. We're done. Thanks for coming down, Dr. Windsor," Blanchett said, holding out a business card. "If you think of anything else that might help, please call me at this number."

Windsor took the card without looking at it, then followed Schwartz into the tavern. On the way he tossed it in a trash can on the curb. Inside, Bud got on the phone to explain everything to his wife.

"I hope you don't think this is your fault," Windsor said after Bud hung up and started fumbling with the coffee maker. "Just because someone is offed in your parking lot doesn't mean you're responsible."

"Squid was nobody's bargain, but no one deserves to die in a dumpster or at least end up in one," Bud said, then gave Windsor a sideways glance. "Did you lie to that cop?"

Windsor waved off the question. "Don't worry about this. By tomorrow the cops will be off to some other murder. No shortage of those these days. The bright side is that the tour companies will be bringing buses through your lot. Old ladies will get out to drink a beer at the last place Squid Gilroy was seen alive. Everything will be fine."

Bud's eyes grew big. "You really think so?"

"No."

"Windsor, you're killing me." They shared a laugh and clinked coffee cups. "So, you want to tell me what this is all about?"

"Not much to tell. Gilroy talked to Stetson. Stetson talked to me. I talked to
Gilroy."

"About what?"

Windsor waited to answer, not sure he wanted to pull his friend into something that was looking more and more like a dead end, now that Gilroy was out of the picture.

"Billy Broadnax. Gilroy was peddling something about Billy not being responsible for Jennifer's death. Said he had proof. I was going to meet him here today to see what he had."

Schwartz looked stunned. "So, you believed him?"

"I don't know what to believe at this point, but my chance of learning the truth may have just ended up in your dumpster."

Bud sighed and gave Windsor a sympathetic look. "You sure you want to relive all of that? Maybe going back to catching fish and throwing them back doesn't sound all that bad."

"You're probably right, but I'm going to give it a few more days."

"Okay," Bud said. "It's your call. Now, is it too early for a shot of Jack?"

"What time is it?"

"Does it matter?" Bud said as he grabbed a bottle off the back bar.

Chapter 15

Two small children wearing only dirty underpants pushed toy trucks around a dusty hole that was a poor substitute for a real front yard. They made high-pitched engine noises as they ran the battered dump trucks through the dirt and into head-on collisions.

On the porch, Enrico DeGarza sat motionless in a water-stained recliner watching them while mindlessly swatting at flies. On a stool next to him was a forgotten bottle of Pacifico. He wore jeans, a tank top, and sandals. Even after a year, inconsolable sorrow on his face. He looked too lost in thought to notice the dusty black BMW parked in the turnout across the narrow asphalt road.

Enrico DeGarza and Windsor never got along that well. Mostly because they had nothing in common other than their love of Jennifer. In most families that would be enough. For Enrico DeGarza it wasn't even close. He was a Mexican immigrant who came to the U.S. illegally to pick beans and strawberries then started a moderately successful yard service business. Years of seven-day weeks mowing, blowing, edging, and pruning earned enough money to support his wife and his two younger daughters. More importantly, it meant he could put his oldest daughter through college and into law school.

Windsor knew fifteen minutes after he got there, he wouldn't get out of the car. That was two hours ago. The old man hadn't moved. Neither had Windsor. The scene at the cemetery is still too vivid and painful. He wished that Stetson had taken his suspicions about Jennifer's death to her father rather than him. The old man wouldn't know what to do about it, but at least he might stop blaming Windsor.

The porch was tacked on to the front of a rundown three-bedroom mobile home on a small lot deep in the farmland of Washington County west of Portland. The lot was little more than a notch carved out of a cornfield with a dirt yard and a gravel drive. The logo on the dusty pick-up next to the house read "DeGarza Landscaping" with a telephone number. The eight-foot-high corn stalks surrounding the house looked like an occupying army that for two months a year blocked any view except out the front toward the road.

Looking at the house made Windsor think about Jennifer and the first time they met. It was six years earlier at a conference on the law, medicine, and the media. She was a fiery defender of the rights of the accused in an era of intrusive journalism. He was there to talk about the ethical obligations of psychologists and psychiatrists who treat people who have committed crimes or testify at their trials. He thought her guidelines for the conduct of lawyers, doctors, and reporters in criminal cases were naive, but her passion enthralled him.

Windsor viewed guidelines of any sort as just that—guidelines. These were developed by weak-kneed editors bowing to buffed-out lawyers. Part of his presentation at the conference included describing the press guidelines as impractical and quaint. He predicted that they would only be followed by reporters when it was convenient and ignored when it wasn't.

The panel's moderator, an aging journalism professor who taught law and the press at the University of Oregon, flew into a rage at Windsor's disregard for the carefully crafted guidelines. "We cannot casually pick and choose which rules we are going to follow and when," he'd said. "You are an anarchist preaching chaos."

"I'm not a journalist, but I've had enough experience with the media to know what will happen," Windsor had fired back. "The days of a few media outlets are over. Now there are hundreds of websites, blogs, and podcasts run by people who know nothing about ethics of journalism and have no desire to learn. It's the wild west out there."

Then came a prophetic outburst that still haunted him. "Let's say there's a serial killer loose in the city. The more people murdered, the greater the media frenzy. Reporters and so-called reporters from all over the nation, maybe the world, are descending on Portland. Each one of them intent on getting a better story than the other guy. They'll have cameras, satellite uplinks, and checkbooks. Conspiracy theories will rule the day. They'll take one look at your press-bar guidelines and snicker about what a charming, peculiar little state we live in. After that, they'll go about their business of violating everything you all agreed to."

"That's the kind of behavior we're trying to prevent." The professor was in full whine.

"Good luck with that, because if you think that any of them are going to stand by with your little booklet clutched to their heart while getting rolled over by their competitors, then you don't understand the world you think your good intentions will fix."

In a confrontation after the session, an outraged Jennifer denounced him as an irresponsible symbol of everything that was wrong with how the media covers crime, especially high-profile cases. She even suggested that psychologists who talk to the media are complicit in impeding the course of justice. Just watching her made Windsor feel ten years younger. She accused him of being condescending. When he agreed and apologized, it broke the ice. Her smile captivated him enough to ask her out. They had dinner that night and sex two weeks later. That was when he learned firsthand that her passion was not limited to the rights of the accused.

A month later they drove fifteen miles from Portland to the little house in the cornfield to meet her parents. Enrico DeGarza wouldn't talk to him. He scowled at Jennifer's mother each time she tried to be polite. The half-hour stay became an eternity. Jennifer left in tears. Between sobs, she apologized to him all the way back to the city.

That was the only time he'd been in the house, but that was enough to know that this time of year the inside would be like a new oven—sparkling clean and hotter than hell. Jennifer's mother would be cleaning while wearing a print dress that hugged her short, wide body. The grief she shared with her husband would be clothed in a white apron stained where she'd wiped her sweaty hands. Her hair would be tied in a bun with a few loose strands that hung in her face to be constantly brushed away. A small radio tuned to a local Spanish-language station would be pumping out mariachi music.

On a broken console record player behind the small Formica dining room table would be a shrine with candles, crucifix, and a beautifully framed photograph of an angelic Jennifer DeGarza, taken on the day of her quinceañera, her fifteenth birthday. Windsor had seen the picture before. It showed her in a high-collared white dress. The flowers in her dark hair matched the ones in her hands. Her smile sweet, her eyes full of hope for the future.

Jennifer was the first American-born member of her family. Two older brothers were scratching out a hard-scrabble life back in Mexico. A third was serving a life-sentence for murder in California. Her two younger sisters had just started high school when Jennifer died.

Windsor didn't recognize the children playing in the dirt. His best guess was that they were his sons' kids. If it was Enrico's job to keep an eye on them, he appeared to have lost interest in favor of a nap.

Even after Jennifer and Windsor were married, Enrico insisted on continuing to pay for her education. Windsor even tried to give her family money or buy them a better place to live. Each time Enrico refused.

"I don't need your money, gringo" the old man had said. "My beautiful Jennifer will be a famous lawyer one day. Maybe even a judge. A Supreme Court judge. She'll remember her family."

Father and daughter were the same—proud and stubborn. He knew that when he married her. He learned more a few years later when the law firm that Windsor's father had started was looking for a new associate. He offered to talk to one of the partners, Jason Todd, about hiring Jennifer. She politely, but firmly, refused.

"I want to help my people and those like them. The underprivileged. Those who are being discriminated against," she told him. Clearly, her goal was to make it on her own rather than at a blue-blood firm that did corporate law for banks, insurance companies, and private utilities.

He'd loved her already. After that he loved her even more.

Windsor sat in the hot car for another half hour. Three times he started to get out, walk across the road, and try to talk to Enrico. He could explain what he'd learned from Stetson and that he was trying to learn more. It was a nice idea but wouldn't matter to the old man. Even though they hadn't talked in a year, it was still too soon.

Instead, he picked up his phone, dialed a number from memory, and left a message.

Chapter 16

Alex Windsor parked the BMW in a pay lot on the corner of SW 2nd and Morrison. He walked a block down the street to wait in line at a food cart for a lamb and beef gyro, no lettuce, and extra tzatziki, to go. Lunch in hand, he walked two blocks east to Tom McCall Waterfront Park. Finding a bench facing the river, he sat down and pulled out his lunch. He ate and waited. Halfway through the gyro, Detective Cassie Terrace showed up with a bento box and an Evian.

"I've missed you," she said, sitting down next to him and kissing his cheek. "It was good to hear your message."

"I wasn't sure you'd come."

"I had to. You're an international man of mystery. Gone for a year, to Tibet apparently, then showing up out of nowhere."

"How'd you know?"

"Don't let those tall buildings behind us fool you. Portland is still a small place full of gossip and rumors. Given your history, you're an A-lister. Celebrity psychologist and …"

"Yeah, I know the rest."

"I'm sorry, I didn't mean it that way."

"It's okay," Windsor said, then asked, "How's Theresa?"

"She's eleven now. Soccer camp for a week then two weeks with my parents in Fresno. She'll be back to start school."

Windsor met Cassie six years earlier when she was still working patrol. She was a single mother with a four-year-old daughter and a dogged determination to be a homicide detective. On a professional level, she was all business. On a personal level, they dated for five months before he met Jennifer, including a passionate weekend in Seattle fueled by coffee and raw oysters.

Over dinner and wine on their first date he learned she was thirty-one years old, had a law degree she earned going to night school while working days as a correctional officer at a state prison for women but never took the bar exam. She used the degrees and the contacts she made during college and law school to change from a career of keeping people behind bars to putting them there. She rose quickly to detective through a combination of brains and record test scores. Being a beautiful Black woman didn't hurt, but it wouldn't have made any difference. Cassie Terrace was all business, a force of nature. Her color wasn't going to hold her back or help her get ahead. She moved to the Homicide Division about the same time Billy Broadnax killed his fifth victim.

He knew she'd been hurt by his decision to marry Jennifer, made worse by his lame attempts to explain why. As a psychologist he should have been able to deftly handle something like that, only he wasn't. After that, they ran into each other a half-dozen times at various court hearings. She was nice, but distant. What was done was done. Until the night Jennifer was killed. Cassie was the third call he made after 9-1-1 and Sam Westlake. He learned later that it was Cassie who drove him downtown the night of the murder and checked him into a boutique hotel.

"So why did you call?" Cassie asked, putting down her lunch and turning to look at him.

"I need some information. Maybe you can help me out."

"This personal or professional?"

"Both, I guess."

"And?"

"Do you think there's any chance that Billy Broadnax didn't kill Jennifer?"

Cassie looked stunned, then put her head in her hands and leaned forward. "Jesus, Alex, anything but that."

"All I need to know is if there was anything about her death that was different from the others." Windsor did his best not to sound like he was begging, when that was exactly what he was doing.

Terrace took a deep breath, the bento box and Evian forgotten on the ground between her feet. "Her death was identical to the previous seven. After Billy turned himself in, he confessed to all of them. He described in detail everything he did, how he did it, and why. Orders from God, he said. Rid the world of wanton women. The whores of Satan. None of it made sense. Not that it mattered. Each victim was killed the same way, including Jennifer. That's why she was named in the indictment along with the others. In a matter of days, Broadnax was gone, never to be heard from again … or so I thought." She reached over to squeeze his hand. "It's been a year, Alex. Don't you think it's time to let it go?"

Windsor took another bite then tossed the gyro back in the paper sack. A half dozen speed boats raced by on the river before disappearing under the Morrison Street Bridge, their wakes nearly capsizing two beleaguered-looking kayakers in flotation vests and safari hats.

"I need to know if it's possible that someone else killed her. Someone who made it look like Billy did it," Windsor said. "Just the remotest of chances. Just tell me what you think."

"Okay," she said. "The first seven murders were strictly random. There was no connection between Broadnax and any of the victims. That means they didn't know who he was, and he didn't know who they were. If there was anything different about your wife's death ... and I mean if ... it's that her death only appeared planned because everyone assumed it was in retaliation for that opinion piece you wrote."

"At the DA's request."

"Yes, but your name was on it, not his. But that's not the point. Billy Broadnax roamed all over Portland's upscale neighborhoods, sneaking through yards, peeking in windows, looking for women who were home alone. He even staked out grocery stores and bank parking lots looking for victims. That's what he told us. They were crimes of opportunity. Revenge was never part of his MO. He could have seen Jennifer at the store or at a gas station, then followed her home. Your house is off the street. No streetlights or close neighbors. It's in one of the only upscale neighborhoods where he hadn't killed anyone. It makes sense he would eventually get there. It was like he was checking boxes. He was going to run out of victims when he ran out of either neighborhoods or pages in the Bible. That's why Jennifer's murder happened the same way as the others."

"Coincidence, then?"

"I know. I know. Cops aren't supposed to believe in coincidences, but you can't rule it out. Either way, it doesn't change anything. Your wife is dead, and Billy Broadnax killed her."

One of the things that made Cassie so attractive was her honesty, even when it was brutal.

"Everything about her murder was precisely the same as all the others," Cassie said. "I don't need to tell you what that looks like. No one else could have killed her because they wouldn't have known all the things he did to his victims. They were things the public didn't know because we held back certain details for just that reason. We made sure of that. I'm sorry, Alex. I can't make it any plainer."

"You really believe that?"

"Absolutely. Those murders tore this city apart. It took months to get past it and I'm still not sure it's behind us. It was a terrible time. Riots, protests, COVID, and on top of that a serial killer loose in the city. Thank God there wasn't a trial. That would have been a circus. The way things worked out, he pleaded guilty and was gone. There's no way I or anyone else want to dredge all that up again."

A bicyclist and two in-line skaters whizzed by on the promenade in front of them. A pack of skateboarders followed, yelling obscenities, and flipping cigarette butts into the river. A half dozen panting joggers brought up the rear.

"How did Billy find his victims?" he asked.

"Like I said, he hung out in parking lots looking for women who were attractive and well dressed. He followed them home then spent several nights watching to see if they were married or lived alone and what kind of schedules they kept. He didn't know any names. Only places. He said he kept a list, but we never found it. He told us he destroyed it just before turning himself in."

"So, he was methodical? Not just mindless?"

"A little bit of both. Methodical in how he selected his victims. Mindless in what he did to them."

"So, of all the women in Portland he just happened to pick one who's married to a psychologist who just called him an impotent momma's boy in print."

"Can't rule it out."

"Is it possible the crime lab missed something at the house that night? There'd been seven murders in fourteen days. Maybe they weren't as thorough as they would've been under normal conditions."

"You were involved with the task force more than I was, Alex. You know what it was like. The crime lab boys were bouncing around town like pinballs. No sooner done with one crime scene than off to another. It got to the point where if one victim looked like the last one, then everyone knew it was another Meat Man murder. We took off from there."

"Then it's possible," he said. "Too many bodies. Too little time. It could have been someone else."

"No, Alex, it isn't possible," she shot back. "Think about it. Two maniacs roaming around little ol' Portland, Oregon, killing women in the same way at the same time. Each a perfect imitation of the other. No. It just doesn't work that way. The crime scene technicians are professionals. They know what they're doing. Things like that don't happen. Billy Broadnax killed them all."

Windsor nodded, reluctant to turn the meeting into a confrontation.

"You think it was all a coincidence. I think it's something more sinister. What if we're both wrong?"

"I'm sorry," Cassie said, she put her arm around him. "I know this is hard for you. I know what she meant to you. I don't mean to be insensitive, but you called me, remember?" She turned toward him, her leg against his, her voice soft but determined. "You've seen all the files, all the evidence. Looked at all the videos. You know what Billy did to those women, what he did to your wife. He was a different breed of serial killer. Talking dogs or space aliens had nothing to do with what he did or why. He wasn't pro-fascist or anti-fascist. He'd never heard of Proud Boys or Black Lives Matter. He didn't play video games. He didn't rape or molest his victims in any way we could find.

"There were those who believed he was exercising power over women for his own gratification. That was way too complex for Billy. He was a brute. He killed for the hell of it. He was smart enough to get away with it for two weeks and dumb enough to not know right from wrong. He did it because he wanted to. He said God told him to do it. Well, that's not any god that I know about. If someone else killed Jennifer, then they would have to be as sick as Billy. I sat across the table from him. Trust me. No two people are that sick. Not in this town anyway and not at the same time. I'm sorry."

"But you just said it yourself. The crime lab boys were all over town. They could've made a mistake. They could've overlooked something."

"Could've. Would've. Should've. Sounds to me like you're trying to convince yourself of something."

"You're right," Windsor said. "Sorry to be a pain in the ass. I was hoping that I wasn't to blame after all."

"Stop that. I told you. Billy didn't kill out of revenge. I doubt he even read your op-ed." There was a calmness in her voice now as she stroked Windsor's back. "Jennifer was just in the wrong place at the wrong time. Don't believe what they told you. The bodies were piling up. The DA and the task force were taking a lot of heat for how long it was taking to find The Meat Man. They blamed you and your opinion piece for Jennifer's death to make it easier on themselves."

"What if I'd never written it? Would Billy still be out there?"

Cassie waited to answer. "I think we would have caught him eventually, but there were still a lot of neighborhoods he hadn't gotten to."

She put her arm through his and leaned against his shoulder. "You care to tell me where this came from?"

Chapter 17

Windsor was almost too embarrassed to tell her. He knew how she would react after hearing that he was putting himself through his wife's death all over again because of some low life. Sadly, he had no choice.

"A guy named Harold Gilroy. People call him Squid. Some sort of private eye."

She sat straight up. "You mean the Harold Gilroy they found in that dumpster downtown this morning? What's he got to do with this?"

"He talked to Broadnax. Says Billy admitted to seven murders not eight. He said he had proof. I offered to pay for it. Never got the chance."

"Proof? Really? Let me tell you something about your friend, Gilroy. He had a handful of priors going back ten years, mostly for fraud and theft of services. Prior to becoming some sort of private eye, he worked in a boiler room peddling alien abduction insurance to the elderly and used cars to farm workers before spending ten days in jail for selling meth outside a high school. We found his car parked behind one of those porno places on SE 82nd. The clerk who identified him said Gilroy tried to buy his thermos thinking it was a sex toy. When they searched his car, they found a crack pipe and a new suit. When they pulled him out of that dumpster, his pockets were full of oxy and meth. That's the kind of guy Gilroy was."

"How'd he die?"

"Beaten to death. Probably with a tire iron or something like it."

Windsor nodded. "Witnesses? Suspects? Motive?"

"Too early."

"Theories?"

"None that involve Billy Broadnax."

"Since I talked to Gilroy the day he was killed one of your guys wanted to talk to me," Windsor said. "I don't remember his name, but I think he was new at this. At least he acted like it."

"Blanchett."

"Something like that."

"So, he questioned you? What did you tell him?"

"Not much. Just that Gilroy and I talked. Just not what we talked about."

"Jesus, Alex. Don't you remember anything I told you? It's not what you tell the cops that gets you in trouble, it's what you don't."

"Yeah, well, I'm telling you. It's sort of why I called you."

"This puts me in a tough spot, Alex. You know I'm going to have to share this with Blanchett."

"I didn't think of that. Sorry, but can you give me some time to figure out what's going on?"

She stopped talking and stared at the traffic moving along the interstate highway on the east bank of the river. "Okay, but not much. And if you find anything, you must let me know. Deal?"

"Deal."

They got up and walked north on the promenade toward what had become a permanent but harmless homeless camp. The nylon tents scattered around the bare ground were surrounded by dismantled bikes, plastic garbage sacks and, in one case, a potted palm sitting in a grocery cart.

"Let me give you some advice,' she said. "Don't make too much of this. Billy's been in jail for a year with nothing to do but listen to those other slime balls in there. All he may be doing is cooking up phony stories so he can get a few hours outside the walls to attend a hearing."

"What about Gilroy?"

"If he ended up dead in a tavern dumpster, then he probably wasn't a model citizen."

"You're right," Windsor said. They crossed Naito Parkway then up Ash Street toward Windsor's car. "I left town not long after the funeral. I don't know what happened with Billy other than he's in prison. At the time all I heard was his name and that he turned himself in."

Cassie sighed. "It was pretty weird. He walked into the bureau with his father and confessed to everything. That was two days before Jennifer's funeral. We questioned him for hours. Everything checked out. Detective Arnett told you all this."

Windsor nodded. "I remember."

"That's why I wasn't at Jennifer's funeral. We were still questioning him and getting ready to file charges. The heat was on to make sure everything went off without a hitch. I'm sorry. I really wanted to be there. I tried to call you, but you'd already left town."

"Thanks for that."

"After that, things moved pretty fast. Broadnax's lawyer convinced him to plead guilty. Judge Hawkins agreed and sentenced him to life without parole. It all took less than three days and out of sight to the television cameras."

"Lawyer?"

"A slick older guy from your family's firm. Strickland or Stockton. Something like that."

"Chandler Stockdale?"

"That sounds right."

"He was at the funeral. So was Judge Hawkins. They didn't say anything about him being Billy's lawyer." Windsor thought for a few moments. "Then, again, we didn't talk."

Cassie shrugged. "Stockdale would have known what was going on. Probably not Hawkins, though. All she did was make it clear that someone reputable take the case so there wouldn't be any criticism that Billy didn't have adequate representation or that he was railroaded somehow. She wanted no grousing when they hustled him off to prison for the rest of his miserable life. Apparently, this Stockdale is above reproach."

"What made Billy turn himself in?"

"His father. Nice old guy from what I hear. I didn't question him. Others did, but I read the reports. He figured out what Billy had been doing and convinced him to surrender."

"So, the evidence from my garage was never used?"

"I know what you're thinking. Don't go there. It's over."

He kissed Cassie on the cheek and thanked her. "I better go," he said. They were standing at a Max stop waiting for a train to take her back downtown to her office.

"Would you mind getting Gilroy's address for me? You can text it."

"Ever heard of the internet?"

"I tried that. Nothing."

"You're not going to let this go, are you?"

Windsor shrugged. "Not right away."

"Okay, I'll take care of it, but you owe me one," she said. "And Alex, you know where I live if you need to talk."

Windsor nodded. "One more thing. If you find anything new when you look at Jennifer's file, will you let me know?"

"What makes you think I'll look?"

"You're too good not to."

Chapter 18

North Earle Street was a part of Portland that didn't show up in the chamber of commerce brochures or on internet travel sites. At best, it was a place to be avoided at all costs if you valued your life and possessions. If it popped up at all it was on the evening news after another senseless drive-by shooting or family squabble that ended in gunfire and the arrival of Child Protective Services. Shots of crime-scene tape stretching across the street, a body under a sheet, and a grieving mother screaming for justice were wrapped up in a two-minute clip, then quickly forgotten.

While only a block long, North Earle Street was a dreary collection of small low-rent houses and a two-story apartment building catering to those life had left behind. Most of the places dating from World War II might have been nice little bungalows at one time. Not anymore. They featured dusty porches, dirty or broken windows, and overgrown yards occupied by cannibalized cars or, ironically, a lawn mower. The only thing more abundant than abandoned shopping carts was the ornate graffiti that covered the boarded-up windows on three abandoned houses. To Windsor, it looked like a permanent stop for those whose goal in life was die in the street or win the lottery, the chances of the former being far ahead of the latter.

In other words, a place known to those who lived there and the police.

The address of Harold Gilroy's studio apartment was at the end of a weed-filled driveway behind a run-down, wanna-be Cape Cod. Flannel bed sheets covered windows from the inside. Not that it mattered because the apartment's front door was propped open with a broom. Strewn across a small patch of dirt-brown front lawn were a half dozen empty boxes and the same number of plastic garbage sacks.

Windsor checked the address again in the text message from Cassie Terrace. If this wasn't the place, then at least he was close. Only one way to find out.

He knocked on the splintered door frame after easing past a rusted-out Buick slumping in the gravel driveway with the trunk open. On the third knock, a large woman in a jungle-print muumuu, black loafers, and white anklets seemed to appear like a phantom from the interior. She was in her mid-sixties, with blue plastic rollers hanging from the ends of stringy gray hair. The bags under her bloodshot eyes dissolved into a cascade of wrinkles that fell across her cheeks, chin, and neck like melted candle wax. Tiny flakes of something white clung to thin hairs on her upper lip. When she approached the door, it was in a practiced walk that was a side-to-side motion apparently designed to prevent her massive thighs from rubbing against each other.

"Is this Harold Gilroy's apartment?" Windsor said, still standing in the doorway.

"He's not here and he's not coming back."

"And you are?"

"His mother."

Windsor looked past her into the cave-like apartment. "I talked to your son before he was killed. I'm sorry for what happened to him. He seemed like a nice person."

"My son was a shit, mister." She paused and gave him a sad, frustrated look. "Sorry. It's been a bad couple of days. Anyway, it was a nice thing for you to say." She squinted at Windsor. "You a reporter or something?"

"Or something." Windsor took a careful step inside the door and glanced around. "I'd only met him a few times, including just a couple of days ago. I've read the paper. The story about his murder made the evening news."

"News for you maybe. A hell of a lot of work for me." She motioned toward the apartment behind her. "Look at this pigsty? I'll be here all-day cleaning this up because if I don't then I won't get the deposit back. Damn landlords." She eyed the apartment once more and sighed. "I don't know why you're here, but I really don't have time to talk."

When she turned and walked away, the dark apartment swallowed her up. Free of any concern that he was interrupting a mother's grief, Windsor jumped in right behind her. Moldy dishes, dirty clothes, empty pizza boxes, and countless pop cans littered the one-room apartment. It all spilled over into a kitchen area that was nothing more than a sink, a microwave, and a cupboard. Gray sheets, a frayed wool blanket, and wrinkled clothes lay balled up in the center of a Murphy bed. Pulled down from the wall, it nearly bumped up against the window on the other side of the room.

The only signs of neatness were the three pairs of expensive, highly polished dress shoes carefully lined up on the floor of a small, doorless closet. On the hangers above it were three suits, each frayed around the cuffs and turned from white to a dingy gray. Windsor imagined Squid sitting on the end of his bed in dirty underwear cooking ramen noodles while compulsively shining his Cole-Haans.

The old woman ignored him, intent on pawing through the drawers of a cheap dresser with a cracked mirror on top.

"Did you know what Harold did for a living, Mrs. Gilroy?" he asked.

"No, and the name's not Gilroy. It's Cowles. Edna Cowles. Harold came from my first marriage." She raised up slightly to look at Windsor. "But whatever he did it probably wasn't anything worthwhile. He was never much to brag about. Too much like his father, the no-good son of a bitch."

"When was the last time you saw him?"

"My husband?"

Windsor took a deep breath. "No, your son."

She stopped what she was doing to think. "Father's Day about two years ago. He thought it was Mother's Day. He never could keep them straight. He called a couple of times since then asking for money. I don't remember exactly when. Not that it matters. I don't have any."

"Did he ever mention who he worked for?"

"You mean recently? No. All I remember is that he told me once he was selling some kind of insurance or some nonsense. If he was, he must not have been very good at it because all he ever wanted from me was money. If you ask me, he didn't have a job. Never did. At least not something most people would consider a job."

"Harold told me he was a private investigator. That ring a bell?"

That earned a snort from Edna Cowles. "The only thing Harold ever investigated were strip clubs and personal ads."

When she bent almost double to pull open the next to bottom drawer of the dresser Windsor took a quick look around the apartment. If there were any clues about who killed Gilroy or why, he was not going to find it in the tangle of soiled sheets, dirty dishes, and polished shoes.

"Did he ever mention anyone named Broadnax?"

"Nope," she muttered, shutting one drawer and bending lower to open another before realizing that the dresser was empty because most of Squid's belongings were strewn around the room.

"Christ," she said, turning to survey the bed and the kitchen beyond. She moved past Windsor to begin angrily stuffing sheets, blankets, and clothes into a green garbage sack. Once it was full, she walked across the room to throw it out the door into the yard.

"Did Harold leave any documents around? Papers? Maybe a laptop? Anything like that?"

Edna Cowles looked around at the mess and shook her head. "Not that I've seen."

"So, you probably don't know if Harold had been out to the state penitentiary recently." When the old woman looked confused, Windsor quickly added, "To visit, I mean?"

That got her attention. "Funny you should ask," she said, pulling an envelope from the pocket of her muumuu and handing it to Windsor. "I did find this on the top of the dresser." She nodded to her right. "It was in among a bunch of unpaid bills. I kept it because it looked sort of official."

Windsor took the envelope. It was addressed to Harold Gilroy and from the Office of the Superintendent of the Oregon State Penitentiary. He opened it, pulled out the letter, and read it while Edna Cowles went back to stuffing more clothes into garbage sacks. In needlessly obscure bureaucratic language, the letter confirmed Gilroy's request to meet with William Charles Broadnax, inmate number 598321D, at three p.m. on July twenty-fourth. Windsor did the math. That was more than two weeks ago.

"May I have this?" he asked.

"Go ahead. It's one less thing to clean up," she said, then paused for a few seconds.

"What did you say your name was?"

"Windsor, Alex Windsor. I'm just an acquaintance. Sorry to bother you. Thanks for your help. I'll let you get back to what you're doing."

She shrugged while surveying the mess that had been her son's life.

Driving out of Earle Street, Windsor passed a van with the Channel 5 logo on the side and a man in the passenger seat staring at a laptop.

Chapter 19

"Let me get this straight, Dr. Windsor," David Weathers, the public information officer for the state Department of Corrections, said. "You want to know if Gilroy was here. Is this a joke?"

Weathers was a defrocked wire service reporter who left behind the long hours, short pay, and hectic workplace for a comfortable nine-to-five job at the prison. It came with health insurance, four weeks paid vacation each year, and a generous public employee pension. When Windsor was still practicing, Weathers had helped arrange visits for reporters who wanted to talk to some of his clients. He was also one of the familiar faces at Jennifer's funeral.

"No," Windsor said. He was at The Ridge with his cellphone and a beer. "I just need to know whether Harold Gilroy visited Billy Broadnax at three o'clock on July twenty-fourth."

"Is this business or personal?"

"Does it matter?"

"As a matter of fact, it does."

"It's personal," Windsor said. "I won't lie to you. But it's big-time personal. It has to do with Jennifer's death."

"Let me see what I can do," Weathers said, then put Windsor on hold. He came back on the line a few minutes later to confirm Gilroy's visit to Broadnax. "It was arranged by a clerk in visitor services. The visit lasted a little more than an hour. No one knows what they talked about. Gilroy left without saying anything to anybody."

"Is Chandler Stockdale still Broadnax's attorney?"

He could hear Weathers flipping pages. "Yes."

"Was it cleared with him?"

Weathers paused. "Not that I can tell."

"How does that work?"

"Well, it shouldn't. Sometimes it happens. It's possible the request went straight to Broadnax. He should have contacted his attorney. Sounds like he didn't."

"Would you deliver a message to Broadnax for me?" Windsor said. "Tell him that Harold Gilroy is dead and that I'd like to talk to him about it. And David, I'd appreciate any kind of work around to keep Broadnax's lawyer out of it."

"Really, Alex?" he said. "You want to talk to your wife's killer. That's not going to go over well. Anything to do with Broadnax is touchy. This is beyond that."

"You know I wouldn't ask if it wasn't important."

It took a few seconds for Weathers to answer. "You know the drill. I need some basic information, then give me some time to figure this out. By the way, who's this Gilroy guy?"

"It's a long story, David, but it's important I talk to Broadnax."

Windsor hung up and shivered at the thought of going face to face with his wife's killer, assuming he was. Not that he had a choice. Gilroy was out of the picture and, presumably, so was whatever evidence he had, if any. The only road left was to go right to the source. That road led right through David Weathers. Now, all he could do was wait.

Windsor drained the last of his beer and motioned to Bud Schwartz for another, then glanced up at the television over the bar. Windsor paid little attention to local television news. He found it superficial and preoccupied with weather, traffic, and gadgets like helicopters, drones, and live shots from unmanned cameras atop buildings with corporate names. He wouldn't have been watching the news at all that night if the regulars at the bar hadn't started yelling when Schwartz's dumpster flashed across the screen.

"That's a damn nice dumpster, Bud," one of the customers said.

"Best I've ever seen," joked another.

"Reminds me of one up on 23rd where I spent the night once," said a third. "It was outside this Italian place. Woke up wrapped in fettucine." That earned a bar full of laughs.

"That's not even the same one," Bud said. "The police hauled the real one away. Evidence, I guess. The garbage company brought one in this morning."

After a lingering shot of the replacement dumpster, the camera showed the front of The Ridge and the small parking lot next door. A beleaguered looking police spokesperson babbled about a perpetrator, a deceased, and an on-going investigation.

Windsor thought the reporter asking the questions and doing the stand-up looked familiar.

"All we know about Harold Gilroy tonight is that he was a private investigator with an obsession for expensive shoes," the reporter said. "Those shoes are missing. That means that the dead man's obsession may have cost him his life. This is Rich Raymond in downtown Portland for Channel 5 News."

Windsor recognized Raymond as the hyperactive reporter in the aviator glasses and safari jacket who dominated the news conferences called by police during The Meat Man murders. Seeing him now, all Windsor could do was quietly groan.

Before the murders started, he'd heard from other reporters that Channel 5 had hired Raymond to up its ratings. Raymond's initial contribution to television journalism was a thirty-minute prime-time special about a night in the life of an underage male prostitute. When the station's ratings jumped and its advertising revenue with it, Raymond went on the hunt for new and more lurid stories. Along the way, he picked up the nickname "Filthy Rich" from a media reporter for one of the city's alternative weeklies.

"Rich, we understand that a name familiar to many Portlanders has popped up in connection with this case. Tell us about it." The question came from an over-caffeinated blonde anchor back in the studio.

"That's right, Jillian. Today I talked with Edna Cowles, the mother of the victim, Harold Gilroy. She told me that Alex Windsor had also talked to her about her son's death. That would be Dr. Alex Windsor, the forensic psychologist whose wife was the Meat Man's eighth and final victim. Many believe her murder was an act of revenge by Broadnax for an op-ed piece Windsor wrote describing the killer as a sexually repressed mama's boy."

"Something tells us we're going to hear a lot more from you about this story," Jillian said.

"You can bet on it."

Everyone at the bar turned to look at Windsor, but he was already gone, vanished out the back door at the first mention of his name.

Chapter 20

The walk from her mother's house to the convenience store was the only time Rebecca Roberts had to herself.

Living at home again was hard enough, but the older her son Danny got the more demanding he became. She loved the little four-year-old, but there were times when she just wanted to be alone. This was it: A fifteen-block walk to work five nights a week. It took twenty or twenty-five minutes, more if she left early and walked slower.

Only this time there was nothing calming about it. Seeing Matthew again had only made things more difficult. Her ex-husband was as demanding as Danny and about as mature. Too controlling, short-tempered, almost unemployable. He hated her blue-dyed hair and her pancake makeup, but who cared? At least he didn't know about her tattoo and where it was. That would have sent him over the edge.

Rebecca couldn't believe that he'd come back to town. It was not a good time. There was Danny, plus she was living with her mother. She had a miserable job working the graveyard shift at a convenience store in a part of town where every customer looked like they wanted to either buy a Red Bull, kill her or both.

Then there was that creepy little private detective who promised her all that money.

She pulled her ex-husband's note from the pocket of her jeans and read it again. The one he had given her when he appeared out of nowhere earlier in the day while she and Danny were playing in the front yard.

"Come see me, baby, please?" he had said before handing her the note. He left without even saying hello to Danny. No surprise there. Because he wasn't Danny's father, he'd always resented the little guy and her along with him.

She'd told him no, she didn't want to see him, but kept the note just in case her resolve melted like it always did with him. She knew the truth but hated to say it: Even life with him would be better than her old room in her mother's house and a shit job. It all made her hate her life even more than she already did.

The ninety-degree day lingered into the late evening. Windows and doors on most of the houses along the street were open in the hope of catching a light breeze to cool things off. Porch lights glowed. Fans whirred. Paunchy working-class heroes and their wives sat on the steps or inside watching television. Others sat in lawn chairs in the front yard drinking beer and smoking dope.

Everything about her life—where she lived and where she worked--was nothing like she imagined. Growing up, she dreamed of handsome men with money, nice cars, and a condo on the river. She would have a good job at Nordstrom or Banana Republic. She would make enough to have an apartment of her own, day care for Danny, and a car. Maybe not a new car, but a nice one—a Honda or Toyota. Now, she was beginning to think that it would never happen. She had made too many mistakes. The time had gone by too fast. It reminded her of the lyrics from an album Matthew used to play over and over again: "No one told you when to run. You missed the starting gun."

On her walk to work Rebecca always tried her best to avoid the vacant lot that backed up against the rear of a discount sporting goods store that anchored a low-rent strip mall. She usually jogged over a block just to be safe, but tonight that would mean being late to work. The manager was always there when the shifts changed. He had already threatened to fire her if she was late again. She wanted to tell him to fuck off, but that would only make things worse. As much as she hated the job, she couldn't afford to lose it. Living at home and having her mother provide day care for Danny she finally had a little money to spend. Nothing like what she made at the receptionist position she had at that psychiatrist's office. That had been perfect. The people were nice. She enjoyed the work. The money was decent.

Then she screwed it up.

Thinking about it only brought up memories of all the other mistakes she'd made, including listening to that weird little Gilroy guy. Just thinking about him made her cringe and hug herself despite the warm night. She wished she'd never met him, never agreed to steal copies of those files he wanted. He made it all sound so easy. They were just copies, he'd said. You're not stealing the originals, he'd said. Just do what I say and in a few weeks you'll have money for all those things you want, he'd said. She could go on dates, maybe meet someone nice. Find a real life for herself.

What bullshit, she thought.

Gilroy had even given her money to tide her over. Too bad she'd already spent most of it believing his line about more on the way. It wasn't. She'd ended up with nothing. She was fired for copying the files. Now Gilroy was dead.

Damn, she thought, why can't I catch a break?

At least she still had the copies of those reports he wanted. She just didn't know what to do with them. She tried reading them but didn't understand all of what they said. She recognized the name Broadnax as someone who killed some people. The rest was complicated psychiatric stuff and some sort of timeline. Gilroy said they were important and worth a lot of money. All she had to do was be patient until he came to get them. That, he'd said, is when the money starts rolling in. Rolling in from where and from who? No one she knew. All she could think to do was keep them in a box in her bedroom and wait to see if anything happened, whenever that was. Probably never, the way things were going.

So, here she was walking through the dark streets of east Portland to a job selling cigarettes and Twinkies to deadbeats.

Afraid of being late to work, she had no choice but to cut through the parking lot. It was only a few hundred feet to the streetlights on the other side of the block. After that she'd be safe and only two blocks away from work. Halfway across the dark lot, she was sure everything would be all right. She didn't notice the car sitting in the dark until the headlights came on and nearly blinded her. She shielded her eyes as the car moved closer. She backed up a few steps, thinking she should run.

Instead, she froze.

"Excuse me, miss. Sorry to bother you, but I'm lost." The man in the car leaned out the window. "I'm trying to find SE Powell. I need to get out to the freeway."

Rebecca couldn't tell his age. He was wearing tinted glasses and a baseball cap with a logo on the front she couldn't see. His voice was older and sort of hoarse, but warm and friendly enough that she relaxed a bit.

"Six blocks north," she said, pointing. "Then turn left."

"Thanks." He started to drive away then stopped. "I'm sorry. I must have startled you. I pulled in here to read my street map. The problem is maps aren't very good if you don't know where you are in the first place."

"The streets around here can be a little confusing," she said.

"Especially if you're just passing through. Thanks again for the help." He started to drive away again, then stopped. "Say, can I give you a lift?"

The encounter with the man in the car had put her even further behind schedule. If he drove her the last two blocks, she'd might make it in time and not lose her job.

"Sure. Thanks." Rebecca walked around to the passenger side of the black Taurus and got in.

Chapter 21

On cold winter nights Windsor would sit in front of the cabin's fireplace drinking whiskey while waiting for the oxycodone to kick in. He tried thinking deep thoughts about paths not taken and what to do with life after causing the death of someone you loved. They were bitter and sometimes enlightening conversations with his inner self that served little purpose other than reminding him of the pistol above the refrigerator and the pills in the bathroom cabinet behind the shattered mirror that made him look the way he felt.

He knew that if he died, it really wouldn't matter. He had a will, but it left everything to Jennifer. The only relative he knew about was the spinster aunt who took him in after his parents were killed. She'd died five years earlier. Sam Westlake didn't need money. With Windsor gone, all Sam would lose was a fishing companion and someone to take care of his dog when he was away from the ranch. Still, leaving him something would be a way of saying thanks for getting him away from Portland and into an icy trout stream.

Maybe what was left of his money and property after the lawyers and accountants were through would eventually fall to Jennifer's family. God knows they could use it. He smiled thinking about the look on Enrico DeGarza's face when he learned he'd just got an eight-figure inheritance. All Windsor knew was that the lawyers would figure it out. Whatever they did was fine with him. Until then he would drink, stare at the fire, and pray for a rising sun to chase the ghosts away.

A lot of those thoughts disappeared when he realized the peace and solitude that comes with standing ass-deep in cold water. It worked to the extent that it took his mind off guns and pills, but only up to a point. There was no fishing at night and hanging out with Sam playing cribbage was no substitute for what restores body and soul. Looking back on it, Arnie Stetson showing up with rumors about Squid Gilroy and Billy Broadnax may have been just what he needed. Something that broke the spiral of highs while fishing and lows while not.

All of that and more explained why he was standing at Cassie Terrace's front door with two bottles of wine.

"Peace offering," he said, holding up the bottles, one red, one white. "I might have been a little pushy earlier today. Besides, you did say if I ever wanted to talk."

She looked at the two bottles of wine. "You must want to do a lot of talking."

"A whole year's worth."

Chapter 22

Cassie Terrace took the two bottles and kissed him on the cheek. "I don't remember you being much of the wine type. Would scotch suit you better?"

Windsor gave her a sheepish nod. "Thanks."

Cassie gave Windsor a smile he hadn't seen since their weekend in Seattle. "Make yourself comfortable," she said, taking the wine, turning off PBS, folding up the file she'd been reading, and heading toward the kitchen. She came back a few minutes later with a twelve-year-old bottle of The Macallan and two crystal whiskey glasses. Windsor took a sip.

"You've upped your game when it comes to scotch," he said. "I remember you as more of the blended kind of woman."

"Promotions have their advantages."

"You should be proud."

She nodded, then quickly changed the subject. "I heard your name on the news tonight." She leaned back against the opposite end of the couch, stretching her legs until her feet rested against his thigh. "Doesn't take you long, does it?"

Windsor shrugged. "It's not the way I want it."

"That reporter, something Raymond. A bottom feeder but he makes money for the station. At least that's the word on the street. I couldn't care less. I watched tonight because I got a heads-up that your name was going to pop up. Other than that, I tuned him out a year ago after the way the station handled Jennifer's murder."

Windsor gave her a questioning look.

Cassie gave him one of those "I'm sorry" looks. "I guess you didn't see it," she said.

"See what?"

Fortified with more of The Macallan, she told him how Rich Raymond claimed that someone had sent him a blurry cellphone video taken in Windsor's garage sometime between when he found Jennifer's body and when the forensics guys arrived. The station hyped it for a couple of days.

"The public affairs people tried to talk them out of airing it," she said, "telling them the video had to be fake. Even the chief and the mayor got involved. The station refused to budge."

"And?"

"Turned out it was a hoax, and not the first time, apparently. After the piece aired, we found out that he had a similar problem back east with staging phony crime scenes. He moved on before being fired. That's how he ended up out here. It looked to us like he was just up to his old tricks again. We complained to the station, but they didn't seem interested in doing much about it. The news director said there was no firm evidence it was fake and, if it was, he blamed Raymond's sources rather than Raymond."

"Apparently he's still covering crime."

"Not with our help. Now, when he calls, we feed stories to other stations. It doesn't always work."

Windsor refused to let the news of the video bother him. "It's television," he said with a shrug. "That's just the way it works."

Sipping the scotch in silence, Windsor tried to control his nerves and not feel like it was a first date. Sam Westlake had been the only person he'd spent any time with during the last year. Being around a woman, especially one like Cassie, felt odd.

He knew so much about her in so many ways.

"So," she said. "Tell me about Tibet."

Windsor smiled and shook his head. "I don't know where that got started. I was never in Tibet. I hate traveling. You know that. I was in Central Oregon." Windsor told her everything about Pine Mountain Ranch. The nights lost in the fog of Bushmills and pills. How he pulled himself most of the way out of the abyss by learning about the river and how to fish. He described the fish he caught: Rainbow trout, Bull trout, and Dolly Vardens.

"The abyss. How was it?" she asked.

"Deep. Dark. Lonely."

"What did you find?"

"Pills, whiskey, a gun, thoughts of suicide."

"What changed?"

"Sam, his dog, fly fishing. I know. Sounds corny, like some Hallmark movie. But it's true. Standing in cold water for hours turned out to be better than putting a gun to my head."

"And now?"

He had to think for a moment. "Let me get back to you."

"Fair enough. I'm just glad you're back." She leaned over to kiss him on the cheek, then quickly changed subjects. "Now, tell me about this cabin."

"Pretty Spartan. One room divided by a half wall. Bed on one side. Living room on the other. Nice fireplace. Functional kitchen. Front porch with a rocker. Great view."

"That's it?"

He thought about describing the shattered mirror in the bathroom and how looking into it made him feel, but he figured that by now she pretty much got the point.

"You don't like talking about it, do you?" When he nodded, she changed the subject. "Any luck getting in to see Billy Broadnax?"

Windsor smiled. "Nothing stays secret for long, does it?"

"Not when it comes to him."

"Broadnax talked with Gilroy. That much I know is true. What I don't know is whether Gilroy was telling the truth about what he learned, or if Broadnax was just making things up. Only one way to find out."

"Talk to Billy."

Windsor nodded then did some damage to the scotch.

A look of sympathy followed her sigh. "And when you do?"

He scanned her face to make sure she wasn't making fun of him. She wasn't. "I'll figure that out when the time comes. He won't be the first killer I've talked to. Just the worst."

"You're not just an objective observer. Aren't there ethical issues in play here?"

"Marginal. Billy's not my patient. All I can do is ask to see him. If he says no, then that puts an end to it."

"I just wish there was something I could say or do that would convince you to forget the whole thing. Go back to your cabin. Fish with your friend."

Windsor knew it was too late for that but didn't tell her. With Gilroy dead, Billy Broadnax loomed over everything—even from the prison where he would spend the rest of his life.

"Care to put in a good word to get me in to see Broadnax?"

"Not a chance."

"Kind of what I thought."

"We went over most of this at lunch," she said, moving closer to him. "You want to tell me why you're really here."

They had been lovers once. He wanted to believe that it had nothing to do with why he was there, but it wasn't working. No way would it work for her. He was lost and lonely. The house on Royal Oak Way empty without Jennifer and forever sullied by what happened to her. It was like living in one of those movies where some couple buys their dream house only to find out it's haunted by a family of murderous demons.

"Do I really have to explain?" he said.

She moved the length of the couch, draped one leg over his knee and an arm around his neck.

"So, this Sam person and you are still good friends?" Cassie said. Her lips were suddenly close to his ear. The memories of their weekend in Seattle drifted back to him along with the faint scent of scotch.

"He saved my life," Windsor said. "He and those fly fishing books he left on purpose for me to find."

"Tell me more about these fish you caught." Her whiskey-scented breath warm against his neck. "What did you call them? Dolly Parton?" She ran a finger down his cheek.

"Not Parton. Varden. Dolly Varden."

"How big are these … Vardens?" Her tongue went in his ear.

"Twenty inches. Maybe more."

"Ooooh. Really?"

"Aggressive, strong, arrogant, but sort of dumb and ugly."

"I know that type." Her tongue disappeared into his mouth.

He took her hand and pulled her up. "Which way?"

She gave him a long deep kiss. "Follow me."

Windsor woke up on the second ring and reached instinctively for his telephone. All he found was Cassie's naked breast—warm, firm, and more than a handful. He had to let go when she sat up on the side of the bed and put her phone to her ear.

When he ran his hand down her back it felt tense. The call was business.

"The lot behind a sporting goods store. Text me the address." she said into the phone. "Give me an hour."

She turned around to lay across Windsor's chest. She smelled of sex and sleep. All he wanted to do was spend the day there with her, getting lost in her, regaining some feeling of humanity.

"Work?" he asked.

"Yes. A young girl. Dead in a parking lot on the east side. But that's not all of it. She was beaten to death with what appears to be a tire iron."

"Just like Gilroy."

"Could be."

Chapter 23

Sitting in parking lots. Walking the malls. Watching. Waiting. Looking for the right woman. She had to buy food at the best grocery stores, carry garment bags out of upscale department stores, drive expensive cars, and live in one of the city's elite neighborhoods. That's when he felt most alive, most in control, most committed to ridding the world of harlots who sleep with money-grubbing sons of Satan.

He'd watched YouTube videos and, as much as he was able, read books. From it all, he'd learned about what happens when evidence is left behind. That's why he didn't molest them, didn't caress their naked bodies, wore gloves. He'd even shaved his head before each killing so as not to leave hair behind. It was all an attempt to protect himself against doing anything that would lead the police to him.

Once he'd chosen his victims, he spent days carefully writing down everything he knew about them. He'd made three lists: What to do, what not to do, and when to do it. Then he memorized each one. Satisfied that he could repeat each step over and over again, he was ready. The hunt began.

The first victim was in some ways both the hardest and easiest. He saw her loading groceries into the back of a Mercedes SUV outside a Zupan's. She was perfect: a long, narrow face, expensive glasses with large, dark frames covering cat-like eyes, a slim figure in a business suit. Her legs long and shapely. Her dark hair in a neat ponytail.

That was the moment. She was the one. It all started with her. He remembered gripping the steering wheel hard as she backed out of the parking spot and drove past him. Now, he'd said to himself, starting the pickup and following her through the city into a leafy upscale neighborhood on the east side of the river. He parked a block away and waited. Two hours later a man got in an Audi sedan and drove away. An hour after that he was standing across the street in the shadows of a towering elm. When the first floor went dark and lights on the second floor came on, he crossed the street and disappeared down a set of steep steps on the side of the house.

After that, he followed his own directions … step by step. Each carefully timed to happen in a rapid-fire sequence. He had written it all down. Just follow the schedule.

Billy Broadnax fought to remember, to savor, every moment of that first night and the ones that quickly followed. Only it was getting harder and harder. The women, the houses, what he did, and how he did it. They were all running together. Since they were all the same, it should have been easy to remember. Only it wasn't. There were too many too fast. He should have taken souvenirs to help him remember, but that wasn't on the lists he'd made.

He always knew that someday he'd be caught and convicted of murder, but eventually the world would realize he was doing the Lord's work. It was all right there in that Bible that girl had given him. Even though he struggled to read it, the very first words laid everything out. Every page a road map. The justifications leaping off the paper at him.

"In the beginning …"

"The Lord saw that the wickedness of man was great on the earth."

"… the earth was filled with violence."

"Let us make a name for ourselves."

"I will make your descendants as the dust of the earth."

"And the fear of you and the terror of you shall be on every beast on the earth."

The words made him accept the fact that he would spend a little time in prison, but only until the lawyers and the judges came to understand what he'd done and why. He would show them the Bible and read from it. Carefully explaining how he'd been guided by God's hand. How what he had done made the world a better place, ridding it of evil and sin.

But he never got the chance.

Now, he was beginning to lose faith. He believed at the time that what he was doing was the right thing. Now he was beginning to think he might have been wrong. He'd been wrong about things before … a lot of things.

It took Billy Broadnax a while to shake the past out of his head and try to deal with the present. He remembered Harold Gilroy as a little guy with shiny shoes, white suit, and ponytail who wrote a letter that said there was a way he could get out of prison. They met and talked, then he disappeared. There were no more letters or phone calls about appeals, court dates or freedom. All he could do lately was hang his head and stare at his prison-issue slippers.

"A doctor named Windsor wants to see you," said the guard. He was standing outside the bars of Billy's cell. "Do you want to see him?"

A pained-looked crossed Billy's face. He no longer liked making decisions. He no longer felt in control. All those mistakes made him afraid to make any more. A year in this place and he was losing all connection to the outside world. He had made decisions before but knew now that they were wrong. Exciting and satisfying yes, but wrong. That's why he was in prison. He knew now that killing so many women in such a short period of time was wrong. He should've waited longer between killings. One a week, maybe, or one a month. Let people forget about one before doing another. That way, maybe no one would have noticed, and he wouldn't be in prison. Only he couldn't help himself. He knew where each one worked, shopped, and lived. He checked them off like items on a grocery list.

Now he was in prison. He hated this place. Everything was bad. The food, the people, the cells, the odors. It was hard to sleep because the lights were always on. Voices echoed off the steel and concrete. Trays rattled in the kitchen. Shouts of "fuck you" applied to everything and everybody. The clothes were all the same. Exercise time too short. Every time he got his cell just the way he wanted it the guards would show up, make him pack it all up, and move him to another one. Other than that, there was nothing to do except sit on his bed twenty-three hours a day. There were books, but he didn't read well. Other inmates had magazines, but they made him feel dirty. He'd had a Bible once but couldn't remember what happened to it. Maybe his father had it.

He didn't miss his mother. She beat him and yelled at him until he got older and bigger. Then she stopped. He did miss his father. He even missed the bed pans at the nursing home where he'd worked. They used to make him sick. Now, he'd give anything to see one again or to sleep on that cot in the little room he liked to call his office.

The only nice thing about prison was Ng. The other inmates call him "femboy" and other names Billy didn't understand. All Billy knew was that he liked Ng because he showed him how to do things he'd never thought of or the girlfriends he had wouldn't do. All Ng asked for in exchange was protection from the white racists and Hispanic gangs. Still, getting out of prison was more important than Ng. That's why he agreed to see Gilroy. Billy also knew that if he wanted out, he would have to make better decisions.

"Well?" the guard said.

"What do you think?" Billy said.

"I think you're a fucking moron, but that's beside the point." He held a form and a pen. "If you want to see this guy, then sign here. If not, then we're done."

"Okay." Billy said, his voice high and childlike.

Chapter 24

Windsor was sitting at a Starbucks in the Pearl District when David Weathers called to say Billy Broadnax had agreed to see him.

"When?" Windsor asked, putting down the newspaper.

"Name it. It's not like Billy has a full calendar."

"How did you pull it off?"

"Billy signed a release form that waived the need to contact his attorney. He just didn't know what he was signing. Let's just call it a work around."

"So, no Stockdale."

"We'll let him know after your visit. He'll raise hell. We'll apologize. Promise to do better. It will all go away in a few days if you get this over with as fast as you can."

"Tell Billy I'm on my way."

"Remember, if you want to get out of there without being shot or locked up don't wear blue," Weathers said, then hung up.

Two hours later Windsor was emptying his pockets, signing forms, being frisked, and walking through a metal detector or two. After that was a series of jail doors. The one in front opened only after the one in back slammed shut. He'd been through this before. Still, the unmistakable sound of metal against metal was always unnerving. It carried a certain finality about it, as if going in carried no guarantee of coming out.

A guard led him into a ten-by-twelve room with concrete walls and a metal table bolted to the floor. He sat alone for twenty minutes wondering what would happen if there was a mix up in the paperwork and he became a permanent resident. He was still contemplating life behind bars when Billy showed up wearing faded blue jeans and a matching shirt with "OSP" stenciled over the pocket. The shirt looked two sizes too big, the pants six inches too short. The shackles on his ankles and the handcuffs on his wrists were attached to heavy belly chains that rattled as he shuffled, penguin-like, in the door. A guard pushed Billy into the chair on the other side of the table. While another guard watched, he used a short length of chain to fasten Billy's handcuffs to a metal ring embedded in the floor. Unable to raise his hands above his waist, Billy sat slightly hunched over, his arms resting on the arms of the chair. The guard checked the chains two more times, handed Billy a plastic water bottle then backed into a corner to stand at attention, his hand on a black wooden club. The other guard left to stand outside the door.

Windsor had spent countless hours wondering what he would do if he ever met Broadnax face to face. What was he supposed to feel? Anger? Sadness? Disgust? Maybe the satisfaction of knowing that someone like Broadnax was going to spend the rest of his life behind bars was enough. Maybe not.

Now, staring down the length of the table at Billy, any emotions he'd held inside for so long refused to well up. Whatever he'd once thought about being alone with his wife's killer now lay dormant. He'd tried talking to Sam about it, but the old man just nodded or changed the subject to fishing. It was Sam's way of saying get over it, what is done is done. Then Arnie Stetson showed up and changed everything. The sharp edge of hatred was somehow dulled. His doubts didn't make Broadnax any less of a killer. It only made Windsor less the vengeful victim.

During the long booze-and-pill-filled nights at Sam's ranch, he'd created a vivid mental image of Billy as a cold, methodical predator capable of unspeakable horrors while eluding police. A shrewd, ingenious killer who carefully stalked his victims and attacked when they were most vulnerable. What he saw, instead, was something short of a grotesque half-wit, one drool away from catatonic. Cassie Terrace said Billy was meticulous in carrying out his crimes. He believed her at the time. Suddenly he wasn't so sure.

Billy was tall, nearly six-and-a-half feet, but thin and wiry. Veins stood out on his forearms and neck. On his shaved head was an ornate tattoo of a fire-breathing dragon, its long tail curled around a naked woman with perfect breasts and flowing dark hair. Snakes tattooed on his forearms disappeared up the sleeve of his prison shirt, reappearing above the collar with fangs and a forked tongue.

Billy reached up as far as the chains would let him to move the water bottle to the left side of the table, stared at it for a few seconds, then moved it to the right side. After a few more seconds he set it in front of him, rotating it a few times until the label was perfectly centered. Then, he repeated it all over again—left, right, center.

Windsor had seen this before in other patients—OCD, obsessive-compulsive disorder: constant and repetitive obsession; unnecessary desires to carry out certain behaviors, or compulsions; unreasonable actions that can't be stopped. Billy had been meticulous in his killing. He was being just as meticulous with a water bottle.

"Who are you?" Broadnax said, apparently finally satisfied the bottle was where it needed to be.

The question could have been as much for himself as for Windsor. Whoever it was for the words came out as a low, guttural mumble through fleshy lips that barely moved when he talked. His half-lidded eyes never left the water bottle except to glance at Windsor or look with confusion at his shackled wrists.

Windsor had seen his share of prison inmates. Most professed innocence. Others accepted their fate, but blamed society. They all tried to act prison-tough because that's how to survive in a maximum-security penitentiary. Any sign of weakness led to degradation. Billy was different. Even after a year in prison, he looked oblivious to why he was there. He didn't seem persecuted or wronged in any way, not even resentful. He just looked confused. Not that Billy's demeanor mattered that much to the rest of the prison population. Every inmate knew who he was and what he had done. Killing seven, maybe eight, women put him at the top of the inmate food chain—untouchable and admired. Whether he knew it or not, Billy Broadnax was an A-list member of prison society. Someone to be revered by the despicable.

"Do you know what happened to Harold Gilroy?" Windsor asked.

Broadnax finally looked up, giving Windsor a blank stare like he'd just woken up. Slowly, he looked around the room, nodding to the guard, then going back to staring at his shackles and fussing with the chains. Windsor asked the question again and got the same reaction.

"He's dead," Windsor said. "Someone beat him to death and threw his body in a dumpster."

Unfazed, Broadnax went back to staring at the water bottle.

Everything about Billy told Windsor that he needed to talk slowly, be as precise in his words as Billy was in where to put his water bottle.

"Gilroy told me before he was killed that the two of you had talked. Would you tell me what you told him?"

Billy leaned forward slightly. "Do you have a girlfriend?" When Windsor ignored the question, Billy said, "I do." An evil smile spread across his face. He leaned back in his chair as far as the chains would let him. His tongue took a lap around his lips. "His name is Ng. God made him what he is. Now he is mine." The guard standing behind Billy shook his head in disgust.

Windsor had dealt with the usual array of psychological conditions: addiction, ADHD, bipolar disorder, depression, anxiety, schizophrenia. His education and training were intended to give him insights into the human condition, ask questions, find answers, give advice. Six years of classes, books, papers, seminars, and videos came back to him: review the crimes, put the killer at ease, gain some rapport, ask questions, get the killer to talk about what happened during the crimes and after.

Blah. Blah. Blah.

Windsor wasn't there to understand Billy Broadnax or cure him. All he wanted to know was did Billy kill Jennifer. Time to get a little tougher, see what would happen, break through Billy's prison-tough patina.

"That's great," Windsor said, "but I'm not here to find out about your love life. Tell me what you and Gilroy talked about. After that you can get back to playing jailhouse rock with whatever passes for a girlfriend in this place."

Broadnax's demeanor changed immediately. The prison persona disappeared, replaced by something that resembled a chastised child. Maybe it was Windsor's harsh tone or that Billy suddenly remembered what he'd done and why he was in prison. Whatever it was, the evil grin was gone. His eyes began darting around the room and out the small window that overlooked a visitors' area. He looked everywhere but at Windsor, who kept his eyes on Billy, not saying a word.

Billy went back to his fascination with the water bottle, moving it around the table, rotating it until it was back in the same place. The handcuffs kept him from taking a drink, which made the whole water bottle thing even stranger, including why the guard gave it to him in the first place. Probably just screwing with him. The compulsive behavior and the instant transformation from convict to child left little doubt in Windsor's mind that Billy Broadnax was more than a serial killer. He was completely and totally insane. Then again, both were pretty much the same.

Chapter 25

Windsor knew enough about Broadnax to give him his own singular place in the pantheon of serial killers. He was nowhere near the likes of Jeffery Dahmer; Joseph DeAngelo, the Golden State killer; or Richard Ramirez, the Night Stalker. His tactics were more along the lines of Peter William Sutcliffe, the Yorkshire Ripper, who killed thirteen women in central England in the late 1970s. To Billy's credit, he didn't rape his victims and he didn't eat them. Good for him, Windsor thought. It was the other things that set him apart.

The first murder was on July thirty-first. A twenty-seven-year-old flower shop employee home alone while her husband played golf in a Tuesday night men's league at a nearby country club. It turned out to be just the start.

The second victim died the same way as the first. Her body discovered by her husband when he returned home from a business dinner.

The third was found two days later in her garage. The last person to see her alive was a box boy who carried her groceries to her car. She was found by a friend who came by the next morning for coffee.

By then, the eerie similarities of Billy's butchery had earned him the inevitable nickname The Meat Man, coined by a distraught police detective during what he thought was an off-the-record interview with a reporter. The name stuck. For the next two weeks, "The Meat Man Murders" dominated the front pages of every newspaper in the region. Predictably, they found their way into national newspapers and on to the networks and syndicated TV tabloids. After that came the blogs, podcasts, and other denizens of social media.

Like the other murders, the fourth and fifth victims came two days apart. Each crime scene became its own all-too-familiar, mind-numbing event. Ropes, rafters, a butcher knife, a page from the Bible stuffed into the body. Then came the sixth and seventh murders with more of the same.

Windsor had seen the photos of the first seven victims in the file he got from the police task force. He made himself look at each one, all the while trying to stay objective. Observe don't judge. Look past the carnage, the blood, the brutality. What was the killer saying? What did he want people to know about him? Why was he doing this? How could he kill without a trace?

Eventually he found the answers. He learned the hard way that it wasn't worth the effort. Now, all that seemed so long ago. Too bad the images seemed so fresh.

"Mr. Gilroy was a nice man," Broadnax finally said. The mumbling was gone, replaced by a thin, high-pitched, almost child-like voice. "He said he could help me get out of here. He said that if I told him the truth about the women that he would talk to the warden. I could go home."

"The truth about the women?" Windsor said.

"Uh huh, especially that one woman."

"What about the women, Billy?" Windsor said, trying to keep the urgency out of his voice. "What did you tell Gilroy about the women?"

Billy turned even more childlike. "'He will punish those who do not know God and do not obey the gospel of our Lord Jesus.' Thessalonians Chapter 1, Verse 8. 'It is mine to avenge; I will repay. In due time their foot will slip; their day of disaster is near and their doom rushes upon them.' Deuteronomy Chapter 32, Verse 8."

Billy reeled off the quotations, cherry picking lines that justified his actions without understanding what they meant, all the while toying with the water bottle.

"They were whores of Satan, you know, living in sin with the Devil's disciples. God sent me messages about them and what I needed to do."

"So, you talked to God?"

Billy shook his head back and forth so hard that spit flew out of his mouth. "No, no, no. I just knew. I just knew. His messages were in the words in The Bible. It was all right there. I read it. 'The wages of sin is death, but the free gift of God is eternal life in Christ Jesus our lord.' Romans Chapter 6, Verse 35."

"Stop it, Billy! You have no idea what you're saying. No idea what it means. Just tell me what you told Gilroy. Tell me something I don't know."

Billy looked around the room again, seemingly still unsure where he was and why he was there.

"He said I didn't kill that one," he said finally. "That's why he came to see me. He said we could make money. Money to get me out of here. All I had to do was talk to some people—reporters or something. He knew all about newspapers and television. He said there was a report that proved I didn't kill that one."

Broadnax's chin rested on his chest, giving Windsor a full view of the dragon tattoo on the top of his head.

"Report? What report?"

Billy shook his head. "I don't know. He didn't tell me."

"Which one didn't you kill, Billy?" Windsor said it slowly, then held his breath.

"Mr. Gilroy said it was the last one. I don't really know. That's just what he told me. I can't remember each one. I wish I could, but I can't. They were all the same. That's the way I planned it. Now I can't tell one from the other."

Windsor ran the victims' names through his head. Mary Louise Donovan, Judith Bleaker, Diane Masterson, Tiffany Milton, Emma McElroy, Alyssa Hart, Mandy Coffee. He refused to keep Jennifer DeGarza Windsor on that list.

Windsor shook the memories from his head, forced back his fears, and leaned forward on the table to get as close to Broadnax as possible. Broadnax smelled like vegetable soup gone bad. Small bubbles of spit foamed at the corners of his mouth.

He backed off when the guard cleared his throat.

"This report," Windsor said. "Did you see it?"

Billy shook his head. "No, Mr. Gilroy told me about it. He said he could get it. That he knew a girl who had it. He could get it from her."

"What girl?"

Billy only shrugged.

"Did this girl have a name?"

Billy moved the water bottle around a few times before answering. "Maybe. I don't remember things too well."

"Do you remember turning yourself in? Going with your father to the police station? Why did you do that? Surrender?"

Billy shrugged like what he'd done was no big deal. "I know. I don't remember much about what happened before that. I just found myself in a cell with handcuffs. I remember telling them everything I know. I was sure they would understand. That it was God." He stared down at his hands for a few seconds. "My dad was with me. He told me everything would be okay. I miss my dad. Do you know him?"

"No, I don't," Windsor said. "Listen carefully, Billy. Did you read anything in the newspaper about yourself that might have made you angry or want to seek revenge?"

Billy looked confused for a few seconds, then slowly shook his head. "No. I don't read newspapers and ... revenge. I don't know what you mean."

Windsor sat back in his chair, taking time to let that sink in. If Billy didn't read the opinion piece about him, then it wasn't the reason he killed Jennifer. Windsor felt relieved for a few seconds. He wanted to believe that he was finally rid of the guilt for Jennifer's death. A year of remorse wiped away in a few seconds. No more dead drift. Then he realized the admission came from the mouth of a deranged killer. He wasn't convinced.

"Are you telling me that you killed seven women, not eight?"

Windsor waited another minute for an answer. Billy slowly moved his huge head up and down. "I think so."

"Are you saying that the last victim was killed by someone else?" Windsor was repeating the question, but he had to be sure. He had to get inside Billy's head, make him remember, make him tell the truth.

Broadnax did the small-child routine again, looking out the window, then down at his shackled feet, then back to the water bottle. "That's what Mr. Gilroy told me."

Windsor was getting frustrated. For all he knew, Broadnax had made the whole thing up in his sick little brain. Lying about how many women he killed wouldn't be the worst thing Billy Broadnax had ever done.

"Can you prove any of this?" Windsor knew the answer before he asked the question.

Billy's demeanor changed suddenly again. The shy child was gone. The brutal killer turned hardened convict was back. "Ain't that your job? Don't mean shit to me."

Windsor leaned back. He wanted to wait a moment to get used to the change in Broadnax. Watching him was like channel surfing. He leaned forward again. "If you didn't kill one of those women, then someone else did. That someone else is free instead of in here with you."

Billy laughed as he turned to look at the guard. "What's one less asshole in this place?" He turned back toward Windsor. "Everything I did was for God, but he's forgotten me and everyone else in this place. There's no God in here. There's nothing. I used to believe in him. I don't anymore. This is all God's fault. He made me do it and then turned away. 'The Lord preserves all who love him, but all the wicked he will destroy.' Psalms, Chapter 145, verse 20."

The guard in the corner tapped the wall with his nightstick. Time was up. He stepped forward to start unlocking the chain that attached Billy to the floor.

"You've got to tell me," Windsor said. "Are you telling the truth? Is there any proof that you didn't kill my wife?"

Billy stood up and stared at Windsor, sneering while shaking his head back and forth. "Gilroy is dead. I can't prove shit."

Chapter 26

The dog never barked because no one ever came to visit. That was fine with Chester Broadnax. The closest thing to a visitor he wanted or needed was the mailman, even though all he ever got were bills, most of them overdue. Molly used to bark when the mail arrived, but stopped when her eyes went bad, and she couldn't see all the way down to the roadside mailbox. So, months ago she stopped barking at the mail truck or anything else. The sign at the gate was doing a good job keeping the peddlers and Jehovah's Witnesses away. Meter readers, Chester had decided, were a thing of the past.

No noise and no visitors meant he could sleep most of the time thanks to cheap bourbon with a splash of water and no ice. The television was on day and night but turned low, so it didn't interfere with his frequent naps. Besides, he'd stopped listening or watching a long time ago, couldn't even remember the last time he changed channels. It was only there for company. Knowing that his only companionship were the voices of strangers coming out of a box made him miss his wife all that much more. Then again, he was better off alone. He and Audrey didn't talk that much anyway, and certainly not about their son.

Six months earlier he'd given up the little patch of land in Washington County where he'd lived with Audrey and Billy in favor of a single-wide five miles southeast of Salem. It sat well to the east of several small, low-cost housing developments in an area where zoning seemed to require one rundown house for every five acres of unusable land. He could see Interstate 5 in the distance and planes taking off and landing at McNary Field.

He also had an unobstructed view of the state prison where his son would probably spend the rest of his life.

Chester drank and ate in the living room, sitting in either a swayback couch or an imitation leather lounge chair with cigarette burns on the arms. Breakfast and lunch were doughnuts and more bourbon. Dinner was whatever can or bag he'd brought back from the store. It didn't matter. Thanks to three packs of cigarettes a day it was impossible to taste anything anyway.

He viewed his trailer as a prison of its own. It sat in the middle of a dirt-and-grass lot. With no trees around it, the uninsulated trailer was an oven in the summer and a deep freeze in the winter. He thought about planting trees to provide a little shade and make the place look more lived in. Of course, trees cost money that he didn't have, and he probably wasn't going to live long enough to see them get more than six feet high.

Other than trips to town, he seldom went outdoors to do anything more than stand on the small wooden porch, smoke a cigarette, and stare across the fields at the prison's razor-wire fences and yellow walls. On days when the sun was out, he could make out the men dressed in blue milling around on the grass inside the perimeter. It made him wonder if Billy was among them. Was he blending in? Was he making friends? Enemies? Did it even matter anymore?

Maybe someday his memory of Billy would be as distant and small as those men inside the prison's wire fences. If that day was coming, it had better get here soon. Then again, dying and forgetting sort of went hand in hand. Until then, he and Billy would have their respective lifetime sentences served out in their separate dungeons within sight of each other.

The combination of heat, bourbon, and no food made it time for another nap. He turned the TV down a notch, laid on the couch, and wrapped himself in the dim murmuring of another afternoon game show.

He'd just nodded off when Molly started barking.

Chapter 27

Alex Windsor turned off the two-lane road onto a dirt track with a strip of brown grass down the middle. It ran for fifty yards between a pair of rusted barbed wire fences held up by moss-covered posts. To the right was a field of thistles and dried grass. To the left was the same thing, only with a view toward the freeway. The light-blue mobile home at the end of the lane sat in the middle of a dirt patch. An uneven cinder block foundation made it look a few degrees off center.

An old Chevy pickup sat under a junk-filled carport attached to one end of the trailer. A dog with a gray muzzle, a limp, and a hoarse bark stood in the middle of a circle of bare ground on the other side of the carport. The barking grew louder and more urgent as Windsor's BMW pulled up next to the front porch.

He was unsure about whether this was a good idea. The talk with Billy had left him shaken and unsatisfied. Billy was clearly crazy, but he could still be right about not killing Jennifer and not reading the opinion piece. The best his training could tell him was that Billy was some sort of malevolent idiot savant, barely able to read and write but capable of plotting an intricate schedule to kill seven women in quick succession. Wishful thinking made him cross Jennifer off the list of Billy's victims.

After talking to Billy, Windsor thought maybe his father could fill in some gaps. It seemed the next logical step. He was with Billy when he turned himself in. Maybe he was with him the two or three days before. Learning that Chester Broadnax lived just a few miles outside of town sort of sealed the deal. He just wasn't sure what kind of reception he would get. If the dog was any indication, things didn't look good.

"What do you want?" yelled the old man who charged out from the trailer.

A lit cigarette occupied one hand. A glass containing something brown filled the other. Baggy pants hung precariously from narrow hips. A wrinkled short-sleeved shirt strained against a protruding belly. A bulbous nose held up a pair of steel-rimmed glasses that were as off center as the mobile home. His gray hair was a long-abandoned comb over.

"This is private property. I don't cotton to no visitors, especially if you're selling something."

Windsor got out, shut the car door, and leaned against it. If the old man was armed with little more than a cigarette and glass, he felt safe.

"Hello, Mr. Broadnax. I'm Alex Windsor. I don't know if you remember me."

Recognition crawled slowly across Chester Broadnax's face. He took a long pull on his drink then waved a finger in Windsor's direction. "Yeah, I remember you. I remember what you wrote about me, you son of a bitch. You said I molested Billy. That was a goddamn lie." He pointed angrily toward the road. "Now get the hell out of here." The tone of the old man's voice started the dog barking again.

"And your son confessed to killing my wife. Does that make us even?"

The old man slumped, the words like punches that took the wind out of him.

"When I wrote that, I didn't know your son was the killer," Windsor said. "Most of what I said about the killer turned out to be true. Some of it didn't. I'm sorry for that, but there's nothing I can do about it now. Besides, I'm sort of retired."

Windsor's apologies seemed to confuse the old man. He set his drink down and leaned on the railing. "If you're not a shrink anymore, then what do you want?"

"Some things have happened that I need to talk to you about. It has to do with Billy and the things he did." Windsor took a couple of tentative steps toward the porch, not sure if the old man's anger was gone. "I need to piece together what happened in those days before Billy turned himself in."

Chester's shoulders slumped a few more degrees as he shook his head in disbelief. "If you're here to talk about Billy, you might as well get back in your fancy car and be on your way. There's been enough misery. I don't want no more."

"I've talked to Billy, Mr. Broadnax. I really need your help."

The old man looked down at the ground for a few moments then went inside, leaving Windsor to wonder if he should stay or drive away. He decided to wait. He was leaning against the car door again when Chester came back. He had a pack of Camel straights and a tumbler filled with more of something brown. He waddled across the small porch on spindly, unsteady legs then pushed a rusty lawn chair up against the weathered railing. The chair squeaked in protest when he half fell, half sat in it.

"You talked to Billy? You saw him?" Chester Broadnax said. His breath came in short gasps. The strain of talking and sitting down at the same time turned his face a pale pink.

"Just a few hours ago."

"How did you find me?"

"The prison has your address on file."

Chester mulled that over for a few seconds then asked, "What did he look like? Billy, I mean. My son."

"The same, I guess. I'd never seen Billy until today, so it's hard to ..." He let his voice trail off, not sure what to say next.

Between gulps from the glass and deep drags on the cigarette, the old man glanced at the prison in the distance. "What did he say?" He sounded like he wasn't sure he wanted to know.

Windsor told him but kept it short. When he got to the part about Jennifer, it elicited a sad shake of the head.

"That's crazy talk," Chester said. "I know Billy killed all those women. I knew it all along. I just didn't know what to do about it. Killing was his crime. Not telling anyone about it was mine."

"Why do you think Billy would admit to a murder he didn't commit?"

"Who the fuck knows, mister? Jesus Christ, he's been sitting over there in that prison for a year knowing he'll be there the rest of his life. Every day the same goddamn thing. He's only twenty-five, you know. Imagine being that young and knowing you're going to spend the rest of your life in a place like that? Fifty? Maybe sixty years? No sunshine. No moon. No clean air. Hell, you're apt to say anything. He was crazy when he went in there. I don't imagine he's gotten any less crazy since."

The rant left Chester Broadnax panting and red-faced. He turned around in the chair to look across the fields to the prison shimmering in the afternoon heat. "Every time I look over there I'm reminded of Billy and what he did. Do you have any idea what that's like? I moved down here to be closer to him, but I've never had the guts to visit him. I'm the reason he's in there. It wasn't like he was going to turn himself in." He took a long pull on his drink and a longer one on his cigarette.

"I suppose I should move away, but ..." His voice trailed off.

Windsor turned around to look at the prison in the distance. He didn't have the heart to explain to the old man that he'd been looking at the wrong prison. Chester had been gazing at the medium-security

Oregon State Correctional Institute. Billy was in the maximum-security penitentiary a few miles away.

Let it go, Windsor thought. If Chester couldn't find the courage to visit Billy, then it probably didn't matter which prison he was in.

"Maybe we better start from the beginning," Windsor said.

Chapter 28

Chester Broadnax turned his attention back to Windsor. "I really don't want to talk about it."

"Look, Mr. Broadnax, no one wants to forget what happened more than the two of us. I wouldn't be here if it wasn't important. I can't do anything for you or your son but knowing what happened to my wife would do something for me. I really need your help."

Chester's rheumy eyes searched Windsor's face. He finally nodded his head. "Have it your way." He took a deep breath and melted further into the plastic chair.

Windsor was still leaning against the car door. If he was going to hear the old man's story, he needed to be a lot closer. He moved ten feet toward the porch, his foot on the bottom step, elbow on the railing.

"As soon as the killings became big news, I knew Billy was the killer," Chester said. "You see, he was always a little … off. For good reason, I guess. He was an awkward kid who was always teased at school. Always came home quiet and angry looking. He didn't say anything. He just went to his room and closed the door. It made my wife crazy. He never did anything she told him. Barely said five words a day. He became stubborn and willful. Refused to do anything around the house. That made Audrey even crazier. Sometimes she'd beat him with a belt." Chester pulled at his lower lip. "You need to understand something. Audrey was raised hardscrabble and never forgot it. Don't get me wrong. I loved her and she was always good to me. That said, she was what you might call a straight-razor-toed woman if you know what I mean."

"And?"

"None of what she did seemed to work, so, at one point, we bought him a computer … one of those laptop things. Got it used from a store in Hillsboro. We were hoping that would give him something to do or, maybe, he would even learn something. Whatever he did with that thing seemed to calm him down a little, give him something else to think about. That was enough for Audrey. She quit whipping him." Chester looked away and shrugged. "Of course, some of that may be that he was getting bigger, and we were getting older."

"You were afraid of him?"

"Damn right."

"Any hobbies?" Windsor asked.

"Billy? You mean other than his computer? Not exactly. We had a shop in the garage with a wooden bench. One day I found him in there doing some half-ass autopsy on a dead squirrel. I didn't think much about it other than it was one more thing to keep him busy. Then I found him doing the same thing to the neighbor's cat."

Chester shook his head and stared off into the distance for a few minutes. Windsor let the moment hang in the air.

"Anything else? Odd behavior? Things like that?"

"You mean other than killing people?"

"Yeah. Before that."

Chester thought for a minute. "Billy always kept his room neat—not just neat, but too neat, if you know what I mean. Everything in its place. Bed made. Clothes folded. Computer sitting by itself on his little desk. He always ate his food exactly the same way. If we were having hamburgers, he'd eat all the meat first, then all the vegetables, then all the mashed potatoes. Sometimes he'd fiddle with his dinner plate, moving it around, then moving it again. It always struck me as weird. When he got older, he'd sometimes disappear for days at a time. To be honest, it was a welcome relief."

Chester stopped for a few seconds to catch his breath. The smoke from his cigarette disappeared in the breeze. The brown liquid in the glass sloshed on his shirt when he started coughing. Windsor watched, thinking that telling the story was draining that last bit of air out of the old man.

"We were living out in Washington County then, different trailer, different location," Chester said, after finishing his drink and throwing the cigarette into the dirt next to the porch. "Turned out he had a girlfriend once. Even moved in with her for a while a few years back. I was against it, but Audrey said a girl might be good for him. Anyway, it didn't work out. She was a nice girl, but not very smart or pretty for that matter. She came to see Audrey and me once. Told us some of the things Billy talked to her about, asking what she thought as if hoping she would like it. She wouldn't say much more than that. Maybe there were sex things. Maybe it was something else. After talking to her, I realized that Billy wasn't right in the head. Never would be. She was scared to death. Can't blame her now."

Chester seemed to lose his train of thought for a moment. He got up, went inside, and came back with a full glass. He fired up another Camel, then looked at Windsor like he just remembered he was there.

"You want to know something strange?" Chester said, then answered his own question. "I figured Billy needed something to do in life. Have a skill. You know, something he could fall back on when he needed work. So, I enrolled him in butcher's school. Even bought him a second-hand set of knives." Chester went back to his cigarette and drink, then just shook his head. "Guess we both know how that turned out."

Chapter 29

Windsor let that sink in for a few seconds. It might be the saddest and most ironic example of the adage "No good deed goes unpunished" he'd ever heard.

"Then Billy began disappearing more and more frequently," Chester said. "When he came back, he'd be in a better mood. He even helped around the house occasionally. I thought maybe he was just getting laid."

"And that's when the killings started?"

"Billy had just disappeared again when I read about that first killing. Right away I thought of Billy. Terrible thing, isn't it? Thinking something like that about your own son right off the bat. Then, after two more killings and Billy still wasn't home, I was sure it was him."

"Do you know where he was during that time?" Windsor said.

"Not really. He had a cot in a storeroom at the nursing home where he worked part time mopping floors, scrubbing bathrooms, cleaning bedpans. That sort of thing. It's in Hillsboro, over by the airport. He stayed there once in a while. I went over to see if he was there, but no one had seen him for several days. The manager of the place was pretty pissed off. She said if I found Billy to tell him not to bother coming back to work."

He lit another cigarette, the third since Windsor arrived, and broke into a brief, but violent coughing spell that moved his pink face a shade toward purple. Windsor could only watch.

"He showed up a day later," Chester said when he'd recovered. "It was the same day as your write-up ran in the newspaper. It was right after the seventh woman was killed."

"You confronted him?"

"I went into his room and showed him the newspaper. He never looked at it. Just grabbed it and wadded it up. Then he changed. You've talked to Billy, so maybe you saw it. He has this habit of acting like a little kid whenever he was caught doing something wrong or felt like he was being scolded. He's done that all his life. As soon as he saw the newspaper, he started acting that way again. It was all I needed to know."

"He confessed?"

Tears filled his eyes as he nodded. "Billy was the only child we had. I was forty-two when Billy was born. Audrey was forty-five. We tried for years to have children, but Billy was the only one. We'd almost given up when we had him. Audrey was hard on him. I won't deny that. She wanted him to be perfect and he was anything but." He paused again. "Maybe people our age shouldn't have children. Messes them all up."

Listening to Chester, Windsor wondered if the old man had ever really talked to anyone about Billy and the murders. Probably not. Who would he talk to? There was no trial, so he never testified. He probably talked to the police, but only to verify what they already knew or what Billy had said in some clumsy way. Most of Windsor's patients were young, none anywhere near Chester's age. He had no experience with those who thought only of their own deaths and how it couldn't get there soon enough. All he could do was listen.

"The harder she was on him the worse Billy treated her," Chester said. "Like I told you, as he got older, we became afraid of him. Audrey and I never talked about it, but I think we both knew that Billy might hurt us. I know I did. Hell, you've seen him. He's skinny, but strong as hell. I don't know where that comes from, but I did know that I wasn't in the best of shape. Diabetes and a bad ticker." He held up the cigarette. "Too many of these damn things. Anyway, I knew that if he ever got really angry at one of us there wasn't much I could do to stop him."

"What did you do after Billy confessed?"

"Nothing," he said with a laugh that was equal portions irony and self-disgust. "Isn't that what any father does when he finds out his son is a mass murderer? Nothing."

"You must have done something."

"Somewhere along the way Billy found Jesus, God, or something like that. I never figured out where that came from. Could have been one of those television preachers. Maybe he met a girl who was religious. Probably got most of it from that internet. He even had an old torn-up Bible that he carried around with him. Every once in a while, he'd start spouting off about a vengeful god, burning in hell, and punishing people for their sins."

"Which people?"

"Best I could tell it was rich people who lived in what he called sinful lives fornicating in mansions. He said they had sex with the devil. Produced demon children that would take over the world. Crazy shit like that. Real crazy shit."

"Do you still have Billy's Bible?"

Broadnax thought for a moment. "You know, I believe I do. There's a box of Billy's stuff in the back room."

"Do you think I could see it?"

The old man groaned as he pulled himself out of his chair and went inside. He came back a few minutes later holding a battered book with "Holy Bible" embossed on the warped leather cover.

"Not in great shape," Broadnax said. "Looks like some of the pages have been torn out."

"Do you mind if I take a look?" Windsor said, moving up onto the porch.

"Sure," the old man said, handing it over.

"I assume Billy was not a great reader," Windsor said.

"Great? No, but he could read. It just took him a while." Chester pointed at the Bible. "It would probably take him all day to read one of those pages."

Windsor opened it to the Book of Genesis. The first fourteen pages had been carefully cut out. Two pages—front and back—for the first seven victims. With one exception: Pages 15 and 16 were still there, solemnly telling the story of Abraham. They were the same pages found on Jennifer's body. They just didn't come from Billy's Bible.

Chapter 30

Windsor stared at the tattered Bible, counting the missing pages a second time while silently running through all the options that would explain why the pages found with Jennifer were still there. Only one made sense.

"Is this the only Bible Billy had?" Windsor asked.

"Far as I know."

"Did the police ask you about a Bible?"

"Nope."

"Can I keep this?"

"I don't know why not. Not doing much good around here."

"You think that's why he killed the women—religion?" Windsor asked.

"Who the hell knows? All I know is that Billy said he was sorry, that God wanted him to do it, and that it wouldn't happen again. At first, he cried and begged me not to call the police. It was pitiful to watch. Then he got angry. Said he'd kill both of us if we told anyone what he'd done. I knew it was wrong not to turn him in, but he was my son. Sick as he was, he was still my son. What was I supposed to do?"

The old man excused himself to go inside again. He reappeared a few minutes later with more cigarettes and another tumbler of brown liquid. He didn't offer Windsor a drink, but he did hold out the pack of Camels. Windsor didn't smoke, but almost took one anyway.

"I know this is difficult, Mr. Broadnax, but I'd like to hear the rest."

The old man nodded. "I knew I had to do something, but I just couldn't call the cops. Not yet anyway. So, I got in touch with the guy I rented the property from. Not here. The place where we used to live out in Washington County. He's a lawyer, so I figured he might know what to do."

At the mention of a lawyer, Windsor stepped forward and bent down slightly. He wanted to look Chester Broadnax directly in the face. "Which lawyer?" he asked. It was more of a command than a question.

"Chandler Stockdale. I'd rented that place from him for twenty years. Told me he bought it back in the 80s as an investment. We could live there with the understanding that it was prime real estate and would be a housing development one day. Fine with me, I said. I paid on time. He kept the rent low if I didn't bother him about any repairs or things like that."

"When did you call him?"

Chester thought for a moment. "The same day. Right after the seventh murder. I told him I needed to talk to him about all those women that'd been killed. He seemed to know what I was talking about. He said to come in right away. So, we did."

"We?"

"Billy and me. Audrey was too broke up. She wanted no part of it."

"I thought Stockdale didn't become Billy's attorney until after he turned himself in," Windsor said.

"That's right, but the way Stockdale explained it he really wasn't Billy's lawyer because we never paid him any money. A retainer, I think he called it. Anyway, he said he was just helping me out as a friend. No charge."

When Windsor moved in closer, Chester became more uncomfortable and nervous. "When did you see him? Exactly?" Windsor demanded.

"Let me think. It was about ten o'clock in the morning." Chester took a long pull on his drink, then stuck the cigarette in the corner of his mouth where it bounced up and down while he talked. "Billy killed your wife that night."

Windsor cringed, but let it pass. "You met Stockdale at his office?"

"Right. In that fancy building downtown. The one they call The Tower, I think. Pretty nice digs if you ask me. You ever been there?"

Windsor ignored the question. "What did Stockdale tell you?"

"He told me I needed to turn Billy over to the police, but not right away. He wanted Billy examined by some sort of doctor."

"Were you in the room at the time?"

"I was for part of it. Mr. Stockdale asked me to leave while he and Billy talked in private like. They were in there for about an hour. When they came out Mr. Stockdale gave me the name and address of this doctor. He said Billy needed to see him right away."

"Do you remember the name of the doctor?"

Chester thought for a few moments. "Not off hand, but I still have his card." He pulled his wallet out and thumbed through a half dozen plastic membership cards—Costco, AARP, Medicare—before pulling out a dog-eared business card. It read: Dr. Bennett Benno, Licensed Psychiatrist. The address was a medical building on NE Glisan Street near Providence Medical Center.

Chester pointed at the card. "Isn't that what you were? A psychiatrist?"

"Pretty much. What did they talk about?"

"I don't know," Chester said. "Billy went in alone. I waited in the truck. He told me later that this Benno fella asked a lot of questions about the killings."

"Do you remember what time it was when you left the doctor's office with Billy?"

"About half-past three, I guess," Lester said. "It took a while to drive home. Traffic, you know. Billy disappeared as soon as we got there."

Between pulls on his drink and cigarette, Chester explained how he called Stockdale late that night right after Billy came home. Stockdale showed up at the house two hours later with Bennett Benno. "They told Billy that the police and the newspapers would eventually find out that he was the killer everyone had been looking for. They said his name and picture would be on television. Reporters would come to the house. The best thing for him and for us was to turn himself in."

"What did Billy say?"

"Nothing at first, but that was Billy. Then he said no, but that doctor fellow knew how to handle Billy. He talked to him real stern like. Even mentioned the Bible. Billy went into that little boy act of his. Then, Mr. Stockdale said things would go easier if he confessed."

"What time did Billy come home that night?" Windsor asked.

The old man thought for a few seconds. "Around ten, I guess. Maybe a little later." Windsor did the timeline in his head. Jennifer was killed some time before nine p.m. That meant if Billy did kill her, he would have had plenty of time to get home.

"That's when you called Stockdale."

Chester nodded.

"And you told all this to the police, right?"

"No."

"Why not?"

"They never asked."

Windsor sighed. "Then what?"

"We stayed up all night—the lawyer, the doctor, Audrey, Billy, and me. We talked all about it. The doctor gave Billy some pills, then a shot of some kind. It calmed Billy down real good like. He stayed that way all night. The following morning the doctor gave Billy another one of those shots. After that Billy and I drove into town. Mr. Stockdale, the doctor, and Audrey followed us. When we got to the police department they stayed in the car while Billy and I traipsed right inside and told them why we were there. The officer, a nice older woman we talked with, seemed kind of confused at first. I guess they don't get many people coming in to confess things. Anyway, I was kind of surprised because I was under the impression that we were expected."

Windsor smiled at the thought of some sleepy desk sergeant wondering what to do when someone claiming to be The Meat Man walked in with his dad and confessed to killing eight women. "And then?"

"They took Billy away. About an hour later this guy in a suit came out to tell me that Billy had been arrested. He said they'd read him his rights and he was in a cell. That's when Mr. Stockdale showed up."

Chester began explaining what happened next, even though it was clear he didn't understand most of it. Best Windsor could tell was that Stockdale had been appointed by the court as Billy's attorney and that there'd be a hearing soon.

"He said everything would be taken care of. He said Billy would be fine. He wouldn't get the death penalty, but he'd be going to prison for the rest of his life."

Chester seemed to be sinking lower into the rusty lawn chair, crushed by the weight of reliving the story. Finally, he flicked another cigarette butt into the dirt, struggled to his feet, and wheezing and coughing, went inside and came back with another drink.

"Audrey and me, we weren't in the courtroom when the judge sentenced Billy," he said, settling back into his chair. "That was a few days later, I believe. It was Mr. Stockdale's idea that we stay away. Something about a lot of reporters. They finally let us see him just before he went off to prison. I think he was still drugged because he didn't seem to understand what was happening to him. I asked him if he felt sorry for killing all those women. He just looked at me like I was crazy. He said, 'No. Why? It was what I believe God wanted me to do.' That was the last time I saw him."

Chester looked at Windsor with droopy eyes. "I know he killed your wife. For what it's worth, I'm sorry. I feel responsible. I don't blame you for hating us, but please forgive me. It was as much my fault as Billy's. I think I did the right thing turning him in. I did the wrong thing waiting so long to do it."

The old man stood up. Windsor walked over and put a hand on Broadnax's bony shoulder. "Don't blame yourself. It's not your fault," he whispered. "We've both been through enough. It's time to move on."

"Thank you," Chester said, tears filling his eyes. "Thank you."

After they shook hands, the old man plopped down in the lawn chair to get lost once more in liquor and cigarettes. Neither spoke for a while. The awkwardness of the moment hung between them like a gauzy curtain.

"Where's Mrs. Broadnax?" Windsor said, hoping to break the tension of the moment.

"She died three months ago. She was never the same. Audrey was Billy's ninth victim. Reckon I'll be his tenth."

Chapter 31

Alex Windsor and Cassie Terrace sat at Windsor's table in the back of The Ridge while Bud Schwartz tended bar and traded lies with stools full of regulars. He was in the middle of another rendition of how his parents—both conscientious objectors during World War II—named him in remembrance of the twentieth anniversary of the dropping of the first atomic bomb.

Cassie turned toward Windsor. "Is Hiroshima really his first name?"

Windsor laughed. "No. I think it's Gerald."

"What's that old saying? Never let the truth get in the way of a good story."

Windsor had called Terrace and asked to meet. When she asked why, all he would say was that it was important.

"Personal, I hope," she'd said.

"No. Business. Strictly business."

Windsor had seen all of Cassie's moods from all angles and positions at all times of the day or night. The one she had when she walked in the door of The Ridge was her game face. It was the one he liked the least. He hoped Bud's story would take the edge off things. It didn't.

"A couple of things," Windsor said. "The girl killed the other night the same way as Squid Gilroy. Anything?"

"Rebecca Roberts. Twenty-six-years old. Divorced with a four-year-old son. Worked the graveyard shift at a convenience store ten blocks from where she lived with her mother. The wounds on her head corresponded with the wounds on Gilroy's head. Probably a tire iron. Maybe a crowbar."

"Same weapon. Same person."

"Could be." Terrace was being careful about what she said. That was the cop in her. She was good. Very good.

"Any connection between her and Gilroy?"

She smiled at him. "So, that's what this is all about. Gilroy. Broadnax. Your wife. I saw this movie a couple of nights ago."

"I know but stick with me. There's a lot going on here."

"And?"

"Two hours after Billy supposedly killed my wife, he was home with his mother, father, Chandler Stockdale, and a psychiatrist named Bennett Benno. They are the ones who talked Billy into surrendering."

"How do you know all this?"

"Billy's father, Chester."

Cassie looked stunned for a second then angry. "Is that what you've been doing? Bothering old Chester Broadnax? Jesus, Alex, haven't the two of you been through enough?"

Windsor didn't want to talk about it anymore. "I've also been visiting old friends." He said it with a sly grin.

Terrace didn't bite. Instead, she looked ready to say something then stopped. "We've made an arrest in the deaths of Gilroy and Rebecca Roberts," she said after taking a sip of beer. "The girl's ex-husband, Matthew Roberts."

"Motive?"

"Jealousy."

"Evidence?"

"Plenty. We found the murder weapon and Gilroy's shoes in the back of Roberts' pickup. He fits the description of a man seen hanging around her house the day she was killed. We found his address in her pants pocket."

"Has he been charged?"

"Not yet. It's with the DA."

"So, I guess that puts an end to it," Windsor said, not believing it for a minute, but relieved that Cassie wanted to consider the case closed.

Instead, she said, "I'm not so sure. It seems a little pat for my taste."

"You mean he's being framed."

"Could be. I just don't know who would do that or why. Any ideas?"

When Windsor shook his head, an awkward silence fell between them that made the constant electronic beeping of the video poker machines that much louder. A cue ball flew off the pool table, careened off the pinball machine, and rolled toward one of the big screen televisions showing a Dodgers-Padres game.

"For what it's worth, I reviewed the file on Jennifer's death," Cassie said, her mood slightly softer. "Everything points to Billy. It couldn't have been anyone else."

Windsor wanted this conversation over. The best way was to agree to everything she said. "You're right. Maybe I'm just wasting my time."

Cassie eyed him suspiciously. "You're doing it again, damn it. Sandbagging me. I'll just give you a word of warning. If you uncover something that shows a crime has been committed, you're obligated to notify the police."

"Well, there is something. I have Billy's Bible. The first fourteen pages are missing. Pages fifteen and sixteen were still there."

"The Bible." Cassie tried not to hide her disappointment. "We missed that. Anything else?"

"I talked to Billy. He said he didn't read my opinion piece."

"You believe him?"

"Why would he lie about something like that? Not that it matters. All that does is make me feel better."

Cassie let it soak in. "So, you think …"

Windsor moved in. She had to understand. "Assume for a minute that Billy is telling the truth—he didn't kill Jennifer. The Bible backs him up if you believe that's the only Bible he had. That raises questions about who killed her and why. Let's start with why. Revenge? I find that hard to believe. Jennifer wasn't the kind of person to do something that would get her killed. It's more likely she knew something that put someone else in danger. That someone killed her. Self-preservation."

"Who would that be?"

"If I knew I'd tell you."

Terrace thought for a moment. Windsor could see the wheels turning in her head. If he'd accomplished nothing else, he'd put some serious doubt in her mind.

"That doesn't explain why her death looked exactly like the previous seven," she said.

"Both Bennett Benno and Chandler Stockdale talked to Billy the same day Jennifer was killed."

"What are you saying?"

"Let's leave it at that for now. Just give me some room to move here, to keep looking."

Terrace nodded. "Okay, but what about this Bible? Where is it?"

"I have it. It's yours if you want it, but it means opening up The Meat Man Murders again."

Cassie suddenly looked both tired and anxious. Windsor knew the last thing she wanted to do was force the city to relive the horrors of a year ago.

"You've leveled with me. I'll do the same. The girl who was killed, Rebecca Roberts, once worked as a receptionist at a doctor's office. Her mother said she was let go but didn't know why. That's why she was working at the convenience store."

"What doctor?"

"A psychiatrist with offices on NE Glisan."

"Let me guess. Bennett Benno."

She nodded. "There's nothing here I can take to the chief or to the DA. They'll listen, nod, then ask for the proof. Get me that Bible as soon as you can. I'll take it from there."

"Done."

"Now what?"

"Benno."

Chapter 32

Alex Windsor had never met Bennett Benno, probably never would. He'd heard of him a few times, mostly from news stories about long-forgotten reports from the City Club but didn't know what he looked like. A quick search of the internet turned up a ten-year-old photo of him dressed in tweed and holding a pipe—the perfect image of a guest for evenings with philosophy professors, aspiring poets, and a Democrat.

The man who came out the side door of his office, turned to lock the door with a key, then walked across the small parking lot looked the same, only older and more bent over. The full head of hair was gray and uncombed but matched the bushy mustache. The sport coat wrinkled. The khaki pants baggy. A well-used leather briefcase hung from one hand. The only thing out of place was the small nylon gym bag dangling from the other.

Windsor knew any attempt to get an appointment with Benno was a waste of time. He didn't know exactly why but had a pretty good idea. It started and ended with Benno's status as Billy Broadnax's psychiatrist and Windsor's as the husband of Billy's last victim. The only other option was to wait outside his office, follow him home, and confront him there. All that took was a couple of hours of waiting in the car until Benno came out of his office.

Windsor started the engine as Benno walked across the parking lot to a red Audi. He got in, backed up, and pulled onto NE Glisan Street. Windsor followed, staying a half-block back as they wound their way west toward the center of the city. The Audi turned north for a few blocks to NE Sandy Boulevard.

Ten minutes later Benno pulled into the parking lot at The Colony, a once-popular watering hole that had fallen on hard times. Windsor knew the place as a dimly lit fern bar with candles on the tables and tuck-and-roll red leather horse-shoe shaped booths. It had worked well for the last fifty years. Not anymore. Its loyal customers were dying off and Portland's hipster crowd, while always on the lookout for the next new thing, had yet to discover it, probably because it didn't serve appletinis. Still, The Colony had three things going for it: a parking lot, great steaks, and a prime location across the street from a state-run liquor store and a high-end wine shop.

Windsor drove by just as Benno got out of the car and disappeared in a side entrance under a neon side that read "Lounge." He did a U-turn, pulled into the lot, and parked two spaces away. He waited a few minutes, then got out of the car and went in the same door. The odds that Benno would recognize him were slim, but even longer thanks to the dim lights. He sat at the first table he stumbled into and waited for his eyes to adjust. When they did, he spotted Benno at the far end of the bar finishing what looked like a Manhattan and eagerly signaling for another.

Windsor ordered a light beer from an over-polite waitress. He nursed the beer while watching the psychiatrist down two more drinks and a couple of pills from a vial he kept in his coat pocket. Several couples came and went while they waited for their dinner reservations. Benno scoped out each one and even gave Windsor a glassy-eyed glance. If it registered, he didn't show it.

Windsor considered sitting down next to him and asking about Billy Broadnax. He was unsure why he didn't. Instinct, perhaps, or he still hadn't sorted out everything he'd learned from Chester Broadnax. Besides, a bar is not the place for that kind of conversation. Certainly not with someone on his third Manhattan. Windsor finally decided to stick with his original plan and follow Benno home.

When the doctor reached for his wallet, Windsor threw ten dollars on his table and went out the door ahead of him. Benno emerged a few moments later showing the visible effects of drinks and pills as he half walked, half staggered across the parking lot. He sat in the car for several minutes staring out the windshield like someone who didn't know where to go or what to do. Eventually he picked up his cellphone, looked at it, then put it away. He sat there for a few more minutes before starting the car and backing out.

Windsor hung a few car lengths behind as he followed Benno down NE Sandy, across the Burnside Bridge over the Willamette River, and into downtown. Windsor assumed Benno was going home but couldn't be sure since he didn't know where the psychiatrist lived. If he turned right off Burnside, then he was in the trendy Pearl District, a hipster hang-out that seemed a good fit for a successful psychiatrist. Further on, if he turned left, it meant he lived in the expensive neighborhood in the hills overlooking downtown. Equally appropriate, but with parking.

Benno did neither. Instead, he drove the length of the street and into the hills on the west side of downtown. Three miles later he turned into a large empty parking lot with dim lighting and white striping.

Windsor parked on the street and watched in horror as Benno got out of his car and walked across the parking lot, the nylon bag hanging at his side.

"Not here," Windsor whispered to himself. "Anywhere but here."

Windsor banged the back of his head against the headrest, then climbed out of the car. When he reached the entrance to the parking lot, the psychiatrist was already heading toward a low hedge that ran up a small incline past neat rows of the closely placed and well-maintained tombstones and ground-level markers.

Windsor waited until Benno was out of sight over a small rise. "Why here?" Windsor said to himself again. Reluctantly, he moved quickly across the lot to the outside of the hedge then started up the incline. He looked at his watch. Almost nine o'clock. A hundred yards away down a grassy slope, a few cars moved along the street. A gentle breeze rustled the leaves on a half-dozen elms scattered among the plots. The odors of freshly mown grass and newly dug dirt filled the air. With the sun thirty minutes below the mountains to the west, what little light there was cast the kind of shadows that made cemeteries eerie and heavy with sad memories.

The hedge, gravestones, and small private mausoleums were all painfully fresh in Windsor's mind. He stopped, straining his eyes to find Benno among the shadows. He finally spotted him kneeling at the foot of a grave and gazing intently at the marker. Windsor moved closer, keeping to the shadows of a stand of trees until he was less than twenty yards away. He watched Benno pull a small bouquet of wilted roses from the gym bag. He arranged them neatly in the center of the grave then sat back on his haunches, moving his head from side to side as if admiring his handiwork. He rearranged the flowers slightly, brushed some dirt off the marker, then sat back to admire his work again. Apparently satisfied, he bowed his head for a few minutes before pulling the gym bag closer.

Windsor thought Benno was reaching for more flowers or perhaps a ribbon of some sort. Then he saw the glint of steel and the distinctive upward motion of Benno's right arm. Windsor froze for a second then started running toward him. As he was about to yell, Benno put the small revolver in his mouth and, without a moment's hesitation, pulled the trigger. With a muffled pop, the back of Benno's head exploded in a thin red mist. Instantly, the psychiatrist crumpled backward onto the damp grass at the foot of the grave.

Windsor fell to his knees, thought he was going to throw up, then fought to gain control. No way he saw that coming. How could he? Now what? He could just walk away, pretend it never happened or call the police and spend the rest of the night telling lies about why he was there. Too bad neither one would work.

Instead, he slowly walked toward Benno's body. The psychiatrist had fallen backwards and to the side. The back of his head had been reduced to bloody gore. Chunks of flesh and bone fanned out on the grass behind him. Blood trickled from the corner of his mouth. His dead eyes open, his face had the look of someone surprised by what happens when you put a gun in your mouth and pull the trigger.

Windsor stared at the body for a few seconds then slowly shifted his gaze toward the headstone where Benno had carefully placed the wilted roses. There was no hurry. Windsor knew what was there. He knew it as soon as Benno disappeared into the cemetery. He knelt, pushed the roses aside, and gently ran his fingers over the name, carefully tracing each of the chiseled letters.

Jennifer Louisa DeGarza Windsor
Born May 26, 1994, Died August 9, 2022

Windsor looked at the date on his watch. She'd been dead exactly one year.

When he finally stood up, he didn't know how long he'd been there. Maybe a few minutes. Maybe an hour. All he knew was that his legs were asleep, his pant legs wet from the grass, and he had relived every day they'd spent together, including the last one. Especially the last one.

Gradually, he brought himself back to the present. The only thing he could think of was keeping Jennifer's name out of it. The press would have a lot to say about a noted psychiatrist killing himself at the grave of Billy Broadnax's last victim.

There was only one thing he could think of.

He carefully rearranged Benno's body, so it was closer to the grave next to Jennifer's. Then he moved the wilted roses. If he was lucky, the police would think the psychiatrist killed himself over the last resting place of Sara Eugenia Browning, born in 1899 and died in 1983. It might work, he thought, if they didn't do any of that hocus pocus with the blood spatters.

He reached into Benno's coat pocket and pulled out the psychiatrist's key ring. He took what looked like the office key off the ring and put the car keys back. Then, he surveyed the scene one more time. It wasn't perfect. Maybe the police would write it off as a simple, run-of-the mill suicide and leave it at that. Then, after spending another few minutes looking down at Jennifer's grave, he walked back to his car.

Windsor had counseled plenty of patients who came to him claiming to be suicidal. Most just wanted attention, someone to listen to their problems, act like they cared, be empathetic. The few that were serious were mired in guilt, grief, or some unfathomable depression. The burden of life so unbearable there was nothing left to live for.

Windsor didn't know which category fit Benno. Not that it mattered. None of them explained why he would kill himself while kneeling next to Jennifer's grave.

He walked back to the car, got in, and drove east toward the city. He stopped at a service station on West Burnside. He told the attendant to fill the tank then went inside, ducked behind the counter, and dialed 911. "Shots fired," he told the operator, then gave the name of the cemetery and hung up. The first police cruiser—lights flashing, siren screaming—drove past just as he pulled out of the station. A second cruiser was thirty seconds behind.

It was some time after one in the morning when Windsor mercifully drifted into a stupor. The telephone rang three different times during the night, but he didn't answer. Caller ID announced it was Cassie Terrace, but it didn't matter. That night, his lover was Bushmills. They wrestled, tussled, and talked dirty to each other until both were empty and spent.

"What have you been doing?" Jennifer asked.

She was sitting in the leather chair in their front room, her arms across her chest, her feet on the matching hassock. Her hair gone totally gray, eyes sunken deeper into her head, fingernails longer and more pointed. Her image faded in and out like a poor signal on an old television set. She was still wearing one of his dress shirts, but now it hung on her like a sheet over a fencepost.

"Trying to find out who killed you and why," he said.

"And?"

"I found out that it wasn't my fault."

"I already knew that."

"I didn't. Now I do."

"It won't change anything," she said. "I'm still here ... wherever here is."

"I know, and every time I think about it, I'm torn to pieces again."

Jennifer seemed to sink deeper into the overstuffed chair as if the cushions were swallowing her up. The wings on the back of the chair looked like arms ready to grab her and pull her away from him again.

"If you learn the truth maybe it will help me rest easier, give me a feeling that I'm somewhere I can be at peace."

"But it won't bring you back to me."

"Nothing can do that, my love. Nothing."

Chapter 33

Ten o'clock the next morning a hungover Alex Windsor sat in his car across the street from the office of the late Dr. Bennett Benno. The scene at the cemetery the previous night still was fresh, made worse by questions about why Benno chose his wife's grave as a place to eat a bullet.

Another dream about Jennifer didn't help things. She was less vivid than in the first dream, closer to disappearing altogether. It didn't matter that what he was doing might help her find peace in death. He was going to do it anyway as much for reasons of his own as for her. Confronting Benno seemed the next logical step.

Chester Broadnax had told him Benno was one of two people to talk with Billy prior to Jennifer's death, even going so far as to help convince Billy to turn himself in. With help from Chandler Stockdale. Stockdale. Plenty of time for him. Right now, he needed to find out what Billy told Benno.

Benno was a doctor. Billy was a patient. Doctors keep files on patients. He needed that file. The key he took off Benno's body would help, but not until he tried something simpler.

He ran his fingers through his hair, straightened his collar, and tried to smooth the wrinkles out of his khakis. Looking as professional as he could considering the circumstances, he got out of the car and walked across the street. Two young, confused-looking women dressed in starched white milled around outside the front door. When he walked by them toward the door with Benno's name on it, a short, bat-faced woman in a nurse's uniform stepped out of the pack.

"Can I help you?" she said.

"I have an appointment with Dr. Benno. My name is Alex Windsor." He reached out his hand. "And you are?"

"Adelaide Milburne, the doctors' office manager."

Windsor looked at Milburne, then at the group of nurses behind her. Two of them started crying while a third comforted them. "I'm sorry. Is there a problem?"

"I'm afraid there is," she said, tears of her own welling up. "Dr. Benno ... passed away ... suddenly last night. Very suddenly."

Windsor did his best to look as sorry and confused as everyone else. "I can't believe it. I talked to him a little after eight last night. He said to come by his office this morning. I'm sorry. I didn't know."

"I know," she said. "It's a shock to all of us. Can you tell me why you wanted to see the doctor?"

"I'm a psychologist. One of my patients is a former patient of Dr. Benno's. He agreed to talk to me about her and loan me her file."

"The patient's name?"

"Blake. Lois Blake."

Milburne thought for a moment. "That doesn't ring a bell."

"I know this is a hard time, but if you wouldn't mind maybe we could go inside and see if it's in his files? I'd really appreciate your help. It's a very complicated case. The more I know, the better I can help Miss Blake."

Milburne pondered, then nodded. He followed her inside, through the waiting room, and down a short, carpeted hallway. Benno's private office at the end of the hall was pretty much what he expected: soft leather furniture, dark walnut bookshelves, biographies of Freud, Jung, and Maslow, thick tomes on psychosis, neurosis, paranoia, schizophrenia, and nymphomania. The rest of the room was dotted with framed diplomas from universities, certificates from professional societies, letters of appreciation from civic clubs, and the obligatory bust of Sigmund Freud. In the other corner was a private entrance that led to the parking lot outside. Next to it stood a four-drawer walnut file cabinet with brass nameplates on each drawer. The top drawer was labeled "A to G", the second "H to M," and so on.

"So, Dr. Benno kept paper files?" Windsor asked, looking at the cabinet. "Pretty old school."

Milburne let out a sad sigh. "I tried for years to convince him to let me get his files in the computer, but he always said no." She looked around the room. "Now I guess it doesn't matter."

"If you don't mind me asking," Windsor said. "How did Doctor Benno die?"

"The police told his wife that it looked like suicide, but it's still under investigation." She shook her head and dabbed at her eyes with a tissue. "I can't believe he would do that. There must be some other answer." Windsor knew there wasn't, so quickly changed the subject.

"What a beautiful family," he said, pointing to one of the photos on the credenza. "Is that his daughter?"

The office manager turned to look at a photo of a mousy woman in her mid-thirties with bad hair, bad glasses, and a mouthful of braces.

"No," she said, "that's his wife."

"Lucky man," he said.

"This is where he did most of his work, saw his patients, and kept his files," Milburne said, lovingly straightening a stack of papers on his desk. "He had a difficult private life. Sharon was his third wife. She's a wonderful woman and very devoted to the doctor. She must be devastated by this."

"Who are the two in the other photo?"

"Those are his daughters. He saw very little of them. His first wife turned them against him after the divorce. They were only six years old at the time. It's such a shame they didn't get to know their father better."

After an awkward few seconds Windsor reminded her of the file he was after.

"Of course," she said, walking over to the file cabinet, pulling open the top drawer, and thumbing through the files to the Bs. She stopped, then started again. "I'm sorry. There's no file here for a Lois Blake."

"Are you sure," he said, crossing the room to stand beside her, watching as she went through the files a third time. She went too fast. He couldn't tell if there was a file labeled "Broadnax."

"Are these his only files?"

"These are the most recent. Just the last five years. The rest are in storage in another room." She sighed. "I'm afraid we've fallen behind when it comes to filing. We're a little shorthanded. The girl who did the filing is … no longer with us. In fact, she was murdered a few days ago in a parking lot not far from here. Her name was Rebecca Roberts. Very sad. She was a sweet girl."

Milburne thumbed through the files one more time. "I'm afraid the file you're looking for is not here. He did keep some files at home. He occasionally did some private consultation outside the office."

"Maybe that's it," Windsor conceded. "I'll have to make do without it. Thank you for your help. I know it's a difficult time. I'll leave you alone. You must have a lot to do."

"Very difficult." Her sigh filled the room.

Windsor sat in his BMW until the parking lot in front of Benno's office was empty. He watched Adelaide Milburne lock the front door, walk dejectedly to her car, and drive away. After waiting a few minutes, he hurried back across the street then around the side of the building. He used Benno's key to unlock the private entrance to his office, ducked inside, and quickly closed it behind him. He pulled open the top of the file cabinet and thumbed through the buff-colored folders, looking for the one labeled "Broadnax." It wasn't there. Thinking it had been misplaced, he rifled through the files in the other three drawers. Nothing. He searched the desk drawers and the stack of papers on the glass-topped desk. Still nothing. He opened the laptop on the credenza, but it was password protected.

If Benno's file on Billy Broadnax existed, he wasn't going to find it in his office.

Chapter 34

"A man committed suicide the other night in the cemetery on West Burnside. It appears as if someone moved the body after he was dead."

Windsor said nothing, straining to hide his reaction from Cassie Terrace's eyes as she searched his face. They were at a picnic table outside a line of food carts near Portland State University. Terrace poked at a plate of red beans and rice while Windsor sipped at a cup of bad coffee.

"Moved it away from Jennifer's grave," she said.

Windsor tried to look surprised. "My Jennifer?"

"Do you know another Jennifer buried in a cemetery on West Burnside?"

Snarky, but he let it pass. "Who was it?" he asked, determined to keep doing his best at pretending he didn't already know. "The victim, I mean."

"That shrink you told me about, Bennett Benno. It looks like he ate a bullet next to your wife's grave on the anniversary of her death."

"How do you know that?"

"Blood spatters don't lie. What I want to know is if you find anything odd about that. And let's not forget that it happened just a few days after you came back to town claiming Billy Broadnax wasn't responsible for Jennifer's murder. I sense a pattern here. How about you?"

"Everybody has to die somewhere." Windsor drained his coffee then toyed with the paper cup.

"Don't do that," Cassie said. The anger in her voice was quick and unmistakable. "I deserve better, especially from you."

"I don't know much more than what I told you the other day," he lied. "Why this Benno guy killed himself and where is no concern of mine."

"The last time we talked, Benno was apparently alive, and you were going to see him. Now he's dead. I don't buy into all coincidences."

"Come on, Cassie. You can't possibly think …"

"No, I don't. I may have been a little hasty in dismissing your ideas about Jennifer's death and what you've given me so far makes a certain amount of sense. But sense is not evidence. There's no way The Meat Man Murders are going to be reopened based on what you have so far, including Benno and where he died. We need an understanding. If you find that a crime has been committed, you're obligated to tell the police. Those are the rules. If you have proof, give it to me and I'll take it from there. If you don't, then just stop."

"I've told you everything I know, but I still need your help. I need to talk to Rebecca Roberts' mother."

"Why?"

"Just a hunch."

"Enlighten me."

"Rebecca Roberts worked for Benno. Now they're both dead. Maybe her mother knows something. Like I said, it's just a hunch."

"This is not your job," she said.

"It is until someone else does it."

"You mean the police?"

"Give me some room to move here, Cassie. If I find anything you'll be the first to know."

Chapter 35

The woman who answered the door had a face as sad as the voice that went with it.

She was in her fifties. Short, curly hair rinsed red. Dark-rimmed bifocals. Blood-shot eyes that looked like they hadn't stopped crying since they found her daughter's body in a trash-strewn parking lot eight blocks away.

"Are you the man who called?" Marian Osgood asked. "Dr. Windsor?"

"Yes."

"I need to see some ID." She reached her hand out. "I'm sorry. Things are kind of … odd right now."

Windsor took his driver's license out of his wallet and passed it through the bars. She looked at it for a few seconds. Apparently satisfied, she handed it back, unchained the door, then unlocked the iron gate. Inside, the house was neat and old-fashioned. The smell of cooked bacon and freshly brewed coffee drifted in from the kitchen at the back of the house. A grandfather clock tolled two p.m. in a deep, somber tone that fit both the house and the reason Windsor was there.

A small boy sitting on the floor in the living room was staging a fist fight between two of the Teenage Mutant Ninja Turtles and the formidable team of Ken and Barbie. He looked up expectantly at Windsor, then, not recognizing him, quickly went back to concentrating on the confrontation between Raphael and a bikini-clad Barbie.

"Danny," Marian Osgood said. "This is Dr. Windsor. Can you say hello?"

Rebecca Roberts' son didn't look up. He said hello in a shy voice, then, in a whisper just loud enough for Windsor to hear, asked his grandmother if he could play in his room.

"You'll have to excuse him," she said after the boy left. "Danny and Rebecca were very close. He doesn't understand where she is. He still thinks she's coming home." She sighed as the little boy disappeared into a room at the end of a hallway. "My husband is a ship's captain in the Merchant Marine. He's on his way home now. Maybe things will be better when he gets here." She used a tissue to wipe away a tear. "I certainly hope so." She put on a brave face. "So, how can I help you?"

"I'm hoping that your daughter may have told you something about her receptionist job with Dr. Bennett Benno."

When Marian Osgood looked confused, Windsor leveled with her, telling her about the death of his wife, Billy Broadnax, and Benno. She listened while sitting on the couch, hands in her lap, tearing at a piece of tissue. When he was done, all she could say was "Oh my. What does Rebecca have to do with this?"

"I don't know. I was hoping you could help me out. I understand it's a long shot, but anything at all might help. Do you know what kind of work she did for Dr. Benno?"

"Receptionist mostly and making copies of files for lawyers and the police. At least that's what she said. I just assumed everything had sort of come together for her. God knows she'd earned it."

"I take it the job didn't work out."

Marian Osgood shook her head. "One day she told me the doctor had laid her off and wasn't going to pay her anymore. That was when she got the job at the convenience store. She said it was only temporary, that she had something else lined up. She never told me what it was."

"When was that?"

"Just a few weeks ago."

"Any boyfriends?"

"Not since her divorce. Her marriage was a kind of love-hate thing if you know what I mean. She never had much luck with men. The divorce just made her even more discouraged. Then there's Danny. He didn't leave her much time to socialize. She had a date every now and then, but none of them seemed to interest her. I think she found it better to avoid them altogether, at least that's what I'd like to think." She sighed, wiped her eyes then poked the tattered tissue in the sleeve of her sweater. "Things just got worse and worse for her. I never thought things would get this bad."

"Do you remember any of the men she went out with recently?"

She thought for a moment. "There was one man that came to see her several times in the last couple of weeks. He was older and sort of … unkempt. I don't think they were involved if you know what I mean. He didn't seem like a very nice person. I think they knew each other from when she worked for the doctor."

"Do you remember his name or what he looked like?"

"Not his name, but I remember his shoes. They looked expensive and highly polished. It was odd because the rest of his clothes looked sort of sloppy. You know, wrinkled with stains on them."

"Did she mention the name Harold Gilroy?"

Marian Osgood thought for a few seconds. "She may have. The name sounds familiar, but I can't be sure."

It didn't surprise Windsor that Gilroy was involved even though what he knew about Squid made him think he was more inclined to peek in Rebecca's bedroom window at night than show up at the front door during the day.

"Did you know her ex-husband visited her the day she was killed?"

She acted surprised. "No. Why? Is he involved somehow?"

"The police think so. He's been arrested and could be charged with her death and with the death of Harold Gilroy. They think the two are connected."

"This Gilroy person. He was the one who came to see her? The one with the shoes? He's dead too?"

Windsor nodded.

She looked surprised for a few seconds before shaking her head, then glancing at her daughter's picture on the mantle. "He always was a hot head." She gave Windsor a pleading look. "Do the police really think Matthew did all that because she was seeing this Gilroy person?"

"They do, for now at least."

"You hear about things like this happening, but you never believe they can happen to you," she said, the tears made a comeback followed by the tissue. "It seems anything can happen to anybody these days. Portland isn't the safe city it used to be."

"You said part of Rebecca's job at Dr. Benno's was making copies of files. Did she bring home any papers from the office?"

"She might have. I haven't felt like cleaning out her room. I'll get around to it, but not for a while. If she did bring anything home, it would probably be in there or in some boxes she stored in the garage."

"Do you mind if I look?"

She shrugged and got up. He followed her down the hall. "I'll leave you here," she said without going inside.

The room was small and neat with a double bed, chest of drawers, and small desk with an office chair. Windsor looked gingerly through the dresser and the desk drawers. Finding nothing, he went back to the dining room to ask Marian Osgood if he could look at the boxes in the garage. She led him out the back door, across a small breezeway, and in the side door of a cluttered two-car garage. She pointed to a cardboard box in the corner next to a set of studded snow tires. When she excused herself and went back in the house, Windsor picked up the box and set it on a dusty workbench. Inside were a half dozen manila envelopes. Five of them contained papers and assignment sheets, apparently from the classes Rebecca took. Written in felt pen on the sixth was "Harold Gilroy."

Windsor opened it and pulled out photocopies of several documents, including a memo, a series of emails, and what looked like a report and a timeline printed on cheap paper with bad spelling and worse grammar. Scanning it gave him a brief glimpse of what the papers were and what they could mean. He slipped them back into the envelope and returned to the house.

"I found this," he said, holding up the envelope. "I'd like to keep it if you don't mind. I can make copies and return it if you'd like."

"If you think it will help," she said.

"Listen, Mrs. Osgood. The police are pretty good at these sorts of things. If they think Matthew Roberts is responsible for what happened, then I'd stick with that until they tell you something differently. I know that doesn't help. I'm sorry."

Marian Osgood nodded, dabbed her eyes with the tissue, and thanked him. "You really think Matthew did it?"

"Time will tell. These things take a while. The police usually get it right, but not all the time. Be patient and let's see how things play out."

Windsor thanked her, then walked back to his car. He put the envelope on the passenger seat and stared at it. The torn-up Bible was one thing, but in the eyes of prosecutors it would probably fall into the category of circumstantial. He needed time to review them but the documents in the envelope could take things to a whole new level.

Chapter 36

Windsor laid the envelope on the dining room table and stared at it. If inside was what he'd been looking for, then everything had been worthwhile. Leaving the ranch. Coming back to Portland. Believing that Broadnax didn't kill Jennifer. Enduring the ghosts in the house they shared together. It would all have meant something. If it didn't and the papers inside were just the jargon-filled musing of a psychiatrist or the random rantings of a low life, then it was time to disappear again. Back to his cabin, Sam Westlake, and fly fishing. Instead, hands trembling, he slowly pulled out the documents and spread them across the table.

The first document was Benno's lengthy psychiatric evaluation of Billy Broadnax. Windsor had written plenty of evaluations just like it. They took different forms, but the language stayed pretty much the same, which meant a certain amount of decoding and reading between the lines. Benno's was no different.

It was dated August ninth—the day Jennifer was killed and the day before Billy surrendered to police. It was written in the form of a memo from Benno to Stockdale and titled *Psychiatric Evaluation of William Charles Broadnax*. The more he read the more he realized that the evaluation was not just an antiseptic, clinical breakdown of a patient, but a twisted road map through the mind of a killer. Having met Billy, Windsor could find little to disagree with regarding his mental state. It was the details that caught his attention. They had more to do with describing how Billy murdered his victims than what kind of psychotic, bat-shit crazy reasons he had for doing it.

Serial killers had never been part of Windsor's practice, mostly because there weren't that many of them and none, until The Meat Man, in Portland. That didn't prevent him from having an enduring interest in who they were and what motivated them. What he did know came either from professional journals, news accounts, documentaries or long talks with the cops and profilers who tried to find them. It all brought him to the conclusion that no two were alike. The mass murderers who walked into classrooms, shopping malls or synagogues left their hate-filled motives scrawled across social media. Theirs was usually a single act of mayhem, unlike the actions of methodical serial killers who carefully plotted each attack. If serial killers had one common denominator it was some deep physical or psychological trauma born in a dark childhood experience—rejected by their mothers, abandoned by their fathers, abused by a priest, a scout leader or all of them. Whatever happened, they grew up tortured and tormented in mind and body. They avoided relationships and feared rejection. Then there was always sexual repression, a go-to motive—at least in the public's eye—for most serial killers.

From what Benno wrote, Billy Broadnax was none of that. He may have been obsessed about God and fixated on "wealthy, unchaste women" when in fact he was nothing more than a brutal killer determined to kill and kill again. All killers need a reason: rich, attractive women was Billy's.

Benno went into a gut-wrenching detailed and anatomical description of what Billy did to his victims. How he killed them and what he did after they were dead. Three sentences and Windsor had enough. He knew firsthand what Billy did to Jennifer.

What surprised him was how meticulous Billy had been. That didn't sound like the dark, brooding figure he'd talked to at the state penitentiary. Neat and tidy didn't square with scruffy and chaotic. It did, however, square with Chester Broadnax's description of his son.

He'd read enough to know that Benno's evaluation of Broadnax was only slightly off the mark from what he'd written in his own opinion piece. Sure, Billy was every bit as deranged as he believed, but nowhere near the drooling monster described by police or portrayed in news accounts. He may well have been an "impotent momma's boy" as Windsor believed, but that had nothing to do with why he killed women. He just enjoyed it. Period.

Windsor had seen enough. Billy didn't kill Jennifer, but she fit the profile.

The second document was a collection of emails between Benno and Stockdale, all of which confirmed what Windsor had learned from Chester Broadnax, including Stockdale's involvement with Billy at least two days before being named Billy's court-appointed attorney. In one email, Stockdale confirmed that he received Benno's evaluation and had read it. His only comment was "Interesting."

Another email was about Benno's decision to hire Harold Gilroy to follow Billy and report on his movements. Benno wanted to know where Billy went and what he did in the hours after he left Benno's office. Stockdale agreed.

The third document sealed the deal. It was Squid Gilroy's hour-by-hour chronology of Billy Broadnax's movements from the time he left

Benno's office until he surrendered to police early on the morning of August tenth. Windsor carefully read each entry, running his finger down the page, digesting every word. This is what he'd been looking for. He just had a hard time believing what it said.

If the chronology was correct, Billy left Benno's office and drove home with his father. Three hours later Billy left and drove to a strip club on Canyon Road in Beaverton. Each entry was time stamped.

8:09 p.m. – Broadnax enters The Climax Club.

8:11 p.m. – Broadnax sits at a table near the stage and orders a tequila sunrise.

8:20 p.m. – Broadnax pays for a lap dance from a stripper named Snap Dragon.

8:42 p.m. – Broadnax orders another tequila sunrise.

9:02 p.m. – He pays for another lap dance.

9:26 p.m. – Broadnax leaves The Climax Club and gets in his pickup.

10:12 p.m. – Broadnax goes through a drive-in window at a MacDonald's in Hillsboro. He orders a burger, fries, and a drink and eats in the parking lot.

10:59 p.m. – Broadnax arrives at home.

The report was signed: Harold Gilroy, Private Investigator.

There was only one conclusion: Billy Broadnax was drinking and getting lap dances at exactly the same time Jennifer was being murdered.

Chapter 37

It was the kind of office the killer always wanted. Not the trailers and make-shift buildings where he'd spent most of his life. Things were better now, but he always felt most comfortable in the cab of a pickup, a bottle of whiskey between his legs.

He had a home office, but it was little more than a converted bedroom with some bookcases, a desk, a computer he didn't use, and a couch for afternoon naps. Nothing like the one he was standing in now with its big desk, massive bookshelves filled with leather-bound volumes, and long conference table with thick, important-looking files scattered haphazardly across its polished mahogany top. But what he really liked were the windows. They covered an entire wall, floor to ceiling. They were tinted so he could see out, but no one could see in. Exactly the way he tried to live his life.

Outside the windows the entire city spread out like a miniature town. The MAX system looked like toy trains running between tall buildings. People moved past the windows in the office building across the street. Placing his forehead against the window, he looked down at the busy street twenty floors below. People hurried for a lunch date or lined up at the ATM directly below him, clutching Starbucks cups in one hand and cellphones in the other. The colorful tents of the homeless camps along the river looked like Easter eggs no one bothered to look for. A block up the street his black Taurus sat parked at a meter that would expire in fifteen minutes. Probably best not to get a ticket, he thought.

"We want it stopped," Chandler Stockdale said. "Four people are dead, including Bennett Benno." He was sitting behind his desk, back to the window, coat off. He looked every bit like a man who expected his orders to be obeyed. "I also think it's time we disbanded our little investment club and begin pretending we don't know each other. We only got involved in this because you said it was a straight-up business opportunity. Now, four people are dead. That is not what we signed up for. I'll draw up the papers. We can all meet and sign them."

The man standing at the window smiled to himself. He knew that sooner or later they'd all get cold feet. All their tough talk would amount to nothing. Not that it mattered. He'd gotten everything he wanted. The sooner he was rid of them the better. It meant more for him just like it was before he made the mistake of getting involved with them in the first place.

"None of this would have happened except for your buddy Benno," the killer said.

"Made worse by your killing Gilroy and his girlfriend. Enough is enough. We are not in so deep that I can't get us out of it. You just need to stop."

"And Windsor?" the killer said.

"Let it go." Stockdale said it in the kind of loathsome voice the killer used to hear on CB radios back in the days before cell phones.

"I don't think that's a good idea," he said. "Windsor's getting closer. He just doesn't know all of it yet, but he'll figure it out. He's talked to that Gilroy character, to Billy, to Billy's father, to what's-her-name's mother. Now he's hanging out with that homicide detective he used to fuck. Think about what all that means."

"But he doesn't have Benno's file. Without that he has nothing."

"You're sure it's been destroyed?"

"I did it myself. Benno told me he did the same thing."

The killer went back to staring down at the people waiting for the ATM, marveling at how easily mindless machines became an indispensable part of everyday life. Not that it mattered to him. He had never used an ATM, preferring to deal solely in cash he took from a wall safe at home. He had a credit card in case of emergencies. It just didn't have his real name on it. Any bills that needed paying would catch up with him eventually.

"You've all waffled around wondering what to do with him," he said. "Time to shit or get off the pot."

"I know, but listen to me," Stockdale said. "We can't afford to take any chances with Windsor. He has a certain celebrity status made greater by his sudden return and connection to Broadnax. If anything happens to him around the anniversary of his wife's murder, the media will go crazy. Let it go. Maybe we can deal with him later when things die down. But not now."

"You're making a mistake. By now he knows most of what happened the night his wife died. He just doesn't have the proof. We can't take the chance that he'll eventually find it."

"We've already talked about this. Go home, forget Windsor, and pull the plug on our investment. Stop the payments. All the money going forward is yours."

The killer didn't argue. Ending their investment club meant more money for him, but that wasn't the problem. It was Windsor. If he learned the truth, there would be hell to pay. He would lose everything. So would they, but he didn't care. It was his own skin that he was worried about.

He'd been parked down the street from Marian Osgood's house when Windsor walked out carrying a manila envelope. He didn't know what was in it, but he couldn't take any chances. Something had to be done. He needed time to figure things out. Killing Windsor now was a bad idea. Maybe in a few weeks it wouldn't be, assuming he had that long.

The killer left Stockdale's office through a private door that opened into a back hallway. "Bedwetters," he mumbled as he rode down in the oak-paneled elevator with the elegant brass buttons, all the while knowing he was on his own. Before reaching street-level, he decided that while they may be ready to give up and risk losing everything, he wasn't. He didn't want to kill Windsor any more than they did, but the options were limited.

Chapter 38

The shackles on Broadnax's wrists, ankles and waist left him little room to do anything other than sit facing Windsor.

"What do you want now?" he snarled, his tone a ginned-up attempt at anger and belligerence.

"I have proof that you didn't kill my wife."

"Great," Billy said. "When do I get out of here?"

"You don't, but it does mean you might have another roommate or two."

Billy didn't respond right away. His bald, tattooed head bobbed up and down a couple of times, then turned to look out the window. Anger and belligerence gave way to sad and pathetic. "I don't belong here. They keep calling me a pervert."

"You are not a pervert. You're worse than a pervert. You're a killer, a merciless, unrepentant killer. Pure and simple. I'm sure that earns you a certain amount of respect in a place like this. Live with it, enjoy it for what it's worth, and quit whining."

Billy glared at Windsor but let the remark pass.

Getting a second interview with Billy Broadnax required Windsor to take another arduous trip through the hide-bound bureaucracy of the Department of Corrections and finesse the requirement not to contact Broadnax's lawyer. It eventually called for another intervention by his friend David Weathers in the public affairs office. It was worth it if Billy could confirm everything in Benno's file, including Gilroy's report.

"Do you remember when your father took you to see that lawyer, Chandler Stockdale?" Windsor said.

Billy nodded.

"You confessed to him that you killed seven women. Is that right?"

Billy nodded again.

"When your father left the room, you were alone with the lawyer. What did you tell him?"

Billy shrank down into his chair, rolled his eyes toward the ceiling, then down at the floor. Windsor had seen this transformation in Billy before. That didn't make it any easier to watch. The tough prison inmate took on a new identity, that of a child. Whining. Sniveling. Baby talk.

"I told him how I did it. How I killed each one," Billy said in a high, almost girlish voice. "He asked a lot of questions. Wrote things down."

"What kind of questions?" Windsor said, intentionally keeping his tone sharp. Billy was on his heels. Best keep him that way.

"Details. Things like that. Then he told me everything would be okay. Then my father came back, and we left."

"And your father took you to see this doctor and you told him the same things. The details. What you did. How you did it. Is that right?"

Billy seemed to shrink more and more into himself. Windsor was moving too fast. He needed to slow down so Billy could keep up.

"I'm sorry, Billy. All of this is very important to me. It's personal. I'll talk slower."

"I'm not stupid."

"Of course not, but I need to know what kinds of questions the doctor asked."

"The same ones and different ones. More details. Ones about my parents. What I thought about women. Why I killed those women. Would I do it again. They were hard questions. I didn't like answering them. They made me feel funny."

"But you told him the details of how you killed each woman, right?"

Billy nodded.

"Just like you did the lawyer, right?"

"Yes."

Windsor stared at Billy for a few moments, watching him squirm to avoid Windsor's gaze. "Anything else you want to tell me?"

Billy thought for a moment. "You still want me to tell you about Gilroy, don't you?" he said.

"That's right, Billy."

"I was with the doctor when that Gilroy guy showed up. The doctor said he would be my friend and protect me. He said I could go anywhere I wanted, but that Gilroy would be somewhere around to keep an eye on me. Make sure I didn't get into any more trouble and to find me if they needed me."

"Needed you for what?"

"I don't know. The doctor didn't say. I should have asked, but I didn't. Everything was very confusing." He looked around the room. "Can I go now?"

"No," Windsor said. "Listen to me. Do you know where you were the night Jennifer Windsor was killed?"

Billy looked confused for a second. "Which one was she?"

"Never mind. Did you ever go to a place called The Climax Club and watch nude dancers?"

Billy's eyes lit up. His tongue did a lap around his lips. "Yeah," he said in a harsh whisper. "I remember this Chinese chick and you know what she did with her ..."

"Don't," Windsor interrupted. "You'll just drive yourself crazy. Did you see Gilroy that night?"

"Yeah, but we didn't go there together. He came later. Followed me, I guess, like the doctor said. He sat at the bar near the door, I think. When I left, he was gone. I saw him outside, sitting in his car waiting for me. When I left, I think he followed me again."

"Where did you go after leaving the club?"

Billy thought for a moment. "I'm not sure. I think I got something to eat. A burger maybe. I can't remember each time."

"Did you drive around? Did you go home?"

"I could have."

"Why not another victim?"

Billy shrugged. "I don't know. I think I thought about it. There were a couple of women that I followed home from the grocery store. One of them lived alone." He paused for a few seconds. "It just didn't feel right, I guess."

"So, you went home."

"Yeah."

Windsor sat back in the chair. Billy's recollection of that night seemed to square with Gilroy's report.

"The doctor and the other guy said I was sick," Billy said. "They said I needed to be in a special place." He looked around with disgust. "They didn't tell me it was this place. It all happened so fast."

Windsor couldn't imagine what kind of place Billy thought he was going to. "You just did what the lawyer and the doctor told you?"

"Yeah."

"And the doctor gave you some pills and a shot of some kind?"

"Both," Billy said. "They made me feel better for a while, but then I got sort of confused."

"Were you confused when you surrendered to police and when you confessed?"

"Probably. I don't even remember how I got there. I just know I was with my dad. He told me everything would be all right." Billy glanced down at his shackles. "I don't think that was true."

"Are you confused now?"

Billy shook his head.

"Then listen to me very carefully." Windsor stood up, put his hands on the table and leaned forward. He looked directly down into Billy's eyes. "I believe I can prove that you didn't kill one of those women, but that isn't going to change anything. You're still a killer. You're still on the hook for seven other murders. I don't know what Gilroy told you, but you're never going to get out of here other than to some other prison just like this one. Different cell. Different roommates. If you're lucky you may go to the courthouse to testify about what you just told me, but you'll come right back here. Is that clear?"

While they traded stares, Windsor marveled at how innocent and guileless Billy seemed. Somewhere in the back of that deranged mind was the idea that prison was like being grounded. Sooner or later his angry parents would relent and give him the keys to the car again.

"So, when am I getting out of here?" It was like he'd never heard a word Windsor said.

"Get over it, Billy. This is where you'll die. This is where you deserve to die." Windsor knocked on the inside of the door to let the guards know he was through. He was nearly out the door when he asked for a couple of more minutes. The guards shrugged and waited impatiently.

"There's one thing I need to know. Why did you do it? Why did you kill all those women?"

Billy stared at Windsor with an odd quizzical look. "It was fun. I liked it. The searching, the following, the sitting outside their house, the watching. Then there was the planning. They all had to be the same. The first, second, third. Each one identical. It made me feel good. Why wouldn't I do it?"

"And you'd do it again, wouldn't you?"

Billy's eyes lit up. "Oh, yeah."

"Now you know why you'll never get out of here."

One of the guards hacked out a short laugh as they took Billy away.

Chapter 39

Enrico DeGarza sat in the same place watching the same two children play in the same dirt yard in front of the rundown double-wide mobile home. The trucks they'd played with on Windsor's last visit had been replaced by two toy train engines. The kids kneeled on either side of the dust pit, sliding the trains through the grit until they collided head on in a cloud of dust, sound effects, and laughter.

Windsor sat in his car across the road still wanting absolution from his father-in-law, but too afraid to walk across the hot asphalt and ask for it. As a psychologist he understood his reluctance. Avoid confrontation. The fight isn't worth the energy. Walk away. Change the subject. Pick and choose your battles. It was all that and more. He needed to be sure he was right and that the old man would understand.

His plan was to tell DeGarza he had the proof that someone else was responsible for his daughter's death. The old man could believe him or not. Either way, Windsor's conscience would be clear. He just couldn't screw up the courage to do it. The old man had never liked him, even less after believing that he was responsible for Jennifer's death. Windsor had felt the same way for a long time. Just not anymore. He could show Enrico what was in the files he'd found. Maybe he'd believe it. Maybe not. He only had one shot at Enrico. He had to make it work. One thing he was sure of was that the old man would ask the same questions Windsor had: If you're not responsible for her death, then who is and why?

Not having the answer gave him the excuse he needed to wait, to drive away, and come back when he knew the truth, all of it. His absolution would have to wait, but not the search for the truth.

He knew the next place to go.

Chapter 40

The law firm of Allen, Todd, Windsor & Stockdale dispensed its high-priced legal advice from offices on the top two floors of a sparkly new twenty-story, glass-and-steel high rise. Most people referred to it as The Tower even though it was nowhere near the tallest building in the center of downtown. Its real name had something to do with the developer's girlfriend, but no one paid much attention except UPS. The office's greatest attribute was a one-hundred-eighty degree view up and down the Willamette River and across to the sprawling east side of the city.

The brass-and-glass elevator opened on to a large, top-floor reception area where a predictably young and attractive receptionist answered the phone with a nasally, "Law Offices." She was seated behind a waist-high, highly polished counter so all he could see was a full head of shiny blonde hair.

"May I help you?" she said with a vacant smile.

"I'm here to see Chandler Stockdale."

"And you are?"

"Alex Windsor."

"Oh." She eyed him more closely, then picked up her telephone. "There's a Mr. Windsor here to see Mr. Stockdale," she said then hung up. "Please have a seat. Mr. Stockdale's assistant will be right with you. Can I get you anything? Water? Coffee?"

"I'm fine. Thanks."

Windsor stayed standing, turning his back on the reception area to look out the window at the unobstructed view of the river as it oozed through the center of the city. Mt. Hood stood out a brilliant white-on-gray against the blue summer sky. The smoked windows acted like a huge set of dark glasses that disguised the persistent heat outside, giving the city the calm, cool look it once craved but now seemed to have lost forever.

He was still admiring the view when a woman in an appropriately gray business suit emerged from one of the walnut doors on either side of the receptionist's desk. The reading glasses hanging from a beaded chain around her neck bounced against ample breasts that were out of proportion to her tall, slender frame. Her luxuriant gray hair was pulled tight into the same bun she'd worn for the thirty-five years he'd known her.

"Alex?" she said.

"Hello, Eleanor. How are you?"

"I can't believe it's you," she said, her face lighting up as she eyed him from top to bottom. "I like the beard, but I don't think you've been eating right. You look ... well ... thin."

Eleanor McNamara was the only legal secretary Alex's father ever had. She was nineteen when he hired her shortly after starting the firm. She worked for him until his death. She might work in a different era now, but he was willing to bet that she still took shorthand and made coffee for Stockdale the same as she did for his father.

"Chandler didn't tell me you were coming by," she said.

"He doesn't know. It's sort of a surprise."

Unfazed, she took him by the arm. "I'm so glad you're back. I've been worried about you." She stopped to hold his hand in both of hers. "Jennifer. How she died. The funeral. I'm so sorry."

He hugged her. "I know" was all he could say.

Eleanor clung to Windsor's arm as they walked along the elegant hallway lined with offices, bookshelves, and work areas for legal assistants and secretaries. The open space at the end of the hallway contained two cluttered desks and expensive leather furniture. Behind one desk was a younger version of Eleanor. A nameplate identified her simply as "Tiffany."

"Wait here," Eleanor said, then disappeared into an office with "Mr. Stockdale" stenciled in gold on the door. She reappeared a few seconds later and motioned him in.

Stockdale's office included a huge desk and an even larger mahogany conference table. File folders, legal briefs, law books, and yellow legal pads covered every flat surface. Stockdale was in shirtsleeves with his feet on the desk, a deposition on his lap, and a telephone to his ear. Always looking the part, Windsor thought, as Stockdale pointed to one of the two walnut-and-leather chairs facing his desk and motioned him to sit down.

"Alex! What a surprise." Stockdale's voice was an annoying baritone cultivated over the years to impress judges and juries but annoy just about everybody else. "I didn't know you were back in town." He gave Windsor a firm handshake. "I never had a chance to talk to you after Jennifer's death. For myself and for the firm, I want to express my deepest sympathies."

Windsor's only stake in Allen, Todd, Windsor & Stockdale was a generous annuity set up in his father's will and paid for by the firm. He knew the income was substantial, but seldom used it for anything other than buying the house on Royal Oak Way. Otherwise, it just built up in an account managed by a firm in San Francisco. Despite monthly statements he rarely opened, he wasn't sure how much money he had. He only knew that it was a lot.

From the time it was established forty years earlier by Gerard Allen, Jason Todd, and Windsor's father, the firm set out to specialize in corporate law. Over time it developed a client list that included two of the state's largest banks, utilities in different regions of the state, and a few insurance companies. The practice grew to include more than two dozen associates, twice that in support staff, and offices in the three West Coast states and Washington, D.C. The firm's success made all three founding partners multi-millionaires. They added to their wealth with shrewd real estate deals and even shrewder investment of the profits. Stockdale joined the firm in the late 90s, quickly rising to partner with his name on the letterhead.

After Windsor's father died, and with the other founding partners getting older, the younger Stockdale assumed the role of the firm's alpha male. It was his idea that the firm branch into regulatory affairs and later into legislative affairs. The prestigious clients lured to the firm by the founding partners still provided the bulk of the firm's income but representing corporate clients before state and federal agencies and the state legislature had rapidly become a highly lucrative business.

The clients Stockdale brought to the firm didn't seem to mind paying high hourly fees, even though most of them had public relations problems rather than legal ones. The massive number of billable hours provided the basis of Stockdale's enduring power and influence within the firm.

Stockdale was in his early sixties but looked younger. Thick, black hair graying elegantly and appropriately at the temples. His health-club tan stood out nicely against the bright white of a starched dress shirt. Regardless of how competent a lawyer he was, Windsor thought, Stockdale certainly looked the part.

"Thanks," Windsor said. "I'll make this short. I want to talk about one of your clients."

Stockdale looked at his watch, frowned, then said: "Of course. Anyone particular?"

"Billy Broadnax."

"Billy Broadnax!" Stockdale said, looking surprised. "I haven't heard that name for a while. I would think that you of all people would want to leave that in the past. To my mind that would be the wisest course."

Chapter 41

Growing up the son of a wealthy lawyer, Windsor recognized Stockdale's tone and manner. It was intended to let Windsor know that he'd been dismissed, free to leave, and to no longer bother him. Windsor ignored it.

"This is a little bit different. There have been some new developments in Jennifer's death."

Stockdale looked indignant. "There is no new information. Billy confessed to everything."

"Maybe then. Not now. I've come across something that may change things considerably."

Stockdale looked at Windsor and waited.

"I have two documents that show you were representing Billy Broadnax before he surrendered to police. That the day before he surrendered you talked with Billy, probably right here in this office, then sent him to a psychiatrist for an evaluation and that you were sent a copy of that evaluation."

"That's right. Billy's father was a tenant of mine at some property I own in Washington County. He's a very decent man. He asked me to help him with Billy's ... problems ... so I arranged for him to see a psychiatrist."

"That would be Bennett Benno?"

"That's correct."

"What kind of psychiatric problems?"

"You know I'm not at liberty to divulge that information, but it should be pretty obvious."

"Did you know that Billy had killed seven women when you first talked to him?"

"All I knew was that his father was worried about it but had no proof."

Windsor let the first lie pass because he knew there'd be more. "Did Benno know Billy was The Meat Man?"

"I have no idea."

"Then you didn't get Benno's evaluation?"

"Not that I recall."

Not a lie, but a lawyerly dodge. "Why did Chester Broadnax want to see you?"

"I've already said more than I should. I really need to go." Stockdale looked at his watch again. "I have an important lunch engagement."

Windsor smiled at him. "Let me guess. The Arlington Club. You know, I'm still a member. Let's go. The first martini is on me. You'll have to buy the next two yourself."

"Very funny," Chandler said. "Now, what is it you want?"

"How come you let people believe that you didn't start representing Billy until after he turned himself in?"

"I wasn't representing him. I was doing a favor for his father. That may be a technicality to you, but in the eyes of the law it's an important distinction. I did no legal work for Billy or his father prior to being appointed by the court. I was not paid a retainer. I didn't hide anything. Had someone asked me, I would've told them. Nobody did."

"Did you give Chester any advice on what to do about Billy?"

"I don't have time for this." Stockdale stood up then stopped. "Let me give you a few pieces of advice, Alex. First, Billy Broadnax is still my client. I don't intend to violate my attorney-client relationship with him, no matter what he did or how long he spends in prison. Second, the judge has placed a gag order on this case, which I've probably violated already just by talking to you. Third, Bennett Benno was a close friend of mine. His death was tragic. A terrible blow to me, my family, and the entire community. I don't know what you're doing, but if you intend to malign his reputation in any way, I would be very, very careful." Chandler shook his finger in Windsor's face. "In other words, don't fuck with me."

Having made his point, Stockdale pulled his coat off the back of his chair and started putting it on.

"Since Billy Broadnax is still your client you might like to know that Benno hired a private investigator to follow Billy. The investigator wrote a report and sent it to Benno. It says Billy was drinking tequila sunrises and getting lap dances at a strip club in Beaverton at the same time Jennifer was being murdered. I also have Billy's Bible. The pages found with my wife's body are still in it. What all this means is that someone else killed her. Any idea who?"

"Of course not. That question is an insult. What you're telling me is nonsense. You need to be very careful with accusations like that." Chandler was using his finger again. "There are legal consequences to making irresponsible comments."

"The private investigator Benno hired was a guy named Harold Gilroy. Squid, to his friends. Ever hear of him?"

Stockdale scoffed and headed for the door.

"There's more," Windsor said. "Benno had a receptionist named Rebecca Roberts. You probably didn't know her either, so I'll fill you in. She was a friend of Gilroy's. Both Gilroy and Roberts are dead, murdered. The police think Roberts' ex-husband did it. I'm not so sure."

Stockdale refused to turn around, choosing instead to stop, frozen in place.

"To top it all off," Windsor said, "your friend Benno ate a bullet in the same cemetery where Jennifer's buried. Just a few feet away from her grave, in fact. You wouldn't care to hazard a guess why Benno killed himself and his choice of locations?"

Stockdale turned around. "No, and if I did, I wouldn't discuss it with you."

"Probably just all a bunch of coincidences, don't you think?" Windsor said, giving Stockdale a sly smile.

"This is all very fascinating, but I need to go. I don't know where you've been for the last year or what you're up to. Rumor has it you've been living in Tibet. If that's true, then I think you've smoked too much of that hashish or whatever they have at those places. What I do know is that if any of what you just said appears anywhere in print or on radio or television you better be prepared to defend it in court."

"I'll leave that to the police, Windsor said. "This isn't over, Chandler. In fact, it may be just getting started."

"Be careful, Alex, very careful," Stockdale said, then reached for the door.

"You know how this works. Sooner or later one of the newspapers or some online news site is going to publish a story that says Billy didn't kill my wife. Then there's always Twitter, Instagram, Facebook, and whatever. To what extent any of that will require a rehash of the Broadnax murders is hard to say at this point, but I don't see any way to ignore them all together. Do you?"

Stockdale's eyes narrowed. "Are you going to be the source for this story?"

"No." Stockdale refused to look at him. "I'd rather wait until some cop leaks it to a reporter. It just won't be the whole story. I'm the only one who has that."

"I'm disappointed. You already know how I feel about what this will do to the community to say nothing of the families of those victims. Do you really want to make them relive that horrible time all over again?"

"Don't lecture me about how the victims will feel," Windsor said. "I am one, remember. Besides, this is about me, not anyone else. I have most of the proof I need."

"Such as?"

Stockdale sat back down, stayed motionless while Windsor described the contents of the documents he found in Rebecca Roberts' garage. If Stockdale was concerned, he didn't show it.

"You realize those are privileged documents," he said when Windsor finished.

"Who cares? By the way, I think you just confirmed that you know of the documents' existence."

"Touché," Stockdale said without flinching. "So, this story will implicate me and Dr. Benno in the death of your wife? Is that what you're telling me?"

"Implicate is a good word. I would imagine that your name and Benno's would be featured prominently in any story since you sent Broadnax to Benno. Finding Benno's body near Jennifer's grave just adds to the mystery, don't you think?"

"How did you get these documents?"

"I have them. How I got them is moot at this point."

Stockdale leaned forward, elbows on the desktop. "Have it your way, but if Billy didn't kill your wife, then who did and why?"

"I've been asking myself the same question. My guess is that Benno killed her then killed himself out of guilt. That leaves the why. Care to hazard a guess?"

"You can't be serious," Stockdale said, feigning outrage.

"Serious enough to make a high-priced corporate lawyer like you nervous."

"Your father was a high-priced corporate lawyer."

"Let's leave my father out of this."

Stockdale shrugged in agreement. "I'm just looking out for the interests of my client, this firm, and the city. I believe justice was done in this case. I helped stop the murders and prevented Billy from being executed. A death sentence would have dragged on for years, each appeal reminding the victims' families of what happened. A life sentence meant locking him up forever and forgetting about him. It also put an end to the media hype that was destroying Portland's reputation."

It was the softball Windsor had been waiting for.

"I talked to your client yesterday. Billy confirmed everything in Gilroy's report. Not only that, but he also told me that he sat right here, in this office, and told you all the gory details. Then later that same day he met with Bennett Benno and he repeated it all again."

"Billy is insane," Stockdale said. He was working hard at keeping up the bemused and condescending look of a confident negotiator, except for the small bead of sweat that rolled out of his perfect hair and down his right temple.

"Then you have nothing to worry about, right?" Windsor said. They swapped stares across the desk. "Listen, Chandler, you knew Billy was the killer before Jennifer died. That means you could've done something about it, but you didn't. I'm sure the bar association would be fascinated by that fact, not to mention the district attorney. You're an officer of the court. You withheld evidence. You know more about these things than I do, but can't you be disbarred for that?"

"That's outrageous. I did my job. I'm above reproach in this matter and I'm not going let you or anyone else distort the truth."

"Then like I said, you have nothing to worry about. Someone will print the story, you'll issue a denial, and that will be the end of it."

It was the perfect opportunity for Stockdale to display the appropriate amount of righteous indignation. He didn't disappoint. "Don't give me that crap," he snapped. "You know as well as I do that things don't work that way."

"And Jennifer?"

"How dare you accuse me of murder or even being involved in one." Only his lips moved as he spat out the words, the rest of his body stayed perfectly still while his face grew redder. "I know a little something about libel and slander laws. You wouldn't dare say this or be involved in printing it. I'm calling your bluff. Take your phony documents and your wild theories to those chicken-shit editors down the street or anywhere else and see what happens. They won't believe a word of it because it's all lies. You've got nothing."

"Okay, let's say they don't believe me. That still leaves me and, according to my calculations, there's an even-money chance that if Benno didn't kill my wife, then you did. I hope for your sake I'm wrong."

"Is that a threat?"

"That didn't sound like a denial."

"Answer me. Is that a threat?"

Windsor paused, more for effect than not knowing the answer. "Yes. Yes, it is."

"I have nothing more to say to you." Stockdale started walking to the door again. Windsor blocked his way.

"Maybe it wasn't Benno. Maybe it was you, Chandler?" Windsor said. The anger in his voice stopped the lawyer in his tracks. "Did you hit her, string her up then slice her open? It couldn't have been too hard to make it look like just another Meat Man murder. You had all the details. How hard could it have been to follow Billy's instructions? Then again, maybe it was Benno and you helped him plan it. Maybe the two of you compared notes, then Benno drew the short straw."

Stockdale backed up as Windsor came at him. "Is that how it happened? What was it like to kill someone? Were Billy's instructions hard to follow?"

Stockdale's back was against the window, his hands pressed to the glass. A small wet spot appeared on the front of his gray slacks. It quickly got bigger.

"You're crazy, Alex," Stockdale said. "I didn't have anything to do with your wife's death. You have no right to come in here and accuse me of anything."

"Why did you do it? What did Jennifer do that you had to kill her?"

He could see himself throwing Stockdale through the window, maybe even going down with him, his hands around the lawyer's throat when they splashed all over the sidewalk in front of the ATM machine twenty floors below.

"Alex, for Christ's sake," Stockdale said. His lower lip trembled, and his pants were wet from the crotch down one leg to the knee.

Windsor knew the lawyer was saying something, but the words seemed faint and far away. Looking down, he saw one hand gripping the front of Stockdale's shirt, the other pulling at his tie. His anger fueled by months of grief and a few days of suspicion. One hard push and it would be over for both of them. Stockdale said something again. There were tears running down his face. His whole body shook.

When Stockdale's voice grew louder Windsor stepped away, moving to the other side of the desk before he lost control again. Once free, Stockdale leapt toward the desk. He hit the intercom button on the telephone. "Get security in here right away."

Windsor's anger left as quickly as it came, leaving him drained and embarrassed.

"Don't ever come near me again," Stockdale said, his voice thin and weak. "You spent too much time in those damn mountains. You're crazy and you're going to kill someone. So just stay away from me."

Windsor was moving toward the door when it opened. An elderly man in a brown uniform stuck his head in. He looked scared and hesitant.

"Show this man to the elevator, Clarence. Then make sure he never comes into these offices again," Chandler said to the old man. "Ever."

In the outer office, Eleanor McNamara stood at her desk, her face a mask of concern and fear. Windsor gave her a weak smile. She mouthed the words "call me" as the security guard escorted him toward the elevator. Heads were popping out of doorways and over the tops of partitions as he walked down the hallway.

The guard stood by until he was in the elevator and the doors had closed.

When the doors opened on the first floor, Windsor stepped quickly across the hall into the restroom. For several minutes, he stood with his head over the sink.

Stockdale's threats and denials still echoed in his head. The lawyer was now off limits. No way Windsor could go back to him, regardless of what further proof he found. There was only one place left to go: Back to the beginning.

Chapter 42

When Windsor walked into The Ridge, Moon Schwartz was in the kitchen angrily slapping together burgers and sandwiches while glaring at Bud, who was supposed to be tending bar. Moon didn't like working lunch times, but reluctantly filled in when the regular kitchen help was too hungover, stoned or otherwise indisposed. Her rare display of bad temper was caused by more than just being relegated to the kitchen on a hot day in August. She also had to endure Bud standing around behind the bar doing nothing more useful than retelling stupid jokes to the collection of barflies who would probably get dizzy and keel over if they left The Ridge for more than two days at a time.

Windsor walked to the end of the bar and pulled Schwartz away from his audience while enduring Moon's icy glare.

"Mind if I use your office for a while. I need some privacy."

"Sure," Bud said, digging the key out of a drawer next to the cash register.

"Everything okay?"

"Fine." Windsor took the key.

The Ridge was housed in a two-story building Schwartz bought five years after he purchased the first-floor tavern. The century-old brick structure had two other street-level storefronts that over the years had been rented out to everything from a computer store to an art gallery. Three of the four offices upstairs were leased to a lawyer who did indigent work, a pay-day loan company, and an insurance agent specializing in high-risk auto coverage. At the back of the building was Schwartz's so-called office. It's where Bud ordered beer, liquor, and food. Moon used it to do the books and payroll.

It was cluttered and cramped with a beat-up desk and a chaotically arranged bookcase full of magazines and catalogs about the tavern business. The only sign of technology was an inexpensive laptop that Bud got as payment for back rent when the computer store downstairs went broke. A framed portrait of Jerry Garcia with a guitar and an elfish grin hidden in a mass of gray beard hung in a place of honor on the natural brick wall over the bookcase.

Windsor cleared away the catalogs on a desk chair then used the laptop to do a Google search for any listings for Benno. He found three. The first was the doctor himself with both his home and office numbers. The second was a Catherine Benno with an address that appeared to be a west-side apartment complex not far from Portland Golf Club. When he dialed the number a woman with a bar-room voice answered. He lied to her about being a reporter working on a feature story about Dr. Benno.

"You've got to be kidding," she said. "You're doing a story about that philandering old rat bastard?"

"I understand that he was a well-respected psychiatrist who was active in community affairs." Her loud cackle made Windsor flinch enough to pull the phone away from his ear.

"Active in community affairs! Boy, you got that right. There wasn't a woman in the community that he didn't try to have an active affair with." The cackle increased a decibel or two.

"Let's back up a bit," Windsor said. "You were his first wife?"

"Second. We had an affair for two years before he got around to divorcing his first wife. We were married for three years, one of which he spent shagging his current wife."

Windsor tried to imagine the man he saw laid out at the cemetery with his brains blown out shagging anyone, but then he hadn't seen Benno on his best day.

"Did you cite his affairs in your divorce proceedings?"

"You bet."

"And he didn't contest it?"

"How could he? I hired a private investigator who followed him around with a video camera. He got some great shots of him through the bedroom window of Sharon's apartment. I've got the videotape here if you'd like to see it. Maybe you could use some of it in your article. If you're into matching cases of cellulite, that is." She cackled again, only this time with a hint of pain thrown in.

Windsor declined before taking a reluctant shot in the dark. "The private investigator wasn't named Gilroy by any chance?"

"No. I think her name was Henderson."

Windsor exhaled. Things were complicated enough already.

He pressed her about Benno's finances. "He seemed to have all the trappings of a man with money. Nice car, a house, and, best I can tell, a thriving practice. So why kill himself?"

"Don't ask me. He lost almost everything when he divorced his first wife. I took what was left when I divorced him. The last time I saw him he was driving an expensive-looking Audi, so he must have been doing all right. Go figure."

"Maybe the money came from his third wife."

"Doubtful. It cost her a bundle to divorce her first husband so she could marry Bennett. The only thing she brought to the marriage was a stack of legal bills. Knowing Bennett, I'm surprised he didn't leave her right then and there."

"So, where did the money come from?"

"I suppose he could've earned it, but that would've been out of character. You might ask his brother. He was Bennett's accountant. He'll probably be at the funeral. To tell you the truth, it doesn't matter. Bennett would have lost everything in that lawsuit anyway."

"Lawsuit?"

"You're a reporter and you don't know about the lawsuit?"

"I've been out of town," Windsor said. "Tibet actually."

With great glee, she explained that six weeks earlier Benno had been sued for sexual harassment by a young woman who went to him seeking treatment of a psychiatric condition caused by her husband's physical and mental abuse. The suit alleged that during the year she was under his care, Benno coerced her into having sex with him twenty-seven times, got her pregnant then paid for an abortion. The suit sought seven million dollars in damages. The woman also filed a complaint with the State Board of Medical Examiners seeking revocation of Benno's license. The first hearing would've been next week at which time the allegations would've become public.

"The woman said they got it on right there in his office during working hours. I told you he was a dirty, rotten rat bastard."

"You believe her?"

"You bet," she said. "That's where we used to go when he was still married to his first wife. I knew Bennett for three months before we ever had sex in a bed."

"Do you think the lawsuit had anything to do with his suicide?"

"Who knows what goes on in other people's minds? I always pictured Bennett dying of a heart attack while humping someone on that office couch he loved so much. He went out with a bang, all right. It just wasn't the kind of bang I thought it would be."

"I take it you didn't see much of him after the divorce."

"He came around once when his wife was in the hospital for a few days. Said he wanted to relive old times while his wife was getting a hysterectomy. What a slime ball. Anyway, I yelled at him so loud and so long that the neighbors called the police."

He asked about the other Benno in the phone book.

"That would be Helen, wife number one. She hated Bennett, but probably not enough to talk to a reporter."

"What can you tell me about her?"

"Not much. Bennett never talked about her or the two daughters they had," she said. "I asked him about it a few times, but he made it clear the subject was strictly off limits. I got the feeling that something happened involving the girls. Knowing Bennett, I could make a pretty good guess what it was, but I can't be sure. You'll probably see Helen at the funeral today, but I doubt you'll see his kids. They never came around when he was alive. I don't know why they'd come around now."

"Which reminds me," he said. "I need to go to the funeral. Will you be there?"

"No. He has two wives to bury him. Three's a crowd."

Chapter 43

Bennett Benno's funeral services were already underway when Windsor found the last spot in the parking lot and walked up to the porch. At the door, he accepted a little card that said "In Memorial" from a meek, solemn-looking man who fit the part of a funeral director. Inside, the long, narrow chapel was half full. Benno's casket sat in front of a small pulpit that was part of a nondenominational altar. Benno lay in one of those Dutch-door coffins with the top half tipped open. The bottom half was closed and covered blanket-like with a floral arrangement. The guest of honor's face was visible in profile, his head resting on a rose-pink satin pillow. From where Windsor stood it was hard to see any signs that Benno had stuck a gun in his mouth and pulled the trigger.

Finding a space in a back pew, he glanced around while listening to a Presbyterian minister groping to explain the religious and spiritual significant of suicide in a graveyard. It was a plausible theory that had to do with the growing complexity of a world that had lost its way and no longer looked to the simplicity of life found in the Holy Scriptures. By the time he finished, the minister appeared to have convinced himself that the demands of a computerized information age had brought down a man already burdened with the misery and grief of the patients he treated.

Windsor was a little skeptical.

He scanned the mourners again, still looking for familiar faces. He spotted Chandler Stockdale sitting on the aisle two rows from the front, next to a woman with short, gray hair. Adelaide Milburne, Benno's office manager, sat three rows away next to three other women Windsor recognized from the day he visited Benno's office. A woeful sobbing emanating from the curtained box on the right side of the chapel told him where the family was seated.

A tall, cadaverous man sang "Amazing Grace" in a deep baritone too big for the small chapel. When he finished, Stockdale walked to the front to deliver the eulogy. In his annoying voice, he described Bennett Benno as a "dedicated healer of the mind, who gave of himself to make this great community of ours a better place to live." He listed Benno's professional and civic honors, acknowledged the bravery of his family in their time of sorrow and tragedy, then told a few stories about their "long and rewarding personal and professional relationship."

When the services ended, Windsor moved quickly out the door to the ivy-covered entryway. He stood to the side, watching people leave. Stockdale emerged a few minutes later. When he saw Windsor, he whispered something to the woman with the short, gray hair. Whatever it was it earned Windsor an irritated look as she walked off.

"You got a lot of nerve coming here after what happened in my office," Stockdale said after making his way through the last of the mourners. "It's obvious that you didn't believe me when I told you not to screw with my friends."

"I'm just paying my respects to a noted psychiatrist and colleague … of sorts."

"Don't give me that," Stockdale snapped. "I want you out of here right now. The man committed suicide. Show some decency, for God's sake."

"You should be glad I'm here. It means there's still a chance I believe Benno killed Jennifer and you didn't."

More and more mourners gathered on the porch behind Stockdale. Their sideways glances seemed to force Stockdale to try even harder to act like they were having a normal, friendly conversation about a dead shrink.

"If you have something, then tell the police or your friends in the press. Just remember that whatever you do I'll see you in court. If you don't, then go back to whatever it was you've been doing for the last year and forget about Billy Broadnax and Bennett Benno."

As the lawyer stomped off, Windsor realized how tired he'd become of Stockdale and his threats. He'd rather take him up on the challenge to see him in court than listen to that loathsome voice again. One thing, however, was certain. He was getting to Stockdale. That was worth the price of admission.

Last out the door was the widow. Sharon Benno wore a thick veil and a long black dress. She was surrounded by other women dressed in matching black who were doing their best to comfort her, but her uncontrollable weeping came out in loud animal-like sobs. They moved scrum-like off the porch, onto the lawn then paused while the widow accepted condolences from other mourners. The only man among them moved away from the circle of black and stepped to the edge of the porch near Windsor. He lit a cigarette and leaned against the porch's cement wall. The resemblance was vague, but enough to give Windsor something to go on.

"Terrible thing, isn't it?" the man said to Windsor.

"Yes, it is. Please excuse me, but you look a little like Dr. Benno. Are you related?"

"I'm his brother, William Benno." They shook hands. "Were you a friend of Ben's?"

"Not a friend. More of a colleague. I'm a psychologist."

William Benno accepted the explanation with a sad nod. "Weird, isn't it?" He glanced at the scene out on the lawn with groups of mourners talking in whispers. "Someone who treats the mentally ill committing suicide. You'd think he would've known something was wrong and found treatment for himself." Windsor did his best to look sad.

"Well, at least Sharon will be taken care of," William Benno said. "She loved Ben very much. I'm grateful he had life insurance and other assets for her to live comfortably."

Windsor replayed in his head the conversation with Catherine Benno. He remembered the part about a dirty, rotten rat bastard. He also remembered her comment about Bennett Benno having no money thanks to two divorces. William Benno had opened the door. No reason Windsor shouldn't walk in.

"Yes, everyone in our profession considered Dr. Benno a very good psychiatrist," Windsor said. "But take it from me, it's not a particularly lucrative one for those who choose to work with a lot of institutionalized people."

"You're right. Shrinks like Ben don't make diddly. Fortunately, a group of friends steered him into some very good investments. I know. I'm also his accountant."

"I wish I had friends like that," Windsor said.

"Yeah. Ben was brilliant, but he knew nothing about money and even less about women. A deadly combination these days. Always has been, I guess. If it hadn't been for Chandler Stockdale, Judge Hawkins, and some other guy we'd probably be dumping Ben's ashes in the river." William Benno thought for a moment. "I'm sorry. I don't mean to sound cynical about my brother's death. It's just my way of dealing with it. I apologize."

"Do you mean Judge Dorothy Evelyn Hawkins? I didn't realize they were acquainted."

"They've been friends for years. In fact, Ben was a frequent guest at the judge's house for dinner. He said her home is spectacular. Have you ever seen it?"

"Once. It's quite nice," Windsor said quickly. "You mentioned another man who helped with your brother's investments. I didn't catch his name."

"I didn't throw it. Apparently, he's a friend of Chandler's and, I guess, of the judge's as well. All I know is that they met during a party five years ago at the judge's home. This other man got all three of them in on the ground floor of some incredible investment. Ben made several hundred thousand dollars in less than a year, more than a million in three years. I suspect more is on the way. Or at least it was. I don't know what happens now. Ben kept everything about it close to the vest. It made me a little suspicious, but, like I said, he assured me everything was on the level. I guess we'll see."

"Who was this guy?" Windsor asked with a smile. "Sounds like someone I need to know."

They shared a discreet laugh. "To tell you the truth, I wish I knew. Ben never told me anything about him or even what the investment was. Believe me, I tried to find out, but he kept everything to himself. I was skeptical until I saw the money he sent me. When he told me it was all on the level, I took his word for it. Whatever it was, it turned his whole life around. He finally had the financial security he always wanted."

"The suicide? Any idea why?"

"All I can think of is that damn lawsuit." William Benno lit another cigarette. "What kind of society do we live in where a mentally disturbed woman can make false charges that drive a well-respected man like my brother to suicide? It's criminal."

"That would be the lawsuit by the former patient. I heard something about that but didn't take it too seriously. Things like that are not uncommon in our profession. Anyone can file a lawsuit. It's making the claims stick that sometimes gets lost."

"You got that right. Everyone remembers what the allegations were. No one remembers when they turn out to be false."

It looked like William Benno was about to launch into a speech about the liberal press, fake news, and the need for tort reform when Sharon Benno and her scrum of mourners moved off toward the limousine for the short trip to the cemetery. One of the women turned and beckoned to Benno.

"Thank you for coming," Benno said. "My brother was a good man." He stepped off the porch and disappeared into the limo.

Chapter 44

In the days before Cassie Terrace and Jennifer DeGarza, Windsor would poke around in the city's nooks and crannies looking for the out-of-the-way places with good food and creative drinks; the kind that never made it on the annual lists of the city's best restaurants. There's nothing like being on a top-ten list to turn cozy into irritating.

While the city was a target-rich environment for restaurants and bars that preferred food over ambience, it was next to impossible to find a place for an intimate dinner, quiet conversation, or a solitary drink. One exception was a Scandinavian-themed place on the inner east side that featured drinks with vodka and aquavit, food heavy on smoked salmon and pickled herring, and fresh-baked rye bread. When Windsor checked the internet, he was relieved to see it had surprisingly survived the pandemic and eased comfortably into post-COVID reality.

At three in the afternoon the place was empty except for a realtor with a laptop showing homes to a couple of confused-looking thirty-somethings. The background music cycled between ABBA, Björk, and Sibelius. A combination of glass, curtains, and partitions made each table safe and secure from everything other than the day-old herring. One upside was an unobstructed view of the homeless camp across the street. Windsor found a table in the corner and ordered a Ketel One on the rocks with the gravlax and rye toast appetizer.

Maybe Cassie was right, he thought while waiting for his order and watching the mumble people outside, maybe he should let it all go. He knew now that he wasn't responsible for Jennifer's death. That was something. He thought about Sam Westlake, the ranch covered in ponderosa pine, the river where he learned to fly fish. A year before, he couldn't imagine himself fishing. Now it seemed like that's all he wanted to do.

The attraction began the previous winter when a succession of snowstorms trapped him in the cabin for a week, making it impossible to get to either the liquor store or the pharmacy. Denied his booze and pills, he was forced to begin looking for other ways to make life bearable. He found it in a book on fly fishing he pulled off the shelf next to the fireplace. It was a clear, crisp night with three feet of fresh snow banked up against the cabin. He threw an extra log on the fire and started reading. He spent the night learning about back casts, clinch knots, improved clinch knots, and blood knots. He read about stoneflies, mayflies, midges, and caddis. He'd learned the differences between dry flies, nymphs, and streamers. He learned about cut banks, tail water, and other places where fish hung out. Mostly, though, he concentrated on the techniques necessary to fish rivers like the one outside his window with its gin-clear water and hook-smart fish.

Over the next few days, he'd ventured out in the cold to spend hours looking at the stream. The books made him see the river in a whole new way. He studied how to break the river down into different parts, each a stream unto itself. The more he read, the more he came to realize that it was something that would occupy his time and offer some solace.

He explained all this to Sam one night over whiskey and cribbage. "Then we best get you suited up," the old man said with an excited smile.

When the weather broke and the road out of the ranch passable, he and Sam drove into the town of Sisters to a fly-fishing store. Putting his trust in the store's crusty owner, Clyde the Guide as he called himself, Windsor walked out after three hours loaded down with waders, boots, vest, rod, reel, line, leader, tippet, an assortment of flies, and four more books on how to fly fish. Sam had acted as the closer on the deal, offering his expert opinion to back up Clyde's recommendations. Names like Simms, Orvis, and Sage rolled off their tongues. They worked him like a couple of old-time grifters, leaving him little chance of escaping with anything less than the most expensive equipment in the store … and plenty of it.

The next two weeks were devoted to teaching himself to cast. During the day, he'd stand knee deep in the snow outside the cabin with a book in one hand and a fly rod in the other, trying to unravel the mysteries of how to cast a weightless fly. At night he'd practice the knots needed to tie a fly on a tippet and a tippet on a leader. Sam, eager to have someone to fish with, nurtured Windsor's sudden interest with long lectures on entomology, which came to the simple philosophy of "Fish eat bugs. Find the right bug. Catch the fish."

Finally, he felt ready. In late January, with another foot of new snow on the ground and Sam away on business in Portland, he put on as many warm clothes as he could find, then pulled on his new waders, boots, and vest. Shiny new fly rod in hand, he trudged across the meadow to the river. He lost a half dozen flies in the bushes along the bank and lost three fish before finally landing an 18-inch rainbow. From that moment on he was as hooked as that first trout.

Now, sitting in the bar drinking his second Ketel One, Windsor thought about driving the three hours back to the familiar and safe surroundings of the ranch. A day on the river with Sam and his homespun wisdom might be just what he needed to clear his mind. He should do it but knew he wouldn't. Not wanting to spare the time was a lame excuse. The truth was it would feel like running away with a job half finished. He was sure that Benno and Stockdale had something to do with Jennifer's death. What he didn't know was why they or anyone else would want to kill her.

Windsor had spent a year of his life feeling little more than self-hate and guilt. No matter how much time he spent fishing, drinking, or staring into the dying coals of a fire in the cabin, he still had to go to bed at night thinking about what might have been. The last few days had convinced him that the year had been wasted ... except for the fishing.

He gave serious consideration to spending the rest of the day in the bar sucking down anything with vodka in it, but eventually forced himself to walk the half block back to his car. He felt the same way as when he arrived: too many lingering questions, too many dark thoughts. What he needed were solid answers. Now, after his two visits with Billy Broadnax, he knew he was missing something, but maybe he knew where to find it.

Chapter 45

Windsor hated basements, none more than his own.

While he couldn't classify it as a phobia, he thought of them as the black holes in which discarded and unwanted items disappeared to spend eternity in gloom and dust. Too bad to keep. Too good for a garage sale. If that wasn't bad enough, the delicate, silver webs that shone in the sunlight seeping through the frosted panes of the ground-level windows gave the cramped room an eerie aura. If there were ghosts in more than his dreams, this is where they would be. Dust floating in and out of the same dim light turned from black to gray to white then back again as it drifted in the stale, stagnant air. Worst yet, cobwebs and grit covered everything. It got in his eyes and flew up around his pant legs with every step he took toward the boxes piled neatly in the far corner like bricks in a wall.

If he was going to find out why Jennifer was killed, maybe the best place to start was with the boxes of files from her law office. All he could hope for was that the answer was hidden among the court records, witness statements, and verdicts of the few hundred clients she represented in her short career, something that might connect Jennifer to either Benno, Stockdale, or both. It was a long shot, but worth a try. Time to get lucky.

If there was an upside, the basement of his house on Royal Oak Way was smaller than his parents' and less cluttered with useless items and the memories that went with them. Fumbling around for the light that hung from the ceiling, he replaced the burned-out bulb with a new one he'd brought down with him. When the harsh light came on, he expected to see or hear vermin scurry away toward small holes in the concrete foundation. When nothing moved except a couple of spiders the size of birds, he swatted them away before inching his way closer to the boxes that contained her files. They were neatly stacked beside the furnace and covered with a dusty bed sheet. He knew some of what was inside: pictures, diplomas, anniversary cards, and other odds and ends of her stunted career and their all-too-short life together.

They were all that remained from the dingy, two-room office she rented over a Middle Eastern restaurant a few blocks from the courthouse. She insisted on paying for everything herself by taking out a small business loan from the bank. She refused to accept any of Windsor's money, getting angry at his suggestion that he even try buying the whole building. She furnished it with modest office furniture, high-end laptops, and the law books she would need. Then she hired a secretary that she shared with a lawyer in an equally cramped space across the hall.

On nights when she worked late preparing for a trial or a deposition, he'd show up with two burgers from The Ridge, a beer for him, and a diet cola for her. Between bites, she'd proclaim the innocence of some new client, no matter how overwhelming the evidence. He nodded in agreement, all the time wondering how long her idealism would survive as a court-appointed defense attorney representing a parade of destitute and drug-addled lowlifes.

After she died, two of her friends from law school came to him suggesting they shut down her practice. Numb at the time, he said yes then forgot about it. He assumed that they sorted out her pending cases, asked the courts for continuances, took on some of her clients, and closed the office. On the morning after the funeral, they brought Windsor the five boxes, explaining that they included copies of files of past cases and those still active, but in need of assignment to other lawyers. Deciding to deal with it later, he found that the cardboard containers fit perfectly with his definition of what belonged in basements.

He found a broom under the stairs and swept the boxes of as much dust and grit as he could. He got most of it off, but despite his best efforts, it still hung in the air, slowly settling back down on the floor. He coughed, sneezed, and waved at the air in front of his face before finally giving up. One by one, he carried the boxes upstairs hoping that somewhere in some obscure file was a clue to who killed Jennifer and why.

He'd just set the last box down when the phone buzzed. He sat in the chair in the front room and answered it.

"I'll get right to the point," Chandler Stockdale said. "I'm going to forget what happened at my office. What I'm concerned about is that you're going to leak something to the media. I wouldn't put it past you. You've done it enough times before. I want you to understand that if what you think you know about Billy Broadnax ends up in the newspapers or on TV it will cause more problems than it solves."

"We went over this already. Nothing has changed. That's not really my concern."

"Actually, it is."

Stockdale launched into a speech about social responsibility, serving the common good, and how dredging up Billy's horrors would bring up past nightmares best forgotten. Windsor passed on the opportunity to debate social responsibility with a lawyer who represents insurance companies.

"Explain to me how the public good is being served by allowing Jennifer's killer to go free?" he asked instead.

"Jennifer's killer is in prison," Stockdale said. "If you have evidence to the contrary, then give it to me. If it's legitimate, I'll turn that over to the district attorney myself. As an officer of the court, I'm obligated to do that."

"That's pretty rich coming from you. Broadnax sat in your office and confessed to killing seven women and you sent him to a shrink instead of to the police."

"That's a lie," Stockdale said.

"I don't think so, but it should be easy enough to prove. We'll just go talk to Billy. Both of us. Together. If not, then how about his father, Chester? I'm sure ..."

"There will be serious legal ramifications if you repeat that allegation."

"So, we're back to that."

"And I mean every word of it."

Windsor considered hanging up. He took a deep breath instead.

"Look, Chandler, something here doesn't make sense. Chester Broadnax calls up and asks to see you about a legal problem. According to Chester, the legal problem was that he'd just realized that his son might be The Meat Man and he didn't know what to do about it. So, he came to you, his landlord, for help. You and Billy talked one-on-one for an hour. You can tell me what it was about, but my guess is that Billy confessed to killing those women. After that, you sent him to Benno for a psychiatric evaluation, during which Billy told Benno the same story he told you, but in greater detail. Now both of you knew what Billy did and how he did it. Not only that, but Benno also wrote you a memo describing Billy's mental condition and what he did to his victims."

"You can't prove any of that."

"Actually, I can, or have you forgotten that I have Gilroy's report? But don't take my word for it. Talk to Billy. Talk to his father. The way I see it, other than the police, only three people knew the details of

Billy's killing spree. One is in prison, and one is dead. That leaves you. So, let's cut the bullshit and you tell me why you've really called."

Stockdale started to sputter out an answer, but never got the chance. Windsor dropped the phone when the front windows of the house exploded.

Chapter 46

The plate glass window shattered, the roar sending glass showering over Windsor's head and into the middle of the front room. A second roar tore the wing off the back of Windsor's chair, inches from his head. Two holes the size of basketballs blew out of the wall across the room about five feet above the floor. Lathe and plaster added to the cascade of glass flying around the room.

Windsor hit the floor, hands over his head, knees to his chest, and waited for a third blast. He didn't have to wait long. The next explosion tore through the back of the chair. A fourth turned a coffee table into kindling. A fifth shattered the brick on the left side of the fireplace.

Windsor stayed curled up for what felt like several minutes but was probably only a few seconds. When nothing else happened, he raised his head slightly and looked around the room. Tufts of white stuffing from the destroyed chair joined the airborne plaster and clung to the shredded leather. The ottoman, the rug around the chair, and the desk across the room were covered in more glass and plaster. Small shards were embedded in what was left of the chair. The glass in the window was all but gone. Only a few large pieces hung precariously from the frame, looking ready to drop and shatter on the sill.

Windsor ran his hands through his hair and across the back of his neck. They came back bloody, but not enough to scare him anymore than he already was. When the sound of tinkling glass stopped, he reached up to sweep a lamp off an end table.

As the room went dark, he moved on all fours toward the kitchen. The glass dug into his hands and cut through his pants into his knees. He got to his feet and did his best Chuck Berry duck walk as far as the door frame. He reached up to turn off the lights in the kitchen.

Light from one of the weak streetlamps cast eerie shadows across the front room and reflected off the shattered glass, lighting up the stuffing and dust that filled the air. He moved to the back door and out onto the small, covered porch. He hunched down and peeked around the corner down the length of the driveway. It was quiet. No one in sight. He crept along the outside of his BMW. By the time he got to the street, a car with its lights off was turning left out of the cul-de-sac. It was a sedan black enough to blend in with the dark gray sky.

Chapter 47

Nothing brings out the neighbors like a few shotgun blasts in the middle of the night. Fortunately, Windsor didn't have many neighbors. Most, if not all of them, had probably lived years without so much as a firecracker going off. Then he moved in.

Windsor was still standing at the end of the driveway watching the black car disappear when the front door opened on the house next door. He watched as the elderly couple he barely knew beyond an occasional wave peeked out their front door, then slowly crept onto the porch. They were wearing matching robes and clutching each other's arms. Lights came on in the only other house on Royal Oak Way.

Windsor walked back toward the house. Stockdale was still on the phone. "What was that? Some kind of explosion?"

"Something like that," Windsor said, "I've got to go."

He hung up and called 911. Several small cuts oozed blood from his cheeks and forehead. More blood seeped from a larger cut on the back of his hand. He tore a paper towel off the roll on the kitchen counter and wrapped it around the wound. He washed his face in the sink, then wiped away more blood with another paper towel, all the time wondering what had just happened. The shotgun blasts had destroyed his front room, but not him. Still, he was shaken up enough that not even a third shot of whiskey helped. Was it a warning? Was someone trying to kill him? Either way he needed to be careful.

He went outside to stand in the driveway and wait for the police. It didn't take long. First the far-off wail of sirens then the flashing lights of three patrol cars speeding into the cul-de-sac. When the first officer got out of his car, he put his hand on the grip of his pistol. Windsor put his hands in the air.

"I'm the one who called. This is my house."

The officer waited until two more cars showed up, then asked Windsor for some identification. A driver's license and car registration seemed to work. Hands came off the guns. Everybody relaxed.

He was still describing what happened when Cassie Terrace showed up.

Chapter 48

In the dream he saw himself hanging by his feet from the garage rafters, the cold, concrete floor just inches away from his out-stretched fingers. A thick mist oozed through an open door. It swirled in eddies that wrapped around his arms and spread across the floor. He could see people standing in the haze pointing at him. Some were laughing. Others just stared, looking either stunned or mesmerized. Not all the faces were familiar. Those that were had a pale, cadaverous look, especially the seven women standing in the background, each holding a knife high in the air.

They walked through the crowd and started slashing at his arms, legs, chest, and stomach. Blood pooled up on the concrete floor. To his right, Cassie Terrace and Jennifer looked on, stone faced. They were wearing long, brown robes with hoods, like monks from the Spanish Inquisition. He wanted their help but couldn't decide which one to call to. As if in response to some silent command, the crowd parted. Billy Broadnax stepped out of the mist. His tattoos squirmed on his skin, the snakes on his arms alive and hissing.

Windsor heard a voice. "Alex." It sounded urgent, but gentle. He sat straight up in bed, suddenly wide awake, sweating, and panting. "Alex. You were having a nightmare." Cassie Terrace put her arms around him, pulled him close, and stroked his damp hair.

They sat in the kitchen drinking coffee. The clock over the sink said four a.m. Cassie acted like she wanted to go back to bed but the look on her face said she was afraid to. Windsor felt content to stay where he was.

"You all right now?"

He nodded and asked for more coffee while wondering if it was too early to fortify it with more Bushmills. At the cabin there wouldn't have been a second thought. With Cassie it wasn't that easy. She wasn't judgmental but drew the line at drinking before dawn.

After Cassie arrived at Windsor's house she hung back, letting the uniforms do their job. It wasn't a homicide, so it was best not to interfere. When they finished questioning him, she skirted the crime scene tape and came into the house through the kitchen door. Windsor was still standing in the middle of his destroyed living room. They looked at each other and then at the mess.

"I think you'd better come home with me," she said.

Windsor didn't argue.

"You told those patrol guys that you thought it was gangbangers shooting out your windows," she said when they were in the car. Traffic was light. Her house was a twenty-minute drive away. "You weren't serious, were you?"

"It could have been. Asian gangs are big right now. Maybe some protestors. Antifa, Proud Boys. No shortage of those around Portland."

"Right. And they cruise the city's high-rent neighborhoods shooting out the windows of upscale houses on secluded cul-de-sacs. Even those rookies back there had a hard time swallowing that."

"Could have been a Manson thing," Windsor said.

She rolled her eyes at him.

Whatever was going on was something bigger, something more complicated than he'd imagined. It also might mean that he was getting close to something. But to what and to whom? Whatever it was, the last thing he wanted was for the police to be involved. They had their suspect in Matthew Roberts. Let them gum him to death for a while. The real killer was still out there.

When they reached her house, Cassie washed his cuts and gently rinsed the glass and plaster out of his hair. When they stepped out of the shower, she dried him off, bandaged his wounds, and took him to bed. They didn't make love. They were both content to let her hold him until he stopped shivering. Then the nightmare came.

"Are you going to tell me what's going on?" Cassie said. Having given up on going back to bed, she poured more coffee for both of them.

What he wanted more than anything was to tell her all he knew, to let it all pour out so she could help him unravel what had happened. If Cassie had been anything other than a cop, he would have. Telling her everything now would put her in a bind. He had to wait until he knew the truth.

"I don't know all of it," he said. "Only pieces. I need time."

During the night, Windsor had convinced himself that the attack on his house was meant to scare him, not kill him. If someone wanted him dead, they would have kicked in the front door, shot him, and driven away. Not knowing who was after him was equal parts frustration and fright. Either way, he wasn't going to let the attack stop him. Someone had a reason to keep him alive.

"If what happened last night had anything to do with this Broadnax business, you'd better tell me," Cassie said. She had slipped into cop mode.

"I don't know what to believe. I don't know who shot up my house or why."

"But you'll keep looking, right? All by yourself. Doing that same Alex Windsor, disenfranchised knight routine of not letting anyone help you. Not letting anyone know what's going on inside that stubborn head of yours." She sat back in the chair and glared at him. "You're a piece of work, you know that. All twisted up inside, but cool and calm outside. It must be lonely in there."

She went back to bed when he didn't answer.

Chapter 49

"This is the ritzy home of forensic psychologist Alex Windsor. Last night around nine o'clock someone fired five shotgun blasts through the front windows, barely missing Windsor and doing serious damage to the inside."

It was seven in the morning, which meant Rich Raymond had busted his butt to get out of bed in time for a live shot from Windsor's driveway.

"Ritzy?" Windsor said, still sipping coffee in Cassie Terrace's kitchen. She'd left an hour earlier for work, leaving behind a note that said he should make himself at home.

"As you'd expect with all this damage, Windsor isn't around this morning. However, he told police last night that the attack may have been the work of vandals, possibly gang members or protestors." Raymond's voice carried just the right amount of skepticism.

Raymond walked a few steps to his right. The sleepy faces of Windsor's elderly neighbors, still clad in matching bathrobes, appeared on the screen.

"This is Luther Ambler, who lives next door to Alex Windsor and was home last night when the attack occurred. Tell us what happened, Mr. Ambler."

Unsure where to look, Luther's eyes darted between Raymond, the microphone, and the camera. "We were in bed reading when we heard these loud bangs, kind of like small explosions. Bang. Bang. Bang. One after the other. Maybe five or six of them. We both sat up and waited, you know, thinking about what it might have been." Luther looked at his wife who nodded in numb agreement. "I remember hearing a car drive away, but I didn't see it."

"And you called the police, is that right?"

"Yes. I wanted to be sure someone called them, but I doubt I was the only one. A lot of lights went on around here after those shots or whatever they were. Things like this don't happen in this neighborhood." Ambler looked at his wife again. "At least they didn't used to."

"Any signs of gang members, vandals, protestors?" Raymond shoved the microphone back in Luther's face.

"I'm not sure what a gang member looks like, but it doesn't matter because I didn't see anyone."

Raymond pressed Luther Ambler about Windsor.

"Seems like a nice enough guy, but we never really talked." Ambler said. "He introduced himself when he moved in. That was eight or nine years ago. I'd see him now and then taking cans out on garbage night, but just to wave at. He pretty much keeps to himself. We met his late wife a few times. She was a very nice, beautiful woman, and smart. Tragic what happened to her. We almost sold out after she was murdered right there in that garage." He pointed off camera. "Haven't seen much of Alex since then. He just showed up a few days ago. Now he sort of comes and goes."

"Any idea where he's been?"

"Tibet is what I heard," Ambler said with conviction. "One of those monasteries where they shave their heads and chant. Ancient religion stuff. Me and the missus, we're Episcopalians. But to each his own, that's my motto." Mercifully, Raymond let the old couple go back to bed.

"Poor Luther," Windsor muttered, making a mental note to go see the Amblers and apologize for all the trouble he'd caused.

"Something extremely odd is going on and Alex Windsor seems to be in the middle of it," Raymond said, then threw in the obligatory background about who Windsor was and why he had become fodder for an early morning live shot from a normally quiet neighborhood. "Windsor allegedly returns from a Himalayan monastery, starts visiting the families of two recent murder victims, then someone shoots up his house. We're not sure why and Windsor has been hard to find. Not only that, but the police also seem to be completely in the dark. From where I'm standing it looks like someone has Dr. Alex Windsor in their sights. Unless, of course, you believe the story about vandals. This is Rich Raymond, live in southwest Portland for Channel 5 Daybreak News."

Chapter 50

Windsor got dressed and called Uber for a ride back to his house. There was a patrol car in front and crime scene tape surrounding the property. He explained to the uniformed cop who he was and that he needed to pick up a few things. The officer nodded and let him pass.

He skirted the mess that was the front room and walked into the dining room. The five boxes he'd pulled out of the basement were still on the table. There were the kind with lids, hand holes on each end, and places to write what was inside. Two of them were marked "Personal." Windsor knew what was in those—framed diplomas and pictures, a gold pen, a crystal desk clock, and take-out menus from restaurants near Jennifer's office. He pushed those aside, saving them for later, if at all. Too many memories best left sealed up.

The other three boxes contained files—A to E, F to J and so on. Most of them would be closed cases, usually court-appointed, with defendants charged with everything from drunken driving to manslaughter. Any one of them could've had some greater significance, but he had no way of knowing which one, if any. He was looking for something that offered any kind of insight into what happened, that could send him off in a direction that would tie everything together.

He opened the box with the first of her case files. He flipped through them searching for anything that looked familiar. He found nothing other than a few names he recognized from the rare occasions when she talked about her cases. It was the same story with the others. Finished, all he could do was stare hopelessly at the pile of boxes, knowing something important might be in there, but unsure which one. Reluctantly, he opened the first of the "Personal" boxes.

As expected, inside were diplomas and other personal items. They were mixed in with framed photos of her family, the dog she had growing up, and her favorite one of the two of them taken four years earlier at Sam Westlake's ranch. Sam had taken it during one of their vacations. They were standing on a bridge with snow-capped Mt. Jefferson in the background. They'd just returned from a walk up the river to where icy spring water gushed out of a crack in the lava landscape. They had watched, mesmerized as water cascaded down a rock ledge to create a full-blown river seemingly out of nowhere. On the way back they stopped to watch Sam fish for rainbows in his favorite back eddy below the bridge. Jennifer seemed hypnotized by the rhythmic back and forth of the fly line and the ease with which Sam manipulated the rod and line as if they were all one piece. She had squeezed his arm and said, "You need to learn that." Little did she know, he thought.

Windsor stared at the picture then put it back in the box, face down.

From the second box he pulled out a couple of day planners made to fit into the expensive leather briefcase he'd given her the day she passed the state bar. He looked through the one from the previous year, occasionally recognizing more cases or clients that had caused her great joy or grief. There were appointments for arraignments, pre-trial conferences, and trials, along with personal dates, such as their anniversary and birthdays of family and friends. It was the appointment for August ninth at three p.m. that caught his eye. It read "Stockdale re Barnes." That would be three days after her death.

Stockdale? Barnes? Why would Jennifer meet with Stockdale? And who was Barnes? He grabbed the third box and started rummaging through files a second time until he found it—a file folder with a blue tab that read "Barnes, Marvin" followed by a case number, 000137. Windsor smiled. The number meant that it was Jennifer's one-hundred thirty-seventh case and that she had been anticipating more ... a lot more. He slowly opened it. His fingers shook. He just wasn't sure why.

In the file were a half-dozen government forms filled out in pen with dates and numbers. Some mentioned board feet of timber. Others dealt with the lot lines that seemed to have something to do with government timber sales. At the bottom of each form was a signature: Marvin Barnes.

The case was unlike any of Jennifer's others, but it didn't surprise him that she never mentioned it. He remembered one afternoon a few weeks before they were married. She'd called him at work and asked him to come down to her office.

"We need to talk," she'd said. When he got there, she made him sit in the chair on the other side of her desk like one of her clients.

"There's something we need to agree on before we get married." She had on her business face and the tone that went with it. "We must keep our professions separate. I need you to agree that I won't refer clients to you, and you won't testify at any trial I'm involved in, especially if it's for the prosecution."

"You're right," he'd told her, even though the chances of either one of those things happening were remote at best.

"Okay," she had said, "then I just won't tell you anything about my cases, except in the abstract. No names until the case is over. Agreed?" He nodded. "And you'll do the same?" He nodded again.

"There's one more thing. I want to keep my maiden name, but just for professional reasons. Anything personal and I'm Jennifer DeGarza Windsor." She came around the desk, sat in his lap and, with a breathy whisper, said: "Do you agree?"

"What if I don't?"

"You will," she said, taking his hand and sliding it under her blouse, "because you know what you'll be missing, mi amor."

The memory made him smile, as much for the moment as for Jennifer's deep-felt and finely tuned concerns about ethics, appearances, and keeping her own name. He knew that was only part of the story. It was more about being her own person and not living in his shadow or anyone else's. She made it that far as Jennifer DeGarza. She'd make it further the same way.

Windsor called Stockdale's law offices, gave a fake name, and asked for Eleanor McNamara, Stockdale's secretary.

"Eleanor, it's Alex Windsor. I need your help," he said. "It's important or I wouldn't ask. It has to do with Jennifer's death."

"I'll do what I can," she said.

"Can you find out if Chandler had an appointment with Jennifer on August ninth of last year? It had something to do with a man named Marvin Barnes."

"It doesn't ring a bell, but I can check. Care to tell me what this is all about?"

"I'm not sure myself. Anything you can learn might help. What I can say is that after what happened the other day, it's probably best not to mention anything to Stockdale. I hope this doesn't put you in an awkward situation."

"Of course it does, but if it has to do with Jennifer then I'll just have to live with it."

After hanging up, Windsor dialed the number for Pine Mountain Ranch for no other reason than wanting to hear Sam Westlake's voice. Everything he'd learned so far was getting too close to the bone. Too many old names and familiar places.

Sam was always good for a bit of home-spun reality and the latest fishing report. At nine-thirty, he knew the old rancher had been up for three hours puttering around the house until the mid-morning hatch that signaled the time to start fishing.

"It's a banker's river," Sam had said more times than Windsor could count. "No sense even being down there much before ten in the morning. Then things are done around three, later during the summer. Don't ask me why."

Windsor had caught plenty of fish before ten in the morning and after three in the afternoon. Sam called it beginner's luck and stuck to his long-held beliefs.

"Fishing has been great," Sam said after answering the phone on the first ring. "The rainbows are taking mayflies like there's no tomorrow."

"And the Dollies?"

"Haven't fished them, but they're in there. I might take a shot at them later today. I got this new streamer from Clyde the Guide down at the fly shop. Not sure it's legal, but hell, it's my land. I'll fish with what I want to. Anyway, I can see them big sons of bitches laying in the shallows gobbling up everything that comes by. Not bugs, mind you, but other fish. Hell, I think a few of them Canada honkers are missing." He laughed at his own joke. "I tried calling you a couple of times, but no one answered at the house. You okay?"

He wanted to tell Sam about the gunshots but didn't have the energy. "I've been staying with a friend. The house isn't quite ready to be lived in yet. Things are a little complicated."

"Anything you want to talk about?"

"Someday but let me sort it all out first. All I can tell you is that I wasn't responsible for Jennifer's death."

"Hell, I already told you that."

"Not in the way you said. This is different. Now I have proof."

"Well, I guess I'm happy for you, son. Sounds like there's a hell of a story behind all this. You'll tell old Sam about it when you get back, right?

"You bet."

"When are you coming back?"

"I don't know yet, but not long."

"But you are coming back?"

"Oh yeah," Windsor said. "In some ways I wish I'd never left."

Windsor hung up. He was staring out the window when the crime scene van pulled up and two men in white hazmat suits climbed up. They were headed up the drive when Eleanor McNamara called back.

"There's no appointment in the book," she said. "It's the funniest thing. After I talked to you, I remembered a call from Jennifer right around that time, the end of July, and I'm sure I entered the appointment in Chandler's calendar. It's just not there now."

"Any back-up calendars?"

"I looked at those too. The appointment isn't there."

Windsor thanked her, hung up, and started searching directory assistance on the internet for a Marvin Barnes. He found an address in Gresham, a suburb east of Portland. The woman who answered the phone mumbled for a few seconds after Windsor asked to talk to Mr. Barnes. Finally, a younger woman came on the line.

"Can I help you?"

"Yes, I'm looking for Marvin Barnes." Windsor thought he'd been disconnected. "Hello?"

"Sorry. I'm still here." Her voice was forced. "Can I ask who is calling?"

"My name is Alex Windsor. My late wife was Jennifer DeGarza. She was your father's lawyer. I'm just trying to tie up some loose ends about a few of her open cases. Is Mr. Barnes there?"

"Marvin Barnes was my father," she said. "He was killed a year ago in a car accident."

Chapter 51

When Arnie Stetson walked into The Ridge, Bud Schwartz was holding court at the bar with the usual suspects and what appeared to be a couple of newcomers who'd wandered in looking for a local IPA and relief from the sun. The early afternoon lunch crowd had left. Things would be slow until the after-work crowd started drifting in around four.

The barflies hung on every word as Bud used both hands to tell some story about a human toe packed in ice inside a Styrofoam cooler he found on the side of the road. "I called the tow truck," he said, barely holding back his laugh.

They were still yukking it up when Stetson filled a stool at the end of the bar and waved at Bud.

"You got a minute?" he asked.

Bud nodded, opened an IPA, and joined Stetson.

"I'm looking for Alex Windsor," Stetson said. "Any ideas?"

Schwartz eyed him suspiciously. "Why?"

Stetson spent the next ten minutes telling the bar owner everything, starting with the offer from Squid Gilroy and ending with what he'd learned about the newspaper's reluctance to touch any story involving Broadnax, Windsor, or The Meat Man Murders.

"It all goes back to the opinion piece Windsor wrote. My publisher was reluctant to run it at first but was all in after he read the part about 'sexually repressed woman hater.' Then Windsor's wife was murdered. Rather than risk the paper's reputation, the publisher let Windsor take the blame. Most people didn't buy it. A few resigned from the paper in protest. We heard that the letters to the editor were brutal."

"Who's this publisher?" Bud asked.

"Alexander Ramsey. I've run into him in the elevator a few times. He was brought in to increase circulation and advertising revenue. That was three months before the murders. After the murder of Windsor's wife, he dreamed up this crazy scheme to run a promotion saying something like, 'We not only bring you the news, we live it.' He wanted to use a picture from Jennifer's crime scene and a mugshot of Windsor with quotes from his op-ed."

"Jesus."

"It gets worse. The centerpiece would be an interview with Windsor followed by ads urging people to buy the paper to read the account of his personal encounter with The Meat Man. An up-close-and-personal kind of thing if you know what I mean. The problem was that he figured all this out before talking to Windsor. When he finally got around to it, Windsor was gone. No one knew where he was or how to get in touch with him."

"So that ended it?"

"Pretty much. When Ramsey learned that Windsor was a well-connected multi-millionaire with roots in the most powerful law firm in the city, he dropped the whole idea. He decided to focus on Broadnax instead, but when Billy quickly pled guilty and was, poof, off to prison, that ended that idea as well. Instead of gaining circulation, the paper lost it. Even some advertisers went south. The whole incident—Broadnax, Windsor, everything—left a bad taste in everyone's mouth. Rumor has it that Ramsey's name is now mud back at corporate headquarters."

Schwartz nodded. "I stopped reading that rag a long time ago. Newspapers aren't what they used to be, including yours. No offense."

"None taken."

Bud went behind the bar, got both of them a beer, then sat back down.

"What was it like?" Stetson asked

"You mean the murders? It was nuts. The place was full every night until closing. Reporters, producers, and cameramen. These really hot chicks from CNN and Fox. The town was scared to death, as much of the newshounds as the killer."

"And when Billy was arrested?"

"Relief, mostly. Especially after everyone realized there wouldn't be a trial. All the reporters left town after that. I was sort of disappointed, myself. That was the best two weeks this place has ever had."

"And Windsor?"

Schwartz shook his head. "I've never known a man more in love with a woman than he was with Jennifer. He was a different person after he met her. Don't get me wrong. He was a great guy before. Sort of a man's man if you know what I mean. When he'd come in people would flock to his table to talk politics or pry some free advice out of him. After he met her a kind of calmness seemed to come over him. He listened more and drank less. Like someone who'd been looking for something all their life and then found it. He called me the day after she died. We only talked for a few minutes. It was like neither one of us knew what to say. The next time I saw him was at her funeral. He looked shattered, empty. That scene with his father-in-law didn't help. Then he disappeared without a word. I was sure that he'd done something stupid, even killed himself. I didn't know where he was, so there was nothing I could do. When he showed up here the other day, it was a load off my mind." Schwartz stopped talking long enough to shake his head. "Hard to believe he took up fly fishing. Never figured him for the type. Well, at least it's not golf. That would really be weird."

"If you believe Gilroy, Windsor wasn't responsible for his wife's death."

The bar owner chuckled. "This is Portland, Oregon, son. No shortage of off-the-wall theories or off-the-wall people. I don't know if what Gilroy was peddling was right or wrong about who killed her. What I do know is that anyone capable of killing Jennifer Windsor can kill anybody."

"That special?"

"Even more."

"You heard what happened," Stetson said.

"His house? Yeah. I can't figure that one out. Windsor's theory about gangs or protestors doesn't make sense to me, but he was there. I wasn't."

"I'd really like to find him," Stetson said.

Schwartz nodded his head slowly. "There is one place you might try."

Chapter 52

The River Otter was a sketchy riverfront bar in a water-front industrial area north of downtown that catered to the hard-hat-and-Carhartt crowd. It served diluted drinks at inflated prices and steaks that tested the best knives and forks. The seats on the booths that looked out over the river through dingy windows were faded and butt worn. A ragged rug covered what had once been a dance floor. It now hosted a karaoke machine and a nightly parade of frustrated lounge singers who showed up after the working-class crowd staggered home.

Arnie Stetson found Windsor sitting at the bar nursing a bottle of beer. The bar was empty except for Windsor and two couples sipping martinis and red wine in one of the booths. The bartender wore an off-white, ruffled-front shirt, a black vest, and bright red bow tie. Business being what it was, he had plenty of time to cut lime wedges, peel lemon rinds, and spear olives. The biggest interruption was a waitress banging back and forth through the swinging door out of the kitchen relaying dinner orders from those brave enough to tackle the menu.

"How'd you find me?"

"Bud Schwartz. He really cares about you. You know that, right?"

Windsor nodded. "We used to hang out at this place on those days when Bud wanted someone to pour drinks for him."

Stetson ordered a local lager and drank it as he worked up the nerve to broach the subject of Billy Broadnax and the late Squid Gilroy. He was just about there when Windsor handed him the keys to the BMW.

"Let's get out of here," he said.

"Where to?"

"I'll give you directions."

Chapter 53

The owners of the four sprawling homes on the dead-end street in the West Hills coveted privacy more than scenery. They didn't need to flaunt their status with houses overlooking the city. They were the winners who grew up in luxury, lived on the riches accumulated through privilege and old money, and reveled in anonymity broken only by sizable charitable donations. Either that or they had sold a forty-year-old tract home in Southern California and moved north.

There were no cars on the streets, no children in the yards, and no sounds emanating from the sprawling homes behind neatly trimmed hedges and elegant brick walls. Even the crickets and frogs used muted tones so as not to disturb the neighborhood's collective beauty sleep.

"Stop here," Windsor said.

Stetson eased the car to the curb then turned off the engine. Windsor glanced around the neighborhood trying to remember what it was like growing up there, to know the people who lived in each house, to play in their yards, eat at their tables, shoot hoops with their sons, and date their daughters. It seemed like a million lonely years ago.

"I take it this is your old neighborhood," Arnie Stetson said.

Windsor nodded.

"Which house was yours?"

Windsor pointed to a white, three-story Victorian home with green shutters on the windows and tall pillars supporting a roof covering a flagstone front porch. Accent lights highlighted the neatly trimmed bushes that surrounded the house. Wisteria wound around a trellis and over the curtained windows. Two Cadillacs and a Suburban commanded the driveway in front of the three-car garage.

"I sold it after my parents died. Some refugees from the aerospace industry bought it. I don't know what happened after that. Maybe someone different owns it now." There was no sadness or bitterness in Windsor's voice. He merely related the facts with neither nostalgia nor passion.

"I used to play baseball over there." Windsor pointed to a large open area between two houses that served as the neighborhood park. Next to the baseball diamond and chain-link backstop were swings and a merry-go-round at the far end of right field. "I used to climb in those trees." He pointed in the other direction at a hillside that dropped off into a less affluent part of town. "The first girl I kissed was behind that hedge." He paused for a few seconds. "Funny, but I can't remember her name."

He nodded toward a laurel hedge that ran between the house where he grew up and a stately old place next door that had all the appearances of the neighborhood dowager. Barely visible through the hedge was the corner of a sun porch on the back of the elegant, ivy-covered, turn-of-the-century mansion. Needle-like spires topped with weathervanes rose into the night sky above a front porch that ran the width of the first floor. The dense hedge that encircled the house looked older than most parts of Portland. Twelve-feet tall and four-feet thick, it lined the entire perimeter of the large corner lot, broken only by the entrance and exit of a circular drive.

Windsor stared silently at the old house, wondering if the inside was anything like he remembered. Was it still a testament to Victorian excess with its ornate wallpaper, antique tables with claw feet, Persian carpets, and cozy sun porch that overlooked a carefully groomed backyard?

"You left all of this to become a psychologist?" Stetson said.

"I started not liking my friends. They were great when we were growing up, but as we got older, they were thinking more about being rich lawyers and doctors like their parents. Maybe take over the family business, providing it made money without much effort on their part. Everything was money with them. They wanted to be pampered and comfortable like their fathers. Marry beautiful, sophisticated women like their mothers. Have passionate lovers with condos in the Pearl District. They just didn't want to work for it. They wanted it all handed to them."

"You figured all this out when you were a kid?"

"Not in so many words. I just knew that I was different than they were. I had different attitudes and different beliefs. They yearned for the status quo. I yearned to cut it down and watch it bleed. Don't ask me why."

"But your father was a fat-cat lawyer."

"I know, but both he and my mother died when I was fifteen. They left me tens of millions of dollars that I inherited when I turned twenty-one. There I was still in high school and on the verge of getting the kind of money that all my friends would spend the rest of their lives chasing. I don't know if they resented me or their parents for not being killed as well. To be honest about it, I really didn't care. "

"Why didn't you become a lawyer like your father?"

"People become lawyers to make money. I already had money. It gave me the freedom to do whatever I wanted."

"So, why psychology?"

"The academic version is that psychology is the scientific study of the mind and behavior. A multifaceted discipline that includes human development, sports, health, clinical, social behavior, and cognitive processes. Blah. Blah. Blah. To me it was a way to understand where people come from, what makes them who and what they are. Including myself."

"Okay. Fine. But why in Portland? Why not someplace bigger, more important, more … relevant?"

"In his own way, my father owned this town when he was alive. He was courted by every politician who wanted to be more than a city commissioner. When I started my practice the name Windsor was enough to lure wealthy clients. It kept the family name in play and greased the skids for me. The difference between me and my father was that he genuinely cared about this place. I really don't. I'm ambivalent about it. I've been successful because I have no skin in the game. People can talk to me knowing that I won't be offended or flattered by what they say. They don't hold back because they know they can't hurt me."

"And Portland?"

"I came back here because it was easy … and I was curious about how my childhood friends turned out."

"And?"

"Some good. Some bad. Some send their children to me."

When a police cruiser pulled up behind them, Windsor turned around. Stetson looked in the side view mirror. A young officer got out of the cruiser and walked to Stetson's side of the car. After asking for the usual information, he leaned down to look in the window. "Is that you Dr. Windsor?"

"Yes, officer," Windsor said.

"I heard you were back. Everything okay?"

"Fine. I'm showing my friend my old neighborhood. We were just leaving."

"Okay. Just checking. Drive safe."

The officer got in his car, pulled around them, and drove away.

They sat there until the patrol car disappeared around the corner. As they started to leave, headlights came up behind them from the other direction. The low-slung sports car raced by them and into the circular driveway of the house next to Windsor's.

"Nice car," said Stetson. "Too bad Porsche Carreras don't go with nineteenth-century architecture."

Windsor glanced back at the car, then at the house.

"You recognize the car?" Stetson asked.

"No. Just the driver. Chandler Stockdale."

"Is that where he lives?"

"No. It belongs to a judge, Dorothy Evelyn Hawkins."

"The judge in the Billy Broadnax case. What do you think that's all about?"

Windsor didn't answer.

Chapter 54

The sun porch always felt cool, comforting, and secure, even in warm summer evenings. As a little girl she'd sleep there during July and August, waking up to the smell of flowers, the sound of birds, and a welcome peacefulness. Most mornings her father would come out, sit on the bed next to her, and read the paper while sipping coffee. Her mother always slept late. Her father worked long hours at the bank, so it was one of the few times they had alone together.

Her father had been tall, with hair so blonde it was nearly white. Every day he'd wear one of his ten dark suits, a freshly starched white shirt, and a striped tie to work. In the spring and fall he'd wear a raincoat. In the winter it was a newsboy with earflaps and camel-hair overcoat with a belt, the collar turned up. At home, it was the same thing minus the coat and tie. Most people thought of him as stern and humorless, but she knew better. During those mornings on the porch, he'd sometimes read the comics to her. They'd laugh together as he imitated Alley Oop or Dagwood Bumstead. Sometimes they'd talk about the news on the front page, especially if it was important.

So long ago, but to her it seemed like yesterday. Other than leaving for school, she'd lived in the same house all her life. That she'd never married only made it seem much more like time had stood still. No husband. No children. No commitments other than work. Nothing to watch grow other than the hostas and dahlias in the backyard. In that house she could always be that little girl on the sun porch, laughing with her father and living in the confidence that it could be that way for as long as she wanted.

Until now. How could things have gone so wrong so fast?

The return of Alex Windsor triggered something deep inside Dorothy Evelyn Hawkins that said everything she'd known all her life was now in danger. No amount of money or privilege could protect her or the rest of them from what she felt was coming. What she knew was coming. At some point she would have to do what she always did—look out for herself. The others would do the same, but that was their problem. All she knew was that when you're all alone you have no one to protect except yourself.

The investment club that had added so much more wealth to what she already had was over. It had all been Benno's fault. She tried to feel bad about his death but could only muster a sense of relief. She never liked him. He had been weak, a sad man living a sad life that even he knew would never end well. The weakness made him a threat to her and the others. He had acted in a way that jeopardized all of them. Now he's dead. Hoping that everything he'd done died with him might be too much to ask.

She never wanted Benno included in their little club. He didn't seem the type to take the risks necessary to reap the rewards and protect future profits. Yet reap them he did. Now it looked like the journey of greed they'd taken together cost one of them his life. Would there be others? She didn't want to find out.

That morning she'd called the office to tell her secretary she wouldn't be in and to reschedule her appointments. It was the housekeeper's day off. She had the house to herself, free to go into the large, country kitchen and poke around until she found what she was looking for. With a pitcher of ice, a tall glass, and a bottle of gin, she curled up on the sun porch, a blanket across her lap and watched the gardener move between the flower beds in the backyard.

All she wanted to do was live out the rest of life in the only place she had ever really known. She wanted her bed, her clothes, her dishes, the rugs on the floor and the lamps on the table. All of it. Forever.

But most of all she wanted their own private angel of death to just stop. No more killing. He'd gone too far. Three people were dead, four counting Benno, and it was all his doing. There were probably more, but she didn't want to know.

She was afraid Alex Windsor would be next. After that, who knows? Maybe that moron from the television station or that disgusting boy from the newspaper.

"He's out of control," Stockdale said.

"Get him under control," she shot back.

They were sitting on the sun porch. The blanket is gone. The sun is low enough to cast shadows across the backyard. The gin bottle empty. The booze fog lifted just enough to understand what was happening and what Stockdale was saying.

"Find him and tell him to call me," she said. "I don't want Alex Windsor killed. I don't want any more people killed."

"What makes you think he's going to kill him? He had the chance the other night when he shot up his house. He didn't admit it. If he's changed his mind, then he will tell us."

"No, he won't! He didn't tell us about the others, and he won't tell us if there's going to be more. That's the way he is. Killing people is his answer to everything. He's gone rogue, damn it!" The tears streaming down her wrinkled face were a product of gin and fear.

"I don't know where he is and he's not answering his phone."

She considered Stockdale too smart for his own good. Managing partner of the largest law firm in the city, big house, fancy car, twenty-something mistress stashed away in a river-front condo. Yet here he was, telling her he had no control of the man who could bring them all down ... if he hadn't already.

"Do you know what's at stake here?" Hawkins said. "Let me tell you in one word: Everything. All we've worked for all our lives is at risk. That little private detective and his girlfriend were white trash. No one will miss them. No one will connect us to them. Windsor is another story. Kill him and all hell breaks loose. Now, find our angel of death and put an end to this."

"I can't make any promises," Stockdale said.

It was all she could do not to throw the empty gin bottle at him.

"Shooting up Windsor's house the other night is just like him," she said. "Nothing was accomplished and now Windsor is all over the news and that idiot television reporter has made the connection between him, Gilroy, Billy Broadnax, and God knows what else." She sipped at her empty gin glass. "I'm having a little trouble seeing the silver lining in all of this."

The hint of panic that crossed Stockdale's face was a crack in his armor of arrogance and self-control. It gave her a sense of satisfaction, but little else. Since they were all going into oblivion, anyway, why not let him lose his dignity along the way. It was like having a good movie on a bad flight.

"I knew he couldn't be trusted," he said.

She marveled at Stockdale's attempt at revisionist history. He was the one who talked her into getting involved in the first place. Then he recruited his friend Benno because the lecherous little psychiatrist was dead broke and needed money, serious money to hear him tell it. Suddenly, Stockdale acted like it was someone else's idea and he was dragged along kicking and screaming.

"Where do things stand?" she asked.

"The last time I talked to him we agreed that we shouldn't meet again and that it was time to dissolve our investment club."

She stopped asking questions. This was getting her nowhere. Stockdale was a mess. Badgering him about Windsor and their angel of death wasn't going to change anything.

"And Windsor?"

"You mean other than he tried to kill me?"

"Tell me but make it short."

While Stockdale described his meeting with Windsor, Hawkins glanced around the room with its neatly arranged books on the shelves, the paintings that went perfectly with the furniture and area rugs. The thought of losing it made her cringe.

She suddenly felt too old and tired to fight. It wasn't how she expected her career to end. She thought there would be endless dinner parties, speeches, and silver serving trays etched with the State Seal. Maybe Dorothy Evelyn Hawkins day at the State Capitol, glowing editorials in the local paper, a cover story in the bar association magazine. Instead, there would only be a gala at the Arlene Schnitzer Concert Hall the next night, which, in reality, was a poorly disguised fundraiser for a local acting company. Apparently, her swan song would be as bait to lure donations to pay for staging plays by Ibsen and Chekov. Best make the best of it, she thought. It might be the only recognition she'd ever get.

"The only thing we have going for us," she said, "is that Windsor has no proof."

Stockdale gave her a sheepish look. "That may not be the case."

"What!"

"Benno and I had a file on Broadnax that included Bennett's evaluation of Billy and Gilroy's report of his movements the night Windsor's wife was killed. We agreed to destroy them. I did. He told me he did, but if he didn't then Windsor either stole them or he got his hands on a copy. Maybe that dead girl had one."

"Jesus," she said. "I suppose the next thing you're going to tell me is that he knows about Marvin Barnes."

"I doubt it. I had an appointment with Jennifer to talk about Barnes. She was killed three days before. I erased it from all the office calendars."

"What about her calendar?"

Stockdale shrugged.

"Let's put this in legal terms, Chandler. This is a god damn fucking shit show."

With a wave of her hand, she dismissed Stockdale. When he was gone, she went back to the kitchen in search of more gin. She was determined to shed no tears for their doomed investment club. Of the three left, she felt like the only one who could see what was coming. All the years. All the hard work. All at risk of being lost for a reason that now sounds like a waste of time: greed. There had to be a way out of this.

Chapter 55

"Judge Hawkins, please. Alex Windsor calling."

"I'm sorry, but the judge is unavailable. May I take a message?"

"Please tell her I called and that I'd like to drop by her office later today."

"Is she expecting you?"

"I'm not sure."

Dorothy Evelyn Hawkins was the matriarch of the neighborhood where he grew up. She lived a cloistered life in the house she grew up in, broken only by the dorm rooms of college in New England and apartments near her law school in Virginia. After passing the Oregon bar, she moved home and went to work at a large Portland firm, toiling in obscurity for a decade doing contracts, wills, and estate planning. When her parents died, they left her their house and a substantial fortune. She bided her time waiting for the right opportunity before running for the circuit court bench. The seat she won was vacant. While the other candidates were far more qualified, they lacked the one thing Dorothy Hawkins had plenty of—money.

Hawkins' true distinction was her deeply held fear of growing old. Well into her seventies now, she tried to hide her age under a wig that always seemed to be turned about ten degrees off center as if she'd put it on and then spun around a few times. The wig was set off by blush, mascara, and lipstick so smeared it looked like she'd applied it in a wind tunnel.

The strong bond between Hawkins and his mother always mystified Windsor. His mother was always happy, facing every challenge with an air of enthusiasm and wonderment. By contrast, Dorothy Hawkins was stern and dark with a cynical outlook on life that Windsor's father said was the result of a life of too much money and too few men.

The local paper closely followed her sometimes convoluted rulings, once going so far as doing a less-than-flattering profile. The reporter who wrote the piece called Windsor, asking for his recollections of Hawkins and any insights into her personality. Maybe out of loyalty to his mother or a sentimental attachment to Hawkins, he declined to say anything beyond a few platitudes about growing up next door to her. He artfully dodged what he was sure was going to be a central premise of the profile: Judge Dorothy Evelyn Hawkins' love of gin.

It was four p.m. before Windsor found a place to park within walking distance of the courthouse. He braved the heat and homeless, both burning up the streets, before taking the elevator to the fourth floor.

"You must be Dr. Windsor," Hawkins' secretary said when he walked in. She was an older woman with a severe hair bun and rhinestone reading glasses perched on the end of her nose.

"Is the judge in?"

"I'm sorry, but she's left for the day. I told her you were coming, but I'm afraid it couldn't be helped. There's an important event tonight and she needed to go home and get ready. I'm sorry. Perhaps we can find some time for an appointment." She thumbed through a calendar on her desk. "Would something next week work for you?"

"This event tonight? Is it something in her honor?"

"That's right," the secretary said. "It's at The Schnitz. It should be a lovely evening. They've decorated the lobby to look like ancient Egypt. The waiters and bartenders will be dressed up like King Tut or Cleopatra. The judge is very excited."

"What time?"

"Seven p.m."

"What's the best way to get a ticket?"

"Call the box office at The Schnitz. You can pick up a ticket at will call. Also, it's tax deductible."

Chapter 56

The Arlene Schnitzer Concert Hall is the cultural and geographic center of the city. Nicknamed "The Schnitz," its vast stage, cavernous auditorium with seats for 2,700, and lavish lobby had played host to events ranging from Isaac Stern to Lyle Lovett. Outside, the restored art deco marquee that once held names such as Gable, Bogart, Lombard, and Colbert dominated SW Broadway, the artery that runs through the heart of downtown. Tonight, the marquee read: "The Actors' Troupe honors Dorothy Evelyn Hawkins. Call now for reservations." After that came a phone number.

Windsor remembered his father describing The Actors' Troupe as a collection of dedicated theater buffs who enjoyed putting on plays by Ibsen, O'Neill, Williams, and lesser-known writers as long as they had something to do with being gay or suicidal. Judge Hawkins was the Troupe's leading patron, which earned her the honor of being the featured guest at this year's annual fundraiser. That meant that anyone with five hundred dollars could hang out with the local theater crowd, eat crustless sandwiches, mixed nuts, broccoli spears, and wash it all down with an oaky, unpretentious white wine from a local vineyard.

For tonight, the traditional ticket booth in the center of the open-air foyer had been decorated to look like The Sphinx. Inside the three sets of double doors, a bank of ushers dressed like King Tut stood ready to give the bum's rush to anyone without an invitation. In the lobby, a concession counter that once sold Milk Duds and buttery popcorn now hawked T-shirts, bumper stickers, and lapel pins promoting the theater troupe and its various productions. Brought in just for the event were two twelve-foot inflatable replicas of the Egyptian god Osiris that proudly, if somewhat precariously, stood at the foot of a wide, gracefully curved staircase that swept up to the balcony. The person responsible apparently overlooked the fact that Osiris was the god of the dead, among other things.

The street in front of the theater had been blocked off to look like opening night of a 1930s-era Hollywood movie. Huge spotlights crisscrossed the sky while guests arrived wearing period costumes and riding in vintage automobiles on loan from a local car club. A half dozen giddy guests looking like extras from *The Great Gatsby* arrived in an antique limo just as Windsor got to the ticket booth. He picked up his invitation, followed revelers from the limo inside, then elbowed his way through a sea of flappers in feather boas and men in tuxedos and spats. He took the stairs to the balcony level, stopping at the first landing to look down into the crowded lobby.

Chandler Stockdale stood near the front door with the same gray-haired woman from Benno's funeral. Both were dressed in business clothes that created the impression of a busy, power couple stopping by to pay their respects to the judge. Windsor recognized the man they were talking to as a member of the state supreme court.

Spotting Judge Hawkins was like finding the queen in the middle of a beehive. Dressed in sequined black with a feathered hat hanging precariously on the side of her wig, she twirled about, graciously accepting the gratitude of the amateurs who put on the plays she helped pay for. The wine glass in her left hand was kept full by what Windsor figured was an eager and attentive member of The Actor's Troupe. With her right hand, she accepted each congratulations and thanks with the appropriate hand squeeze, hug, and air kiss.

Windsor spotted Malcolm Goodly, the so-called theater critic for the city's alternative weekly, oozing his baby fat between the paying guests to get as close to Hawkins as possible. He knew it would never dawn on Goodly that he was watching a seasoned politician masterfully working a crowd of fawning donors. After watching her for a few minutes, Windsor fought his way back down the stairs and across the lobby. Time, he decided, to find out how much Judge Hawkins knew about Billy Broadnax.

"Congratulations, Dorothy. It's a beautiful event."

She turned toward him ready to greet another well-wisher who had sneaked up behind her. "Alex! Oh my god, is it you?" She smeared her lipstick on his cheek in what was intended to be a kiss then slipped her arm under his. She began introducing him to the nearest group of fawners. "This is Alex Windsor, everybody. Dr. Alex Windsor I might add. I've known him all his life. His late mother and I were the best of friends. Isn't that right, Alex?"

All eyes turned to Windsor. "That's right," he said, then whispered in her ear. "I hate to bother you at a time like this, but I really need to talk to you."

Hawkins gave the onlookers an awkward smile before whispering, "This is not a good time. Couldn't we have lunch? Perhaps early next week?"

"This is about Billy Broadnax."

Hawkins' face went cold and blank for a moment. Windsor thought she was going to slap him, but instead turned toward her admirers. "Excuse us for just a moment," she told them and escorted Windsor to a quiet corner behind one of the towering statues of Osiris.

"What's wrong with you? You know better than this! I'm not going to discuss that case under any circumstances and certainly not here." Her voice was the firm one she used with young attorneys who dared challenge one of her poorly thought-out rulings from the bench. "You're welcome to come by my office. We can catch up on where you've been and talk about old times. But I have nothing to say about that case."

"I think you better make time. This is about more than Broadnax. It's also about Bennett Benno, Chandler Stockdale, and how my wife died."

"I'm sorry, Alex, but I'm very busy. Please, call my office tomorrow. I'll let my secretary know. I have no idea what you're talking about, but we can discuss it over a nice, quiet lunch."

With that, she turned away. Her spidery hand slipped out from under his arm, and she was immediately swallowed up by a new crowd of well-wishers. Malcolm Goodly gave Windsor a perturbed look. "I thought you were in Tibet," he said before falling back into place at the judge's side.

Chapter 57

The Chrysler New Yorker pulled into the circular driveway a little after midnight. It bounced off the curb a couple of times before screeching to a halt at the end of the cobblestone walk that led to the old house with its big porch and towering spires.

Judge Dorothy Evelyn Hawkins got out, carefully tucking the crystal serving dish she'd been presented at the fundraiser under her arm. Her wig had slid over to one side of her head, clinging there like a rare species of moss. She carefully negotiated the steps then stood at the front door fishing in her beaded purse for the house keys.

The wine at the fund-raiser had given her gas and each small burp reminded her why she preferred something stronger. It was time to make a dent in the Bombay Gin, she thought, providing she could find her key and her shaking hands allowed her to insert it in the lock. The encounter with Alex Windsor had unnerved her. She knew it would happen sooner or later, but it was astonishing that he'd show up at an event like that. What happened to his manners and sense of propriety? He was always a precocious little shit. Even if she wanted to talk about that monster Broadnax, which she didn't, to think she'd do it at an event like that was impudent. Something had to be done. She'd waivered about whether to kill Windsor. After all, they did have a history. Tonight, though, was too much. Enough was enough, she thought, poking the key at the lock twice without luck and was about to try a third time.

"Nice party, Dorothy."

The voice that came out of the shadows at the end of the long porch didn't startle her. His impudence knew no bounds.

"I thought so, too," she said without taking her eye off the keyhole. "It was nice of you to attend, despite your rude behavior. I hope you understand how totally inappropriate that was." She stabbed at the lock again, missed, and gave up in disgust. She put the keys back in her purse and turned toward him.

For the last hour, Windsor had been sitting in the porch swing rocking gently back and forth. How many times had he sat in the exact same place watching his mother and Dorothy Hawkins drink iced tea on warm summer afternoons? He remembered thinking how elegant they looked, regal almost. They talked in a way only women can talk. He couldn't recall anything they said, only the way they said it; hanging on each other's words, spending an hour talking about the same subject, sharing life experiences as if they were recipes for Bundt cake.

At the far end of the porch, beyond where she was poking at the door lock, loomed the towering hedge between their two houses. He could just see the peak of his parents' home, his home. If the hedge were a foot or two shorter, he could see the window in his bedroom where every morning for most of the first fifteen years of his life, he'd woken up and looked out into Dorothy Hawkins' carefully manicured backyard. He knew that around the corner of the house there was a gap in the hedge with a squeaky wooden gate. When he would come home and his mother wasn't around, he'd go through that gate to find the two women always there, always talking, smiling, laughing.

He lost touch with Dorothy Hawkins after his parents were killed and he went to live with his aunt in Bellevue, Washington. She'd send a card and check for a hundred dollars on his birthday and Christmas. When he graduated from high school the check was for five hundred dollars, followed by more that helped sustain him through college and the start of graduate school, not that he needed it. His parents had left him more than enough to pay for college, graduate school, and to get his private practice up and running. Still, her sporadic payments showed up every few months. Since opening his own practice, he'd talked to her several times in their respective official capacities as judge and expert witness. She'd greet him warmly, but she was clearly disappointed that someone from her part of town would stoop to a profession as common and unrewarding as psychology, particularly the only son of her dearest friend. Windsor could sense it and kept his distance.

He invited her to the wedding. She didn't come, instead sending a set of antique silverware that came in a scarred mahogany box. When Jennifer opened the lid, the brilliant twelve-place serving set glistened against the box's purple velvet liner. She had never seen anything like it in her life. Windsor recognized it from his childhood. It belonged to his mother.

Dorothy Hawkins never looked young. As a child he saw her as perpetually old, even though she and his mother were the same age. Maybe it was her spidery fingers or her bird-like frame. When she bent down expecting a kiss on the cheek, he'd do it as fast as he could, then quickly pull away. She smelled of moth balls and perfume. The first time he read *Hansel and Gretel* he thought of her tossing him into an oven.

Now, watching her poke at the door lock, the memories came back in vivid detail. "We still need to talk, Dorothy."

Giving up on the door, she walked toward him, the serving dish still secure in one hand. With the other she pushed the wig back up on top of her head as she shuffled along the wooden porch. Away from the glitter and glitz of the theater lobby, Hawkins' step had lost its bounce, her dowager's hump more pronounced.

"You were always such a determined little boy, Alex," she said. "No surprise, I guess, that you turned into a determined man."

She half fell, half sat on the opposite end of the porch swing. They swayed back and forth together, listening to crickets, frogs, and the far-off rumble of freeway traffic.

"The day your mother came home from the hospital after you were born, we sat right here just like this. We talked about what great things were in store for you. She was so proud. And I was so envious. She had a wonderful husband and a healthy, beautiful son. It was the only time in my life that I wanted to trade places with someone."

Watching her sink back into the swing's soft cushions, Windsor wondered if she would suddenly disappear, leaving behind nothing but a black sequined dress, a purse, and the crystal serving dish. A Cheshire cat with a frown instead of a smile.

"Tell me about Billy Broadnax and your friends Stockdale and Benno," Windsor said.

"Alex, sweet Alex." Her exasperated sigh came out like air from a leaky balloon. "Where do you get these ideas?"

"Let's just say they fall into my lap. That's what happens to little rich boys, isn't it? Things just fall in their laps, and they get richer, have more things, marry perfect women. Funny how much luckier rich people are than people without money. Look at you. A multi-millionaire who made hundreds of thousands more investing money in a scheme that just dropped into your lap. And not just you, but Stockdale, Benno, and some other guy as well. Remarkable, isn't it? By the way, who is this other guy?"

The old woman's profile against the dim light from the street never changed. She stared straight ahead like the neon-replica of The Sphinx at the entrance to The Schnitz.

Chapter 58

"What happened to you?" Judge Hawkins said, turning to give Windsor one of those withering looks that had scared the hell out of him as a child. "What made you so resentful of authority and tradition? Was it your parents' death? Is that what made you the way you are? You could've done so much with your life. Instead, you spend it talking to juvenile delinquents with bad attitudes and rich parents. You sit in prison visiting rooms talking to killers, picking their brains as if there is something there worth learning. You write opinion pieces for that silly little newspaper that ended up getting your wife killed. You turned your back on the very things that made you what you are, that fed you, clothed you, and educated you. You were one of us. Not one of them."

The word "them" came out like she was talking about the slugs that chewed holes in the leaves of her Hosta. Windsor knew that if she could listen to her disdain for all things outside the comfortable confines of the West Hills, she could answer her own question.

"I'm not resentful," he said. He wanted it to sound like a simple denial. Instead, it came out defensive.

"Then why choose a profession like psychology with all its mumbo-jumbo? Those ridiculous theories like Rorschach tests and repressed memories. Nonsense. All of it. Not only that, but you took up with that colored gal at the police department. Then you married that Mexican farm girl? Was it to mock us? Was it your way of rebelling against all that we are, and you should be?"

Windsor should've expected that from her. Attaching false motives to the way he lived his life was a lot easier than trying to understand it. She could brush off his actions as the irresponsible deeds of a wayward son, a black sheep. All the evidence she needed was viewed through filters built up over a lifetime of wealth and privilege. He had to be wrong because she never was.

"That's pretty rich coming from someone who never woke up next to anything other than an empty gin bottle."

She looked hurt for about a second. "Is that the way you talk to your patients?"

"You're not a patient, but maybe you should be."

"There's that impudence again. It's getting a little tiresome."

"Call it what you like, but you are way off base, Dorothy. What I did with my life and who I did it with has nothing to do with you, my parents, this neighborhood, or money."

"Would you have done it if your father and mother were alive?" she asked. "I don't think so. John and Margaret would never have tolerated the way you've lived your life, the way you've squandered your heritage. I know how much money you inherited, and I know what you did with it. Nothing. It just sits down there with that accountant in San Francisco getting bigger and bigger while you live like a hermit or a hippie or some useless thing up in those mountains. Where was it? Tibet? Ridiculous. It's wrong, Alex. Wrong to tear down, ridicule, and turn against what they worked so hard to build and be a part of."

"Maybe it needed to be torn down and ridiculed." He was being defensive again. "Nothing, good or bad, survives cynicism and suspicion. Maybe you should look inside your own heart and question your own beliefs before you question the beliefs of others. Are the motives of the people you seek to analyze and debase really any different from your own?"

Windsor resisted the urge to run down the list of local notables suspected in a litany of shady land deals, influence peddling, child abuse, and wife beating. Others fell into the category of smells bad, but still legal. In the early days of his private practice, he'd heard all the stories about the shortcomings of the city's wealthiest movers and shakers. He could see now that the rumors didn't go unnoticed and, if what he believed about Benno, Stockdale, and now Judge Hawkins was true, they were still going on.

"I'm not here to talk about me, us, or them. I want to know about Jennifer and about your little investment club with Benno and Stockdale. About how Billy Broadnax is part of whatever's going on. If everything you said about the altruism and well-meaning intent of the rich and powerful is true, then tell me the truth."

She glared at him, a look he had seen before as a kid. "What are you talking about?"

"Billy Broadnax did not kill Jennifer. My guess is Benno did, but don't hold me to it. Not that it matters. I have proof that it wasn't Billy. What I don't know is why. What I don't know is about that little investment club of yours and how he was somehow involved. Tell me! Tell me the truth!"

"There's nothing to tell. What's done is done. Don't let what happened to her destroy you as well."

"Don't patronize me. I'm not your Japanese gardener. I believe you know who killed my wife and why. You may as well tell me, because you know I'll find out one way or the other. Why, Dorothy? Tell me, damn it. Let's end this right here, right now."

Hawkins ran a finger along the edge of the serving plate. Stared at her reflection in the polished silver. Her face turned empty and hollow. "You're wrong, Alex. Billy confessed and I sentenced him to life in prison."

"Benno and Stockdale knew all about Billy before Jennifer died."

"And I was somehow involved?"

"You hustled him off to prison to cover up what they did to her and why."

"What I did was the best for everyone. Billy. The victims' families. This community."

"Who benefits from hiding the truth?"

She ignored the question. "You said you have proof. What kind of proof?"

"Enough. There's more and I'll find it. You know that so why not save me the trouble. The truth, Dorothy. The truth."

Hawkins' head moved up and down in the shadows at the end of the swing. Windsor couldn't see her face anymore, only her outline and the shimmering of her sequined dress in the dim glow of distant streetlights. He knew now that the real Dorothy Hawkins had died with his mother. The woman sitting next to him was like an ancient tomb once filled with the mysteries and wonders of long ago. Now, looted by time, holding only stale, rancid air.

"The truth you're looking for isn't here." Her voice didn't say resignation, it screamed it. It was the voice of defeat at the hands of life and the compromises it took to meet its demands.

"There was truth here once when my parents were alive," Windsor said. He was pleading, afraid to let the moment slip away, afraid to let her slip away. "There must still be truth in the home of my mother's best friend. Truth in the home of a judge."

"Don't lecture me. Some things are more important than truth."

"Such as?"

"Survival."

The old woman pulled herself out of the porch swing and tottered slowly toward the front door. "Let what happened stay buried with all those you and I loved so much. Let that be the truth."

"You know I'm not going to let that happen."

"No. You probably won't, but you should. You really should."

Watching her finally open the door, Windsor stayed on the porch swing running her words through his head.

Chapter 59

Bud Schwartz stood behind the bar entertaining the boys who came in a little after nine each morning to drink the beer they needed to work up an appetite for the burger and beer they'd have at noon. He was in the middle of a story that Windsor had heard at least a dozen times before. It began with, "There was this young priest ..." and ended with, "No Father, that's just the way the light's shining on it."

Rather than ruin Bud's moment, Windsor got his own coffee from the pot at the end of the bar and took the morning newspaper to his table in the back to see what didn't get written about that day. Halfway through an editorial on the blight of gang graffiti, the door opened to let unwanted morning light creep reluctantly into the dark bar. Windsor glanced at the outline of a man backlit by the harsh morning sun. He watched as the man ignored the regulars at the bar and headed straight for Windsor's table. On the way, he took off his aviator glasses, hanging them into the breast pocket of his safari jacket.

"Rich Raymond, Channel 5 News," he said when he reached Windsor's table. "You're a hard man to track down."

"Not hard enough, apparently," Windsor said, ignoring Raymond's extended hand then looking around for Raymond's ever-present cameraman. "Where's your pack mule? Tied to a light pole outside?"

"This is strictly off the meter, but I'll tell him you said hello."

"You're wasting your time. I don't know why you find me so interesting, but I have nothing to say to you or anyone else."

Raymond looked back to the bar as if he expected service. Windsor waited for him to snap his fingers so he could watch Bud bounce him out the door and into the street. Instead, Raymond got up and came back with a glass of cola.

"Level with me, Dr. Windsor. These murders, Gilroy and his girlfriend or whatever she was. Benno's suicide at your wife's grave. It all has something to do with Billy Broadnax, doesn't it?" Raymond waited while Windsor continued to ignore him.

"And that shooting at your house the other night. Gangbangers? Protestors?"

"Really? Not in that neighborhood."

"I really don't care what you believe." Windsor glanced over Raymond's shoulder at the bar. Bud was making a motion like he was throwing someone out the door. Windsor gave his head an imperceptible shake. Bud shrugged and went back to pouring beer and telling stories.

"I suppose putting you on camera to talk about your year in Tibet is out of the question," Raymond said. "Probably the same story as why you're back in town, right?" Windsor answered with a cold stare. "Well, you leave me no choice. Since you're a psychologist you'll understand where I'm coming from on this." Raymond leaned across the table as if Schwartz and the four guys at the bar could hear him or cared about what he had to say. "Either you tell me what's going on or I run a story tonight about Billy's psychiatrist blowing his brains out at your wife's grave. Not only that, but I'll also quote a reliable source that says Benno's body was moved after his death. After that is a lot of background about Billy, your wife, the opinion piece you wrote. It all makes for a hell of a good yarn, don't you think?"

"You really are a bottom feeder," Windsor said and got up.

The lyrics to Dylan's *Subterranean Homesick Blues* still circled the walls in the men's room where Windsor sought asylum. Better cooling his jets there than feeding Raymond into Bud's deep-fat fryer. He read the lyrics, looking for inspiration, but gave up because the verse didn't include the phrase, "Kill the little asshole."

Windsor knew he was getting close to the truth. He could feel it. He just needed to learn more about what he already knew. The last thing he wanted was a Rich Raymond special that would summon reporters back to town just when he needed more time. He washed his hands and stared at himself in the mirror looking for answers.

"Okay. You win," Windsor said when he got back to the table. Raymond was drinking his cola and watching the big screen television in the corner. The Cubs were losing to the Braves in the first game of a daylight double header. "I'll tell you everything and I'll go on camera to talk about Tibet and why I came back." Raymond gave off an oily smile and started to strut while still sitting down.

"All I want in return," Windsor said, "is to keep my wife's name out of this and two more days to wrap up loose ends. After that, the story is yours."

"So, it does involve Billy?" Raymond could hardly contain himself. "What is it? More victims we didn't know about?"

"You'll have to wait. Take it or leave it."

"Is it worth it?"

"Guaranteed."

Raymond engaged in what passed for thoughtfulness. "It's tempting, but I have to say no. Two days is a lifetime in this business. I don't have to tell you that. How about you tell me right now what you've found out so far and we'll work together on the rest."

"How about you give me the two days and I'll throw in an on-camera interview with Billy Broadnax?"

The look on Raymond's face said everything. If he were some trout, he'd be hooked. "You can do that?"

"Sure."

"Done," Raymond said. "We meet right here, eleven in the morning, two days from now. We'll do the interview right here at your old table. It'll be a nice touch and good strokes for the owner. After that, we'll go see Billy."

"Just to make sure things don't go bad," Windsor said. "The deal's off if you do one more story about me, my wife, or the Gilroy-Roberts murders. Not only that, but I turn in your snitch. That means you'll lose a great source in the police department and the odds are you'll never get another anywhere near as good. I should do it anyway for him telling you about Benno."

Raymond looked stunned then hurt. "He's not a snitch. He's a source."

"Stop. His name is Peter Marcini, a forensic expert who's been leaking stories to reporters for years. But since you're new in town you probably wouldn't know that."

"Benno's suicide? Did you move the body?"

"Doesn't matter who moved it. Benno is dead. He killed himself and you're not going to do anything about it, right? An interview with Broadnax is worth its weight in gold. It's your ticket out of here. Seattle at least. Maybe LA. So don't blow it because of a story about the death of a second-rate shrink in a cemetery. Marcini will never go on-camera, which means you have nothing but a useless, run-of-the-mill story using unnamed sources that most people think don't even exist. Even the wire services won't pick that up. Think about it. You've got me over a barrel. Pick up your winnings and call it good."

"How do I know I can trust you?" he said.

"You can't," Windsor said, "but if you get suspicious then go ahead with the Benno story."

"And if I do, the deal is off."

"Right."

"I'll see you in two days," Raymond said, then got up and left.

Chapter 60

Chandler Stockdale stood at the window of his office gazing at the dull green slopes of The Cascades sixty miles to the east. He preferred the coast, especially when Portland turned hot. On the other side of the Coast Range, it was thirty degrees cooler with thick fog clinging to the shoreline. Each year when the temperatures in the Willamette Valley soared into triple digits, an invisible wall went up somewhere in the low mountains, preventing cool air from working its way east and leaving Portland locked in an oven. Fog would creep up the coastal rivers to hang in the trees like sentries welcoming those seeking sanctuary from the heat. Two miles from the beach, the fog would be thick enough to require headlights and windshield wipers. At the beach it was an impenetrable gray line out beyond the last set of waves. Stockdale thought about driving to the coast, to his house on the spit at Siletz Bay. Maybe he'd stand on the beach hoping the fog would slowly swallow him up.

"Desperate times call for desperate measures," he mumbled to himself as he picked up his phone. He wasn't stupid enough to put the number on his speed dial. Not that it mattered. After dialing it thousands of times over the previous five years he had it memorized.

"We were wrong," he said when the familiar voice answered. "We need your help again."

"So, I'm forgiven for shooting up his house?" the voice at the other end of the line said. The taunting tone brought Stockdale back to reality.

"That was stupid. It didn't work."

"I take it you want something."

Despite wanting to forget about being attacked in his own office, Stockdale gave a brief, sanitized description of his meeting with Windsor. He still felt like everyone in the firm was looking at him. At least he'd kept an extra pair of slacks in the closet.

"Bottom line is we believe he's telling the truth about having Benno's file on Billy," Stockdale said. "I'm afraid he may also know about Marvin Barnes."

"How?"

"I don't know. Maybe the appointment was on his wife's calendar. It wasn't on mine. I made sure of that."

"I could search his house, but odds are those files aren't there. If he's smart—and he is—he'll have them with him." He paused. "Only one way to deal with that. Do I have her majesty's blessing?"

"Never mind about her. She'll be fine with whatever we do."

"If he learns all there is about Marvin Barnes, then we won't have to do anything. He'll come to us. I'll take it from there."

When the line went dead Stockdale called the other number he'd memorized. "He'll do it."

Dorothy Evelyn Hawkins hung up without saying a word.

Chapter 61

Windsor didn't know much about the City of Gresham, other than it did its best to fight off the random gang violence that oozed out from the City of Portland. In fact, Windsor had never been there. His job, home, and hangouts pretty much kept him on the west side of the Willamette River. If he ventured to the east side, it was because Jennifer wanted to explore some dive bar, eclectic restaurant or overlooked food cart. Now, driving around Gresham trying to find the home of Marvin Barnes' widow was testing the limits of the car's navigation system.

What he eventually found was a house on a street so new that Windsor had to call the fire department to locate the address. The Barnes' ranch-style house was one of a half dozen recently completed homes in a development that appeared to be in the vanguard of the urban sprawl heading east toward the mountains. The house sat in the middle of a row of home sites, empty except for red-and-white realty signs stuck in among vibrant dandelions and thistles. Down the block were the two other completed houses, both identical to the Barnes' home. In the distance, carpenters with hammers and saws worked on three more homes in varying degrees of construction.

Windsor rang the bell and waited, glancing out at the new hydro seed lawn that still looked like soggy cardboard, but drying nicely in the mid-day sun. He rang three more times before a woman who looked to be in her fifties and dressed in a frayed red robe with matching slippers finally answered the door. Short brown hair clung to her forehead and the back of her neck. A few stray strands fell across vacant, blood-shot eyes that focused on a point about halfway between them. On one hand was a very old Pekingese with a bark that sounded like a smoker's cough.

In the other was something that looked like a gin and tonic. The woman sipped absently at her drink, staring at Windsor with glassy eyes as he explained who he was and why he was there.

"So, you knew my husband?" she said.

"No, but I'd like to know about him."

"He's dead, you know." Tears immediately filled her eyes.

"Yes, I do know and I'm sorry."

She thanked him with a nod then invited him in over the hoarse protests of the Pekinese. Leaving him in the front room alone with a day-time television talk show that appeared to have something to do with cross-dressing businessmen, she shuffled off toward the kitchen. After two or three awkward minutes, she came back with a fresh drink. With her was a younger and more attractive version of herself. Tough as it was, Windsor pulled himself away from the talk show.

"I'm Matty Barnes. This is my mother," the younger woman said, guiding the older one into a recliner in front of the television. "Can I help you?"

Matty Barnes wore hiking boots, faded jeans torn at the knees, and a Black Lives Matter T-shirt. Long, dark frizzy hair framed a round face with faint freckles, thin lips, and tired-looking eyes that matched her mother's. He guessed her age as mid-twenties, the same as Jennifer when he first met her.

"I'm Alex Windsor. We talked on the phone the other day. My late wife was your father's lawyer. I found his file in the boxes sent from her office. There was something in the file having to do with the Forest Service and log scalers."

Matty Barnes looked bewildered as he tried to explain the logging scaling scheme without suggesting that Matty's father was involved in it. He made it clear, however, that he might have known something about it.

"In all honesty, it's a fishing expedition," Windsor said apologetically. "I'm hoping your father might have left some papers behind that will give me a clue about what, if anything, was going on."

At the mention of her husband's name, Mrs. Barnes stirred slightly, and her eyes began filling with tears again. With one hand, she reached for the Pekinese sitting obediently on her lap. With the other she snatched the drink from the coffee table. The dog growled deeply when Matty gently took the drink away then motioned Windsor to follow her into the kitchen.

"You'll have to excuse my mother. She hasn't been the same since dad was killed. Occasionally, she just starts crying. And it's been more than a year."

"I understand," Windsor said.

"You said your late wife was my dad's lawyer."

"Her name was Jennifer DeGarza. She was murdered about the same time your father was killed."

"Murdered?"

"The Meat Man."

"Oh my God," she said. "I'm so sorry."

They sat at the table in the well-lit kitchen drinking lemonade amid the stainless steel of the matching refrigerator, gas stove top, and oven. The sliding glass door at the rear of the kitchen looked out onto a small cement slab that served as a patio surrounded by more freshly sprayed hydro seed. A few feet beyond, a wood retaining wall held back a steep, weed-infested embankment.

"My father hired your wife. For what? I can't believe he'd do that and not tell me or my mother. Was he in trouble?"

"I'm not sure," Windsor said. "That's why I'm here."

The girl mulled that over for a few moments then asked him to follow her to the garage.

"My mother bought this house and moved in last month thinking that new surroundings would help her get over daddy's death," Matty Barnes said. "Their old house was the only one they'd ever lived in. They moved in the day they were married and never left." She glanced toward the front room. "Moving was really my idea. I'm not sure it was a very good one."

"Whatever your father did, if anything, we'll get it sorted out. I just need to know if you have anything that might help me figure out what's going on. It's important to me."

"Okay. There might be some things in the garage."

Standing in the stifling heat of the two-car garage, she pointed to several wooden orange crates under a tool-covered workbench. "I haven't had time to go through them. I don't know what's there."

"Mind if I look?"

"If you think it will help," she said. "I'll open the doors and try to get some air in here. You'll have to excuse the mess. We're still unpacking."

The heavy wooden crates were marked "Dad." Windsor gently pulled the first one out and set it on the workbench just as the garage door went up. It made it easier to see but did little to cool things off. Matty went back inside and returned with fresh glasses of lemonade. She didn't offer to help. He couldn't blame her. She probably felt the same way he did going through Jennifer's belongings. Instead, she watched as Windsor carefully combed through each of the crates. In the first two, he found old tax returns, bank statements, pension statements, and property tax bills. In the third box, he found a file with the names of four companies handwritten on the outside. Windsor didn't recognize the names, just what they did. Inside were copies of the same forms he'd found in Jennifer's files plus a hand-written letter signed by Barnes.

Windsor glanced through the letter then read it more closely a second time. In it, Barnes described his career and credentials as a timber cruiser and log scaler, which Windsor knew meant his job had something to do with either the mystery of determining how many board feet of timber there were in a stand of trees or how many were in the logs that came out of it. It was what followed that caught his attention.

The rest of the three-page letter outlined a hypothetical scheme to cheat the federal government by any number of schemes. He wrote that it was "possible" to bribe a log scaler or timber cruiser to deliberately under-report the amount of board feet in a tree, inflate the number of defects in a log or list high-value trees as a less-valuable species. Regardless of the method, the scheme meant less money to the federal government and more money to the logging companies that had the contracts to cut the trees and sell the lumber. The letter never said whether such a scheme had actually occurred.

"Is that something?" Matty Barnes said.

"Could be." He slipped the letter and the forms back into the file. "Can I keep this? I'll return it if you'd like."

She nodded, still looking confused about what was going on.

Windsor pulled a second file out of the same box. He opened it thinking it might be more information about Barnes' hypothetical scheme. Instead, it was filled with packets of hundred-dollar bills still in their wrappers. Matty gasped as Windsor slowly pulled out the money and stacked it on the workbench.

"There's at least twenty thousand dollars here," he said.

"Where did it come from?" The look on her face was what you'd expect watching someone pull thousands of dollars out of an orange crate like a rabbit out of a hat.

"Why did my father have it?"

Windsor forced himself not to look at her. He had his theories, but nothing he wanted to share with her, at least not yet. "There were some company names on the other file. They might be a good place to start."

"But my father never worked for any companies that I know of." She looked anxiously at him, then at the money. "He was always self-employed. The Forest Service paid his fees."

She was starting to get it, he thought. "How did your father die?"

"At work. He was cruising timber on Forest Service land in The Cascades. His truck went off a cliff along a logging road." She stared at him, mouth open, tears in the corner of her eyes. "Do you think he was part of some scheme? Something illegal? I mean, the money ..." There was a sudden anger and resentment in her voice. It was aimed at him. He couldn't blame her. A stranger showing up out of nowhere, finding papers and money. Ample reason to be suspicious.

"You think this is bribe money, right?" she said. "You think he was involved in something illegal."

She'd gotten it. He wanted to let her down easy. The girl and her mother had been through enough and he didn't want to be responsible for more.

"That's one explanation, but there's no proof," he said. "If it is true, though, maybe he wanted out and that's why he contacted my wife."

Tears welled up in Matty's eyes. She looked at Windsor, then at the money again. Finally, she sat down on the steps, put her head down, and sobbed. Windsor stood still, feeling helpless and uncomfortable. Maybe there were words for a time like this. Psychologist or not, he didn't know them. Considering his own past, grief counseling was not his area of expertise.

"Do you think he was killed on purpose, that he was murdered?" she said, raising her head. A look of horror mixed with the tears on her face.

Windsor's silence was answer enough.

"My God," she said. "This can't be true. It's all a mistake."

"There's always that chance." Windsor sat down beside her. "I don't have proof of anything involving your father. I just think you need to be prepared. At least until we know the whole story."

She put her face in her hands and started sobbing again. After a few minutes, she looked at Windsor and wiped her eyes with the back of her hand.

"I'm sorry," she said. "This has been a difficult year."

"No apology necessary."

"I can't tell my mother about this. It would kill her." She looked over again at the money on the workbench. "What should I do with that?"

"Don't do anything, for now. Put it in a safe deposit box then wait until I find out what really happened. You're right about not telling your mother anything until there's proof."

He kept the file but returned the money to the envelope and handed it to her. She held it in her hands, stared at it, then stood up and walked back in the house. Windsor followed her into the kitchen and out to the front room.

Mrs. Barnes was still in the recliner, guarded by the ever-vigilant Pekinese. As Windsor left, the dog raised its head, growled once and then went back to sleep. The old lady never moved.

"Don't leave that money lying around," Windsor said. Maddie still had the envelope in her hands. "Put it somewhere safe. I'm serious."

Windsor left, walking back to his car hoping that whatever happened in the next few hours, Matty Barnes and her mother would come out alright. The money he'd found was a start. He stared out the windshield and put the envelope in the passenger seat, knowing that he had more of what he needed to learn who killed Jennifer.

Chapter 62

On the way back to the city, Windsor stopped at an east side dive bar known for its array of local beers and Philly cheesesteaks. He ordered one of the first but passed on the second. The place was empty except for a liquor control inspector explaining to the bartender the dos and don'ts of recreational marijuana in a state-licensed bar.

Taking his beer to a table in the corner, he pulled Marvin Barnes' letter from the manila envelope and started reading it again, looking for clues as to whether there were truths hidden among the hypotheticals.

Windsor was a city boy, which meant he knew as much about the timber industry as any average Oregonian, given that the federal government owned two-thirds of the state, much of it timber land. Stories of how those who cut down those trees tried to cheat those who owned them had for years been the source of numerous rumors and conspiracy theories. One of the local papers or television stations would investigate it from time to time, producing inconclusive stories that no one read or watched.

Along with forms and a letter, Barnes' file also contained a printout of a series published by the city's only daily newspaper on the status of the timber industry in a post-COVID world. It was written by a reporter named Will Brunner and included a short sidebar story on an investigation by the U.S. Attorney's Office into exactly the kind of scheme Barnes described in his letter. The story didn't mention who was being investigated or how much money was involved.

Windsor knew Brunner from his days covering health care and wanted Windsor's take on mental health coverage by Medicare and Medicaid. They'd talked on the phone several times and met at least twice for beers at The Ridge. Windsor checked the time. Brunner might still be at work. He scrolled through the contacts on his cell phone and found Brunner's number.

"Dr. Windsor," Brunner said, taking the surprise call in stride.

They exchanged small talk with Windsor giving a vague explanation about being back in town for business. Brunner said how sorry he was about Jennifer and apologized for not being at her funeral.

"Apologies accepted. Thanks."

"So, I hear you've been in Tibet."

"Not exactly, but close. Listen, Will, I need your help with something I'm working on. You got a minute?"

"Sure. I owe you that. What's up?"

"Timber cruisers and log scalers. You wrote about them a couple of years ago, I think. Who do they work for?"

"Private contractors hired by the Forest Service. The goal is to make sure the public isn't cheated out of any revenue."

"Are they honest?"

"Pretty much."

"Meaning?"

"There have been investigations, but no one has ever been charged. I could never get the names of those under suspicion. Best I could tell, the cases were so weak the feds didn't want to mention any names. Probably a smart move since no one has been indicted for anything."

"How does it work?"

Brunner explained that some logging company pays off a scaler to intentionally misrepresent the value of the timber whether it's standing or on a truck. "The inaccurate reports are given to the Forest Service, which then bills the logging company for the lower amount. The logging company happily pays the bill knowing it's sitting on several million board feet of free timber. The timber is then turned into lumber or plywood and sold for millions of dollars."

"Ever been proven?"

"No. It could be some conspiracy theory dreamed up by environmental groups or government watchdogs for the benefit of a few reporters. Best I can tell, log scaling appears to be more art than science to me, but there's a lot of math involved. Not my strong point. The only way to catch someone is if the estimated amount turns out to be significantly lower than the actual amount. What usually happens … allegedly … is that it comes in within or just outside the margin of error. Innocent errors aren't a crime, at least not in this case."

"Ever hear of a guy named Marvin Barnes? Could have been a timber cruiser or log scaler or both."

"No, but you might check with the Forest Service. If that's his job, then chances are they've heard of him."

"How about a lawyer named Chandler Stockdale representing logging companies?"

"Everyone knows Stockdale, but I've never seen his name attached to the few court cases I've run across. To be honest though, it's been a while since I've had time to look into it. Care to tell me what's going on?"

Windsor begged off and hung up after promising to fill Brunner in when he knew more.

Chapter 63

The file footage made for great television—vivid and brutal.

Rich Raymond's favorite was the shot from the helicopter hovering over the naked body of a woman dangling from a tree outside her house in an upscale northeast Portland neighborhood. She hung from her feet, blonde hair and arms hanging down to the ground. Cops and technicians circled the body before someone mercifully covered the scene with a plastic tarp.

"Who said helicopters don't have a place in journalism," Raymond said to himself.

He sat alone in an editing room preparing the background footage that would accompany his taped interview with Billy Broadnax that Windsor had promised. For his part, Raymond intended to keep his word to Windsor about not doing any more stories about him. Now it was Windsor's turn to deliver. With any luck at all, in forty-eight hours Raymond would air the first-ever interview with Billy Broadnax, the infamous Meat Man. By the next day, he'd have a thirty-minute, hell, sixty-minute special report in the can and ready to air in prime time. Until then, he needed to contact the families of the other victims, get screenshots of some newspaper headlines, and comb through more archive footage.

But it was the interview with Broadnax and the special that went with it that would be his ticket out of Portland to a major market. It had to be perfect. He would set up the special with a little background about death with shots from each location. He would intersperse interviews with Billy, shots from each murder scene, and quotes from the family. So far, he had twenty minutes of usable video, some of which had been shown before and some which he could hype as "never before seen." He even found several clips with Windsor standing in the background during one of the DA's press conferences. That might come in handy in case Windsor reneged on his promise to go on camera.

Trusting Windsor went against Raymond's instincts. Psychologists were never good subjects. Too much hocus-pocus about the internal workings of the human brain, triggers, and suppressed memories. Guys like Windsor looked down their noses at television news, convinced there was no way of doing serious journalism in two-or-three-minute segments.

"Let's see what he says after an hour or half-hour special," Raymond muttered.

Given that the payoff was an interview with Broadnax, Raymond decided that Windsor was worth the gamble. He was willing to risk the possibility that someone who dismissed television news as a cynical, superficial medium obsessed with ratings could still tell the truth. Even if Windsor did weasel out of his promise, there was still the story about Benno's suicide at the cemetery. Raymond could do things to that story that would make the arrogant Windsor wish he'd been a little more cooperative. He could always trot out the phony video of Windsor's wife hanging from the rafters in his garage. That would show him.

He fast-forwarded the videotape to the part where one angry sheriff's deputy tried to wave the helicopter away while the crime scene technicians scrambled to hide the body.

"This is great," Raymond muttered. "Look at those fools. Welcome to the twenty-first century, boys."

After watching another hour of video that produced a few more worthwhile clips, Raymond went to his cubicle at the back of the Channel 5 newsroom. The yellow legal pad on the desk contained the list of questions he planned to ask Broadnax. They were about each murder, his actions during the crimes, and what was going through his mind as he killed each woman. He thought about showing the videotape to Billy during the interview, asking him to comment on each one. "Okay, Billy, here's the woman you strangled, strung up in a tree and eviscerated with a butcher's knife. Tell me what your thinking was in this one?"

He liked the idea, made a few notes to himself, then, just to be on the safe side, called Windsor's house to make sure they were still on for tomorrow. When he got no answer, he tried The Ridge where Bud Schwartz said he hadn't seen Windsor since around noon.

"He told me you'd be in around eleven in the morning to interview him," Bud said. "I'll be waiting with some coffee. Even ordered some fresh doughnuts."

Raymond hung up, still suspicious that Windsor would really come through.

Chapter 64

Plywood still covered the front window, but at least the walls had been patched, the destroyed easy chair replaced, and the front room cleaned up. The odor of fresh paint mixed with the smell of freshly brewed coffee. For some reason the house was feeling like home again. Still, Windsor knew it would never be the same without her.

He looked out the window at a sky laced with gray clouds creeping eastward from the coast. In the last two hours, the temperature had dropped into the high seventies. By dark, he thought, a warm rain would start falling and end before morning.

The change in the weather reminded Windsor of Sam Westlake's untested theory that fishing improved when the barometric pressure was high and got worse when it was low. If he was right, then there was no need to rush back to the ranch any time soon. Maybe he'd wait a few days, keep his eye on the weather then decide to leave town. The trail that started with Harold Gilroy and led to Bennett Benno, Chandler Stockdale, and Dorothy Hawkins might end with the owners of the four companies. With any luck at all, he'd know everything soon. The only remaining question was what he would do with what he'd learn. He had a vague plan—one that would get him back to the ranch fishing by the time the barometer rose again.

He skirted the still-unfinished front room into the small spare bedroom that served as an office. He sat down, stared at the laptop for a few minutes, then fired it up. Somewhere on the internet was the information he needed to learn the truth. He had a sense of what that truth was, and it scared him.

On the corporation commission's website, he typed in the name of the first company, then waited. Slowly, the screen filled up with financial and other information about Three Sons Logging and Lumber, including the list of corporate officers. He read through them, then stopped before reading them again.

He typed in the name of the second company, Pine Canyon Forestry. Same result. Ponderosa Properties. Same thing.

The last pieces of the puzzle fell into place. He stared at the screen thinking that his insides were being ripped out. He knew how it felt. It had happened before. No way it could happen again. He was wrong. So very wrong.

Chapter 65

Arnie Stetson finished two beers while he waited at The Ridge. The clock said a little after five p.m. Windsor was late despite insisting that they meet as soon as possible. He was about to order a third beer when Windsor came in the back door looking drenched and distracted in a Barbour jacket, floppy hat, and rain spattered khakis.

"Sorry I'm late," he said, sliding a manila envelope across the table. Stetson's name was written on the front. "This is Friday night. You can do what you want with what's in there. All I ask is that if you print something, wait until Monday at the earliest. If it takes longer, that's fine."

"What is it?"

"You're a smart guy. Read it. You'll figure it out."

"Why the cloak and dagger?"

"You'll see."

Stetson turned the envelope over in his hands and looked across the table.

Windsor's eyes were distant, the voice that came out of the tight lips low and calm. His words precise, to the point. There was no room for Stetson to misunderstand what was expected of him.

Windsor was showing a different side than their first meeting at the ranch. He looked like someone who had peered into a mirror and seen his own fate. When Bud Schwartz appeared with a beer, Windsor waved him off and asked for coffee instead.

"Does this have to do with who killed your wife?" Stetson said.

"It's self-explanatory. Just read it and follow it where it leads you. The story will write itself."

"And you?"

"I'm not your source for this."

Windsor left before Schwartz returned with the coffee.

Cassie Terrace found the manila envelope taped to the front of the television when she got home from work a little after six. Her name was written on the front in Windsor's unmistakable scrawl along with a note. "C - read this, but please give me until Monday at the earliest. Love, AW."

She poured a glass of wine, sat at the kitchen table, and tore open the envelope. It took an hour to read everything. Another hour to figure out what it all meant. After that she tried calling Windsor. No answer at his house. Same with his cellphone.

When she called The Ridge, Bud Schwartz said she'd missed him by two hours, but suggested calling Arnie Stetson.

"What kind of mood was he in?" she said.

The phone went quiet as if Schwartz was deciding how to answer. "Dark. Like the old days after Jennifer. I think he's gone again."

Chapter 66

The summer storm born somewhere over the Pacific Ocean was tracked by satellites and fawned over by farmers and television weathermen as it approached the coast. By the time it reached Portland, the pent-up rain came straight down, rattling car tops and tin roofs. Leaves burned brown by days of hot weather clogged storm drains, turning intersections into koi ponds. The BMW's wipers were in hyperdrive. Headlights and taillights glistened off the dark asphalt. As traffic slowed, Windsor sped up. He didn't care. Dying behind the wheel seemed only slightly worse than what faced him.

The rain lasted for forty-five miles south on Interstate 5 then petered out east of Salem, leaving in its wake an annoying, lingering drizzle. By the time he'd driven the twelve miles to the City of Stayton, even that had disappeared along with any traffic other than the occasional headlights headed in the opposite direction. He rolled down the window to let the cool air fill the car and chase away the musty dampness. He fiddled with the radio, considered putting on some music, but settling for the sound of tires on the wet pavement and the hiss of a passing car.

Beyond Stayton, the small towns along the highway turned from struggling farming communities into abandoned logging towns, some still ravaged by a previous year's forest fire. The two-lane road hugged the north side of Detroit Reservoir then up the west side of The Cascades. He steered the car through the gentle curves along the North Santiam River. At one point a deer darted across the road fifty yards in front of him. He thought he saw a coyote but wasn't sure. Sneaky bastards.

All the time he made a mental checklist of things he'd done and still needed to do. Ugly as it was going to be, the end was in sight.

Everything he knew about Jennifer's death and Marvin Barnes' log scaling scheme was in the hands of the two people who could do the most about it. By now, they'd read the documents and knew enough to follow the same path he had. All he needed them to do was give him the time he'd ask for. They didn't know it, but it was the time he needed to put an end to everything.

The original set of documents was in an envelope on the front passenger seat, right next to a printout of the corporate officers of the four companies, Benno's evaluation, and Gilroy's report. He knew the contents by heart and hated every word of it. He wanted to throw the file out the window, pretend it never existed. Too late. What Cassie Terrace and Arnie Stetson would do with what he gave them was out of his hands. There were other things that were not. Those things were his business—business that had to be taken care of. Tonight.

By eleven p.m. he'd crossed the summit of The Cascades and headed down the east side toward central Oregon. Stars hung in a clear sky, blinking on and off as he passed trees lining the twisting road. At a little after midnight, he turned down off the highway, drove another ten miles then onto a dusty, one-lane track. He stopped the BMW fifty yards short of a closed gate. He sat inside, the window down, thinking. Alternative scenarios and other plausible explanations had been running through his head ever since he left Portland. He ran through them one more time. He reached over and picked up the documents on the passenger seat, shuffling through them hoping that he'd overlooked something. One last chance to see if he had it all wrong. One last chance to say it was all a misunderstanding, turn around, and drive home.

But there was only one explanation. The initial anger at himself for having missed the obvious had disappeared along with the rain and the miles of highway behind him. Now he just wanted answers. Only one place left to get them.

Leaving the headlights off, he drove slowly down the road, stopped, and got out to open the gate. It swung back with the rusty groan he remembered. There was a time when he would have stopped, got out, and shut the gate behind him. Now, he really didn't care.

Even during the darkest hours of clear moonless nights, the stars gave off enough light to see the huge trunks of the towering Ponderosa pines. The wind was up, sending the familiar scents of pine and smoldering campfires drifting by the window. The faint insect and animal noises made it as quiet as it ever got. The ticking of the BMW's engine as it cooled after the long, nonstop drive over the mountains provided the only unnatural sound.

In the dim light, he followed the narrow dirt track as it wound over and down a small hill into the meadow. The outline of the cabin where he'd spent the better part of the last year stood silhouetted against the night sky. He parked in the gravel strip at the end of the cabin's cluttered porch, got out, and stared across the meadow. The river entered the meadow from behind and to the right of the cabin. It flowed in a gentle arc for a half mile before disappearing into a distant stand of trees. The gin-clear water was broken by occasional riffles that turned into long, wide, silky stretches. Fat cattle still grazed on one side of the river. Ill-tempered geese still pecked at the grass on the other. Lost in the darkness was the bridge that crossed the river about halfway down. On damp mornings, when he'd walk down the river to fish, he'd think of the geese and cattle as opposing armies carefully watching each other across the water, afraid of some sneak attack.

It was too dark to see the series of rugged, tree-lined ridges that rose above and behind the ranch house. The perfectly formed snow-capped peak of Mt. Jefferson was little more than a faint shadow against the night sky. It didn't matter, though, because the scene was etched in his mind. At one time he couldn't wait to get back, wade in the cold water, and feel the fly rod in his hand. Realizing that he really didn't care anymore made the night and what was to come that much blacker.

Fifty yards below the bridge is where he'd caught his first fish. It was on a cold morning in March. He had the river all to himself. The twenty-seven-inch Dolly Varden hit his line with a splash then took off toward deeper water. Unsure how hard to pull on the thin line, he let the fish walk him downstream to just short of where the river narrowed and picked up speed. He held the fish into the current, hoping to tire it out the way Sam had showed him. Slowly, he started reeling, only to see the fish take off again, but upstream and against the current. Another twenty minutes and he was able to grab the exhausted fish by the tail, hold it in his hands then gently take the hook out. He let it go and watched it swim away with the current.

That was six months ago, but he still remembered every second and how the moment squared so perfectly with how he'd lived his life: experiencing a moment of triumph totally alone. Standing thigh-deep in cold water on a frost-bitten morning convinced him that maybe he could get past what had happened.

Now he wasn't so sure.

He'd started the year losing a wife and lover. He would end it being betrayed by a friend. Yet, the self-destruction brought on by the first was oddly missing from the second. The new pain was different. Not as deep and less permanent, but still agonizing.

He walked along the dirt road that skirted the meadow, passing a moss-covered pumphouse and the abandoned truck with a tree growing through the roof. House lights flickered in the distance. Standing in the shadows of overhanging trees, he saw a Porsche parked next to the house and people moving around inside. The feeling of betrayal was almost too much. He turned around and walked away, head down, knowing what he had to do.

The cabin's door was unlocked. He stepped inside, closing it behind him. Even in the dark he could tell that everything was as he left it. The books still on the shelves, the fly-tying material on the table, the half empty bottle of Bushmills on the counter. The gun on top of the refrigerator.

He put the envelope on the kitchen counter then reached for the small revolver. It felt heavy and foreign in his hand. When he slipped it into his coat pocket the way it banged against his hip when he walked was both annoying and reassuring.

He built a fire, letting the kindling catch before putting a log on top. He turned on all the lights, fired up the stereo, and cranked up the volume. He opened every door and window. With the place the way he planned, he grabbed the Bushmills from the shelf over the sink and went outside. The best view would be from the porch, so he sat on the top step and waited.

The light from the house lit up the road below him. Smoke from the chimney curled out over the meadow. The music carried eerily on the night breeze. Pink Floyd's *Dark Side of the Moon*. A few sips of the whiskey didn't do much. A calmness had already come over him. Minus a few details, he knew the truth.

There was only one thing left to do.

"God damn it, Sam. What have you done?"

Chapter 67

Sam Westlake listened while Chandler Stockdale put on his best lawyer act. Stockdale was coatless, tie loose at the collar, shirt tail hanging out in the back. A cigarette in one hand was balanced by a glass of scotch in the other. His normal baritone had been chased away by an even more loathsome whine that had repeated the same thing over and over since he and Judge Dorothy Evelyn Hawkins had arrived two hours earlier.

"Killing him is the only option we have left. The longer we wait, the closer he gets to the truth, if he isn't there already. With him gone there's nothing but the word of a dead man. I said that when he came back to town and I'm saying it now. Besides, you were supposed to take care of this, Sam. That's why you convinced him to come here in the first place. Better late than never, huh?"

Hawkins sat on the couch with the glassy-eyed stare of the disinterested. She rattled the ice in her glass as a signal for the obedient Stockdale to put his summation on hold long enough to fetch her another gin. The judge had started out the evening in the familiar role of passive observer and omnipotent ruler. She'd broken her silence once to announce that no matter what happened, the end had come. She mumbled something about steps being taken at her request which might provide her with enough protection. It would end her career as a judge but keep her out of prison. Having proclaimed their doom and her salvation, she returned to the task of drinking herself into a stupor.

Sam knew Stockdale was right but argued with him anyway. Stockdale brought that out in people.

"He's a lonely, bitter, stir-crazy drunk who thinks someone other than that sick fuck in prison killed his wife," Sam said. "I made sure he had easy access to every kind of booze and drug. It's not my fault he's still alive. Not that it matters. Given what he's been doing since his wife died, it shouldn't take much to destroy his credibility."

"What about the papers? What about the files he has? What if he made copies? What if he knows about Marvin Barnes?" Stockdale was whining again. "Jesus, what if he tells that cop girlfriend of his or some reporter?"

"So what? No one can back him up. Barnes, Gilroy, and that girl are all dead. I made sure of that."

"And those documents?"

"Just convince some judge they're phony. You're a good enough lawyer to do that," Sam said in a tone more convincing than he really felt.

When Stockdale looked to Hawkins for help, Sam thought she was going to mutter something like, "I'll take it under advisement." Instead, she stared at the ice cubes in her fresh drink like they were talking goldfish.

"But he can still make trouble. A lot of people have been destroyed with a lot less evidence than what Windsor has," Stockdale said. "It's up to you to take care of him. You talked us into this scheme. You owe it to us."

"I don't owe you shit," Sam shot back. "Nobody held a gun to your head to make you sign on. I presented you and your friends with a scheme to get richer than you already were. You all jumped on board."

"But what are we going to do?" Stockdale slumped down in an overstuffed leather chair and held the glass against his forehead.

"Let me take care of this my way. We're not screwed yet." Westlake said.

Sam tried to remember exactly when he knew that things would eventually fall apart. It could've been the dinner party at Hawkins' house a year earlier. It was over a plate of Petrale sole that he realized people were going to die. He didn't know how many or how soon. Then that newspaper reporter showed up at Windsor's cabin. After that he was positive that things were headed in the wrong direction. The only question then was how many dead bodies it would take to get there.

Sam glanced around at the familiar surroundings. A small fire flickered in the large fireplace on the far side of the room, flanked by a battered recliner and long couches covered in colorful Indian blankets. Art signed by Georgia O'Keefe and the mounted head of a bighorn sheep covered one wall. A half-dozen prized shotguns and rifles were stored upright in a glass-and-oak case in the corner. A carefully preserved bamboo fly rod in a shadow box occupied a place of honor over the fireplace.

The way things were going made him wonder what would happen to the house and everything in it. He'd bought the property thirty years before because of the fishing, eventually building a home on the ridge overlooking the river and the meadow. He'd designed it himself and supervised the driving of every nail. The wood was the best his mills could produce. He wanted it to be a place to spend time with family and friends. Instead, he spent most of the time there alone. He remembered how excited his wife had been when work on the house began and how her death before it was finished left a hole in his life that he could never fill. His sons had little time for fishing or the long trip out from Bend to visit him. When they weren't preoccupied with running his various businesses, they were thinking about spending Christmas in Hawaii playing golf.

It never occurred to him that Windsor taking up residence in that old cabin on the other side of the meadow would help fill a void. But it did. The reasons behind why and how he lured Windsor into the mountains only made things that much more difficult. He didn't plan it that way. In fact, he started out determined to do everything possible to help Windsor destroy himself with booze and pills. What he found instead was a younger version of himself. Destroying Windsor meant destroying a part of who he was.

The whole thing was a mess—a mess that was all his fault. Now he had no choice.

Tired of Stockdale's whining and Hawkins' drinking, Sam went out onto the deck where Maggie lay curled up on a blanket near the door. When she saw him, her tail banged happily against the side of the house in a dog's oblivion to a master's problems. After a few minutes, Stockdale came out to stand next to him. He had just started again about the need to kill Windsor when Hawkins appeared at the door.

"Get back in here and fix me another drink," she yelled at the two men. Her lipstick was smeared, her wig askew. Her eyes beneath the heavy liner and mascara could barely focus. "If my life and career are going down the shitter, I don't want to face it sober."

"No danger of that," Sam muttered.

As Sam watched his spoiled and pampered co-conspirators, the blackness of his future came over him again. If there was a way out, he would have to find it by himself.

It was then that he saw the lights and heard the music drifting over on the smoke from Windsor's cabin. It brought with it a message that immediately told him what he had to do.

"Pack up and get out of here," Sam said to Stockdale then pointed toward the front room, "and take her with you."

Stockdale looked offended and then angry. "Why? We haven't resolved this yet."

Sam went inside, took one of the shotguns from the case, and returned to the deck to gaze out across the meadow as he shoved two shells in the chambers. "It's resolved, Chandler. You win. Windsor dies."

The lawyer looked confused then followed the old man's eyes. "What's that music? Where's it coming from? It's weird. Did I hear an alarm clock?"

"Lock the door and throw away the key. There's someone in my head and it's not me," Sam muttered to himself.

"What are you talking about?" Stockdale looked more confused than ever. "What is it you're not telling me? What is happening?"

"It's Windsor," Sam said, using the shotgun to point at the cabin. "He's here. I told you he'd come to us eventually."

Stockdale finally noticed the cabin lights that were dim and diffused by the thin smoke that had settled on the meadow. "My God! Are you sure?" There was both fear and awe in the lawyer's voice. The old logger didn't bother to answer. He finished loading the gun and locked the barrel in place. "Then he knows everything. He knows about me, about the judge, and now he knows about you."

"No shit, Chandler," Sam said. "Now do as I say and get the hell out of here."

The lawyer obediently gathered up the judge, carried her out to the driveway, and lowered her into the Porsche. The old woman stirred once but remained in her gin-induced coma.

Everything would end tonight and both of them would miss it, Sam thought. Just as well.

Chapter 68

Windsor was sitting on the porch when he heard a powerful car engine start up. Across the meadow a set of headlights came on then fanned across the distant trees before heading off in the direction of the main road. Despite the distance and the noise of flying gravel, there was no mistaking the throaty roar of Stockdale's Porsche. It never dawned on Windsor that Stockdale and Hawkins would be at Sam's house. Not that it mattered. There was only one person he wanted to see. Let others take care of Stockdale and Hawkins.

When a second, less powerful engine roared to life, Windsor went inside to turn off the music. He returned to his place on the steps thinking that if Pink Floyd wasn't weird enough then total silence was. It just wouldn't stay that way for long.

The clouds that had rolled in from the west were like a patch of black cotton covering a vast expanse of bright stars. With the clouds came a cold wind that sent tinder-dry needles helicoptering out of the pines in front of the cabin. The sounds of the car engines sent a handful of geese into the night sky. The rest craned their necks to look around before settling back down in the grass. The cattle on the other side of the river paid no attention.

Windsor watched as the second set of headlights moved down off the distant ridge, disappearing then reappearing as they moved slowly toward him through the trees that skirted the meadow. The dim beams bounced up and down as the truck navigated the washboard road. As they got closer, he could hear the squeaking protest of worn shock absorbers. The lights followed the gentle curve of the meadow until they were directly to his left. A few moments later, Sam's battered pickup braked to a noisy stop in front of the cabin. The old logger got out with a shotgun nestled in the crook of his arm.

"Is that you, Alex?" he said. The gun was pointed off to the side but poised to swing around and fire.

"Who else?"

Sam lowered the gun and walked toward the cabin. "Mind if I sit down?"

Rather than wait for an answer, Sam climbed the eight steps and lowered himself on to the top stair next to Windsor. He propped the shotgun upright between his legs with the barrel pointed at the night sky. The combination of harsh shadows and soft light from the cabin made the wrinkles in Sam's face appear deeper and darker, like a piece of fruit left too long in the refrigerator. His eyes looked tired; his shoulders slumped. The hands that gripped the shotgun still looked strong, but now had a slight tremor. His voice thin and strained. Even from a few feet away he sounded like someone talking into a tin can at the other end of a long, tense string.

"You want to walk me through this?" Windsor said.

"It's a long walk." Sam toyed with the triggers on the shotgun.

"I think we have time."

"I'll try not to mince words. We're too good of friends for that."

Sam waited for an answer or at least an acknowledgment from Windsor that they were still friends. He wasn't going to get it.

"I guess you've figured out what me and my highfalutin' friends have been up to." Sam rested his forehead against the barrel of the gun and stared down at the stairs. "That means you're probably going to tell that newspaper reporter friend of yours. Probably that cop girlfriend of yours as well. Maybe both. I can't let that happen. I hope you understand."

"You mean you have to kill me?"

"Afraid so."

"I knew that, but I came anyway. That must tell you something. I couldn't care less about your little scheme or how much money the four of you pocketed before Marvin Barnes got cold feet. I need to hear the truth from someone who knows it. I think you owe me that much."

Westlake nodded but continued staring down at the stairs, with his forehead on the gun barrel. Windsor thought how easy it would be to reach over, pull the trigger, and hope Sam's head disappeared. He'd feel better, but still not have the answers he wanted.

"Of all the lawyers in Portland, it never dawned on me that Marvin Barnes would hire her," Sam said. "I didn't even know he'd gotten cold feet and wanted to come clean."

"Stockdale was supposed to meet with Jennifer to talk about it. She didn't make it."

"Meeting with Jennifer was Stockdale's idea." Sam banged his head against the barrel of the gun. "The biggest mistake I ever made was getting hooked up with Stockdale."

"Then why did you?"

"The boys and I ran that log-scaling scam for years without a hitch, along with a bunch of others. We did it all through different corporations that Stockdale helped us set up. Then we hit a rough patch. Housing market down. Environmentalists locking up timber land. I needed money, fast. I went to Stockdale; told him I could double his investment in a couple of years. He agreed. Paid full boat to buy in. Probably ending up making ten times what I owed him. Getting the judge and that shrink involved was his idea. After that everything went to hell." He motioned toward the dark meadow. "I've been dumber than those geese out there."

"Why Stockdale?"

"I'd hired him about ten years ago to sue a lumber yard back east that refused to take delivery of three boxcars full of two-by-fours. It worked out well. I got my money back plus damages and Stockdale got his fees paid."

"And the others?"

"Stockdale's idea. He wanted to stay in good graces with the judge. Benno was a childhood friend with money and women problems. They got in on it for next to nothing. Most of what they earned came out of Stockdale's end."

"And Barnes was part of it?"

"Had been from the start. I'm not sure he knew about my so-called partners, not that it mattered."

"His death was no accident, was it?"

"No," Sam said sadly. "But it had to be done. Marvin made a lot of money on these deals over the years. I thought we were friends, but for some reason he just went south on me. Got religion, I guess, or he thought he was smarter than he really was. Could be the feds caught on. Anyway, we didn't know until after he was dead that he'd hired a lawyer. By the time I found out it was Jennifer, things had gone too far."

"So, Benno killed her and made it look like Broadnax did it. Have I got that right?"

"Benno had the most to lose. He was in debt and being sued by one of his patients. The four of us talked about what to do. Killing her was one option, but none of us took it seriously. That's God's truth, Alex. None of us wanted to go there."

"Except Benno."

"Benno and Stockdale. They cooked up the whole idea after that crazy Meat Man walked into their offices. Swear to God, Alex, I had no idea what they were going to do. We talked. They acted. I didn't know anything about it until it was over. After that Stockdale arranged everything. Billy turning himself in, confessing, the judge sending him away." Sam shook his head. "You know what? I think that little shit Benno enjoyed killing her. I think he relished recreating Broadnax's murder. After that he acted like nothing happened. He even went with Stockdale that same night out to see Broadnax and his folks. Together, along with some strong sedatives, they talked Billy into turning himself in."

As numb and hurt as he was by Sam's betrayal, Windsor could feel his urge to lash out slowly disappearing. Knowing the truth and the details that came with it drained all the anger out of him. He'd come for knowledge, not revenge. At least not yet.

"Then things changed," Sam said. "It was like walking in the woods then suddenly realizing you're lost. You'll do anything to get out and worry about the consequences later."

"And Billy was your ticket out, hand delivered by his father," Windsor said. Sam didn't answer. He didn't have to. "I've got to hand it to your partners. Framing a serial killer for murder was ingenious. No one would care if he killed seven women instead of eight. Billy didn't know the difference. Just plead him guilty to everything and let your good buddy Judge Hawkins give him the life sentence he deserved. Even spared him the death sentence so you could take credit for cutting a humane deal and spare the victims' families years of death sentence appeals. After that, slap a gag order on the DA and wait for things to die down."

"Give Stockdale the credit for all that," Sam said. "The guy's a pain in the ass, but he's one smart, slippery son of a bitch."

"But it wasn't his idea to offer me this cabin so I could drink myself to death. You own that one, Sam. I was no danger to you or the others if I was up here with my head in a bottle, all the time blaming myself for what happened to her even though you knew it wasn't true. Hell, Sam, you were even nice enough to leave a loaded gun in the room in case I mustered up the courage to shoot myself."

Windsor's anger was back, punching at his insides, making him squeeze the gun in his pocket. It was a poor match for Sam's shotgun, but he was long past the point of caring.

"I won't lie to you," Sam said. "That was the plan. For a while there I thought it was going to work. Each day I came over here expecting to find you with that gun in your mouth."

"Sorry to disappoint."

"You didn't."

Chapter 69

The wind kicked up again and brought another flurry of pine needles down out of the trees to rattle on the tin roof over the porch. More geese hit the skies. Smoke from the cabin's chimney disappeared over the river. More clouds rolled in, blacking out all the stars and plunging the meadow into total darkness. There was nothing to see except the lights of the ranch house.

"Tell me about Gilroy?" Windsor said.

"Benno hired him to follow Billy. We didn't find out about it until later. We told Benno to destroy the report and make sure there were no copies, but the fool didn't do it. At least not right away. Can you believe that? He kept Billy's alibi in his files, for Christ's sake. Benno insisted that Gilroy turn over all copies of his own report. Even paid extra to make sure."

"Then Gilroy figured out he had given away a gold mine."

Sam nodded. "Gilroy didn't know until later that the man Benno sent him to follow was The Meat Man. That's when he set his sights on Rebecca Roberts. He met her on one of his visits to Benno's office. He sweet talked her into rifling Benno's files. When she found the Broadnax report, he talked her into making a copy. Then he tried blackmailing Benno and promising to cut her in on it. It didn't go over well. The log-scaling scheme had Benno back in the money. He wasn't about to lose everything to a pair like Gilroy and Roberts. That's when Benno finally got around to destroying the files."

"He called you, didn't he? Told you about Gilroy and Roberts. You killed them and framed Rebecca Roberts' ex-husband."

Sam picked up the shotgun and pointed it toward the meadow. When he pulled the trigger, Windsor almost yelled, not that anyone would've heard him over the sound of a couple of hundred angry geese rising out of the meadow and honking their way into the darkness. The echo disappeared into the surrounding mountains. "Benno never should've been in on this in the first place," Sam said. "The guy's life was a mess and he couldn't be trusted."

"But why kill Gilroy and Roberts?"

"Loose ends. Gilroy was strictly small time. The girl had no idea what she was involved in. They didn't know it, but they were as much a threat to us as they were to Benno. He tried paying them for a few months then stopped because he needed the money to defend himself against the malpractice suit. When the money stopped, Gilroy threatened to sell his story to the highest bidder. Gilroy probably figured he was safe because he only had Benno to worry about. Not finding out about me or the others cost him."

"How did you know Gilroy didn't tell me everything?" Windsor asked.

"I didn't, but it was pretty clear that he told you enough to get you started."

"So, you followed me back to Portland?"

"Had to. I knew something was up when that reporter came out here. Anyway, Gilroy was greedy. He needed money. I figured he gave you some sort of ultimatum about paying for the story or he'd take it to someone else. I knew killing him would just make everyone that much more curious, but I really didn't have much choice. Like I said—loose ends."

"Does that include shooting up my house?"

"Sorry. I was trying to scare you. Guess that didn't work out either."

Sam opened the shotgun, ejected the spent shell, and inserted a new one from his coat pocket. Windsor could hear the geese honking overhead as they circled the meadow waiting to return to their usual spot near the river.

"How long have you known?" Sam said.

"About you? Earlier today. I found Barnes' files. There were receipts from your companies and twenty thousand in cash. A search of the state corporation commission website told me the rest."

The two men sat side by side for a few minutes. Sam glanced up at the sky and pronounced that rain was on the way. "It'll keep the fire danger down. Maybe the boys can get the crews back in the woods again. These dry summers can be expensive. A little rain means money in the bank."

"What about the girl's husband, Matthew Roberts?" Windsor said.

"That stupid little shit just happened along at the right time. I stole Gilroy's shoes to make it look like robbery, but they came in handy. Isn't it amazing how many things went right and yet here we are?"

Sam stood up, walked down the steps, turned around, and pointed the shotgun directly at Windsor's chest. "You know how I felt about her, about the both of you. If I knew Benno was going to kill her, I would have done something. I swear it. She was one hell of a woman, Alex.

I'm sorry. So sorry. Benno acted alone, but the truth is that we're all responsible."

Chapter 70

When the last pieces fell into place, Windsor sat silently with his finger on the trigger of the gun in his coat pocket. If he fired through the fabric, Sam Westlake would be dead in an instant. Maybe he'd have time to fire the shotgun, but he'd still be dead, and he'd know who killed him and why.

But he couldn't do it. He refused to let the knowledge of what happened to his wife drive him over the edge. Her death didn't do it. Neither did the illusion that he was responsible. Now, knowing the truth only pulled him further back from the precipice, rather than hurling him off it. Sam's fate lay in the hands of others. Windsor had what he came for.

"Benno was the only one of us that really needed the money," Sam said. "He was the one with the most to lose if we were found out. We could use that for leverage to keep him in line. Eventually it all caught up with him, gnawing at him to the point that he killed himself. Doing it next to Jennifer's grave was a bit dramatic but worked out pretty well for the rest of us. We knew, or at least I did, that we'd have to kill him someday anyway. He saved us the trouble."

"That's cold, Sam."

"I know. Once things got started … well. Anyway, there's one other thing. I know it's a relief to learn you weren't responsible for Jennifer's death. But that's not completely true."

"What do you mean?" Windsor's head snapped up.

"We thought she was going to tell you about us, about what she'd learned from Barnes. You know, pillow talk. That sort of thing. Once you knew, we figured you'd take the story to your old sweetie at the police department or one of your newspaper friends. It turns out she didn't tell you. We didn't know that until she was dead. You wouldn't have called me that night if you knew. Who you were and who you knew was part of the reason we even considered killing her."

Windsor felt like a knife that had been pulled from his heart was suddenly plunged back in again with a full twist. His hand found the gun. His finger on the trigger. "So why didn't you just kill me as well. Why wait until now?"

"There's really two answers. If you were killed too soon after Jennifer, people would get suspicious, especially your detective friend. Billy was already in prison, so there was no killer around to blame for your death. So, we let you live as long as we could, hoping you'd do the job for us. That's why we spread the story that you were in Tibet. If you never came back, people would think you were lost somewhere in the Himalayas."

"And the other?"

"You've been a hell of a friend. You don't know what it was like up here before you moved into this place. Lonely with just me and that dog. It felt good to have someone to talk to and fish with. We had some great days down there on that river. Some of them the best I ever had. Too bad you didn't just stay up here where I could keep an eye on you. Too bad that reporter got you all riled up."

When Windsor stood up, Westlake took a step backward and raised the shotgun to keep it pointed at his chest.

Windsor wasn't really listening. He'd heard enough. He could do little but stare at Sam. For the better part of five years, they had been friends, nearly inseparable during the last year. He and Jennifer stayed in Sam's cabin, walked around his ranch, had dinner when he came to Portland. He was one of the first people Windsor called after it happened, and among the first to show up at his house.

Windsor knew that old Sam Westlake. He didn't know the one standing in front of him with a shotgun.

"God damn it, Sam!" The anger Windsor had held inside came out all at once mixed with his disgust at Westlake and what the old man had done. "You pitiful old fool. You got sucked in by a group of soulless, amoral fat cats and for what? How much money do you need? Or Stockdale? Or Hawkins? All of you had made it. You got yours. Now you're just a bunch of rich old assholes who thought it would be fun to rip off the federal government for money you didn't need. The next thing you knew people started dying. Jesus, Sam, what was the point?"

Westlake pondered the question. "Do you know why a dog licks its balls? Because it can. We did it because we could. Because we had the power and the knowledge, the connections, and the ability. It was the joy that came from playing the game, not cashing the checks. Hell, Alex, I'm seventy-nine years old. How much time do I have left?"

"Was killing part of that game? Did you and your friends get a kick out of killing people when the game went bad?"

"Things just got out of hand." His voice was barely a whisper and tinged with remorse. "But in the end, we'll win. We have all the cards.

We got the money and the lawyer and the judge. What more do you need these days? That's the way things work."

It sounded to Windsor like Westlake was trying to convince himself.

"No, you won't win." Windsor said. "The police and the newspaper have everything. I gave it to them before I left Portland. Benno's file on Billy, Gilroy's report, emails between Benno and Stockdale, Barnes' letter to Jennifer laying out your little scheme. Before long, you and your friends are going to be front page news. At best you're looking at a criminal trial. At worst a civil suit that will leave you nothing. You'll end up in jail or broke, probably both. Nice going. I hope it was worth it."

As Sam stared at Windsor, the barrel of the gun sank toward the ground. The big man's shoulders seemed to collapse.

"You really gave them everything?" The quiver in Westlake's hands worsened until the shotgun waved back and forth at the ground in front of the steps. "I was afraid of that."

"You can kill me, but it won't do any good," Windsor said. "Dead or alive, you're out of business, permanently. You killed to hide a secret. That won't work anymore. The secret's out. It's over."

Windsor turned his back on Sam Westlake and walked up the stairs. When he got to the top he looked down at the old man, who suddenly seemed smaller and more distant. Sam took another step back and wrestled the gun upward. When it was pointed at Windsor again, he pulled back the hammer.

"Fuck you," Windsor said. "Everybody I've loved is dead. My parents. Jennifer. Now, you're dead to me. So, shoot and we'll fish in hell."

Sam put the gun to his shoulder. They stared at each other for several seconds before Windsor went inside and closed the door behind him.

"You'll never prove any of this," Sam yelled at the closed door. "You know we'll get off. We have too much money. They'll never convict us. People like us don't go to jail. Don't you understand who we are? We're the winners, and we always win."

Windsor watched through the window as the taillights of Sam Westlake's pickup disappeared down the road toward the river. He went back outside to stand on the porch while the truck turned around at the end of the road and came back by the cabin. The pickup slowed as it passed, Westlake's arm resting on the open window. His head turned toward Windsor for a few seconds, then went back to looking out the windshield and drove away.

The pickup skirted the trees along the meadow and back to the ranch house. He saw the taillights go out. The slamming of the truck door echoed back across the meadow. When the lights inside the house went dark, he knew it was time to leave. It was over for him. Everything was now in the hands of Arnie Stetson and Cassie Terrace. In a few days the world would know everything about Sam, Stockdale, Hawkins, and all the murders. Billy Broadnax's name would resurface for a few days then disappear again back to where it belonged.

He was still sitting on the porch when Maggie showed up. "You better stay here, girl," Windsor said.

She climbed the stairs, laid down on the top step and let her feet hang over the edge. She whimpered then put her head down. Together, they stared out over the meadow. They were still there when a shotgun blast echoed across the meadow, sending the flock of geese back into the sky, honking angrily. Maggie's head came up, she whined, then laid back down. Windsor rested his hand on her head.

"Good choice, Sam," Windsor said.

Chapter 71

Billy Broadnax didn't return to the front page of the local paper until Tuesday. The story was held for a day while Arnie Stetson nailed down the details of Sam Westlake's suicide. When it did run, it said that Jennifer DeGarza Windsor was killed to cover up a conspiracy to rip off the federal government for millions of dollars in timber revenue. It named Benno, Stockdale, Hawkins, and Westlake as the ones behind the conspiracy. The story cleared Broadnax of Jennifer's death, citing unnamed sources that identified Bennett Benno as the killer who made it look like another Meat Man murder.

The story was built on the copied documents from Bennett Benno's office, files from Barnes' garage, the string of emails between Benno and Stockdale. The rest came from Windsor, including details of what Sam Westlake told him before putting a shotgun in his mouth, pulling the trigger, and splattering himself across the deck that overlooked his beloved river.

Other than mentioning his role in The Meat Man murders, Stetson never used Windsor's name, identifying him to readers only as a source familiar with the events.

In the days before the article ran it was read and reread by editors, lawyers, and, ultimately, by the publisher himself. Stetson had worked on the story continually since reading the contents of the envelope Windsor gave him. The night before it was published, a nervous and exhausted Stetson sat in Alexander Ramsey's office, watching as the publisher read the final draft while rocking back and forth in his big leather chair overlooking the press room. Ramsey read it twice, never making an edit mark or asking a question. In the end, he picked up the phone, called the executive editor, and simply said, "Run it."

When the story appeared in print, it caused the expected furor that lit up local TV news and brought the print tabloids back to town and to The Ridge. Bud and Moon Schwartz poured enough beer and cooked enough greasy burgers to finance another month-long sojourn to Taos with a stop at Burning Man. Stetson endured no less than a dozen interviews with local and national reporters, including an irate and bitter Rich Raymond, who was left to chase the story along with everybody else while grousing about being duped by Windsor.

Within days of the initial story, Stockdale and his lawyers were meeting with the police and the district attorney to arrange a deal that would eventually put Stockdale in a comfortable federal prison in Florida for eighteen months where he could rake sand traps at a golf course on a nearby military base.

Reporters packed the courtroom the day Stockdale was sentenced. Both his air of superiority and his wife were gone by the time he stood before the judge and mumbled "Guilty, your honor" at the appropriate time. As part of the deal, Stockdale confessed everything about who was involved in the numerous logging schemes, who killed Jennifer, and why. He portrayed himself as an unwitting accomplice who was dragged into the scheme against his will. Since two of Stockdale's conspirators, Benno and Westlake, were dead, it was difficult to prove anything different.

Even though she wasn't directly implicated in Stetson's initial article, Judge Dorothy Evelyn Hawkins resigned from the bench and left town the same day the story appeared. Her house went on the market the next day while she took up residence in an exclusive, gated community in Palm Desert. When she was ordered to return to testify before a grand jury, Hawkins entered the Betty Ford Clinic after retaining a lawyer whose expertise was insanity defense. She eventually pleaded no contest to fraud and conspiracy charges involving the timber scams and was sentenced to probation for five years. She would die a few weeks later of liver cancer.

After interviewing Windsor, the DA dropped all charges against Matthew Roberts, ordered his immediate release, and gave him a letter of apology. Roberts left town with a pocket full of business cards from the personal injury lawyers eager to represent him in a false arrest lawsuit against the city.

Jennifer's family filed a multi-million-dollar wrongful death suit against Stockdale, Hawkins, and the estate of Sam Westlake. After several weeks of negotiations, played out against a backdrop of ongoing news accounts of the whole affair, the attorneys for both sides reached a settlement. It left Jennifer's parents with more than enough money to move out of the trailer house in the corn field.

To pay the settlement, Westlake's sons put Pine Mountain Ranch up for sale. Windsor moved faster than the half-dozen other buyers and by the time the snow melted the following spring, he was living in Sam Westlake's ranch house. Weird as that might seem, it was a pretty nice place. Owning it seemed to bring things full circle.

Cassie Terrace's embarrassment over her insistence that Windsor was on a snipe hunt and that Matthew Roberts killed Gilroy and his ex-wife, didn't last long. She joined Windsor at the ranch for a two-week summer vacation where they sat on the deck drinking wine while watching Theresa play soccer on the lawn with a barking Maggie acting as goalie. In the evenings she would sit on the riverbank watching him fish, amazed when he landed a twenty-six inch Dolly Varden.

Billy Broadnax died on Christmas Day of the same year, stabbed more than three dozen times by a gang of Hispanic inmates. Some inside the prison believed Billy wanted to die and that yelling racial slurs at them was his way of committing suicide. The majority opinion, however, was that Billy was too dumb to know that people from Mexico didn't like being called "spics" and "greasers."

Billy died while efforts to get his case reopened on the solid grounds of inadequate representation were just getting under way. Stetson wrote a lengthy profile of Billy, but his editors reduced it to a handful of paragraphs that ran inside the Metro section.

Four people attended Billy's funeral in the prison chapel, Windsor, Stetson, Chester Broadnax, and a Catholic priest, who asked God to have mercy on Billy's soul.

Windsor doubted God ever got the chance.

The following winter, Stetson sent Windsor a clipping from the paper's business section. It was a story by Will Brunner about Matty Barnes and her mother donating twenty-thousand dollars to the Nature Conservancy to help purchase stands of old growth trees and save them from being logged.

"There's a certain symmetry to this, don't you think?" Stetson wrote in the margin.

Chapter 72

On a cold, clear day in December, Windsor drove to the modest bungalow in a quiet neighborhood in the City of Hillsboro that Enrico DeGraza had purchased with the settlement money. He sat down with Enrico and his wife, explaining everything to them, showing them all the documents that laid out the truth about how Jennifer died and why. When he was through, all three of them were in tears.

The next day Windsor and Enrico met at the cemetery on West Burnside at Jennifer's grave. Windsor stood back, watching Enrico kneel to place flowers on the headstone along with a silver-framed photo of his daughter. The old man bowed his head, softly recited a prayer in Spanish then crossed himself.

When Windsor helped him up there were more tears and more regrets.

"I'm sorry for all the things I said." Enrico wiped his face with the back of his hand. "I was wrong. Please forgive me."

Windsor put an arm around his shoulder. "There's nothing to forgive. You were right at the time. Everyone knew there was evil out there. We just didn't know what kind."

Enrico wiped his face again, glanced one more time at his daughter's grave then looked at Windsor. "Gracias ... son."

Right after New Year's, Windsor called Arnie Stetson and asked him for a ride to the airport. He was leaving that night for a few weeks in Mexico to escape the cold and the memories.

Only the vengeful Rich Raymond had done a story on Windsor's involvement. It was more speculation than news that went pretty much unnoticed amid the din of conflicting stories by a dozen different news organizations about who knew what when. But when two other reporters started asking about him, it only added to Windsor's desire to leave.

"I thought I'd try my hand at some deep-sea fishing," he said. "Marlin, sailfish and something called Dorado."

Standing in the driveway of the house on Royal Oak Way, Windsor handed Stetson the keys and asked him to live in it until he got back and longer if he wanted.

Stetson eagerly agreed, especially when Windsor said it was rent free.

"When I get back, I'll probably spend most of my time at the ranch," Windsor said. "All I ask is that you pay the utilities and keep up the yard. I'll take care of the rest."

Stetson couldn't resist asking more about what happened the night Westlake killed himself.

"How did you know Sam wouldn't shoot you?" Stetson said after Windsor described the events of that night.

"I thought he would. I just didn't care what he did. I just wanted it over with, one way or the other."

"Why do you think he didn't kill you?"

"I've wondered about that. He'd already killed three people, five if you count his role in the deaths of Jennifer and Benno. So, there was no reason not to kill again. I think, though, in the end Sam realized his life was over one way or another. I'd like to believe that our friendship meant something to him. My death wasn't going to stop you from publishing a story that would destroy him. It wasn't going to stop Cassie from opening an investigation that would lead to his arrest. Maybe he spared me because killing me wouldn't change anything. He was finished and so was his scheme.

"You know what I think really killed Sam? Getting involved with people like Stockdale, Hawkins, and Benno. For all his money, Sam was still a dumb old logger who wanted to be liked and respected by people he thought were better than he was. By the time he found out they weren't, it was too late."

"You think he invited Stockdale and the others into his log-scaling scam just to impress them, to be part of their crowd?"

"That might have been part of it. He said there were other reasons, but I believe that he was in awe of who they were and flattered that anyone like them would allow an old boy like him to hang out with them?" Windsor shook his head. "Pretty sad, isn't it?"

"And Billy Broadnax?"

"Bad as Billy was, Sam, Stockdale and the others were worse. Billy didn't know better. They did. Billy didn't care about money. That was all they cared about."

"I hope you didn't believe what Sam said about killing your wife before she told you about what they were up to," Stetson said. "You can't blame yourself anymore."

"I know," Windsor said. "They were wrong, and eventually I'll be alright with it. It was their greed and arrogance that killed Jennifer. Not me."

As they shook hands, Stetson got a brief glimpse of the rarely seen shy-and-embarrassed Alex Windsor.

"You know, Arnie. I didn't think too much of you when you showed up at the cabin that day. I was wrong. I'm sorry for that. I resented you for finding me and forcing me to face what really happened." When Stetson started to say something, Windsor stopped him. "I just want to say thanks."

"Are these better days?" Stetson asked before putting the car in reverse and backing out.

Windsor looked up the driveway at the house. For a moment he imagined Jennifer dancing across the windows in the dining room, then into the front room and back again. Her hair swirling around her face, her smile. Always her smile.

"No," he said. "Never."

~*~

The chair seemed to let her go. The arms and the wings on the back pulled away to let her float up and slowly disappear. Her skin was not as pale. Her eyes no longer dark coals. Even her fingers were less spidery.

"It seems you figured things out," Jennifer said. "How did that go?"

"Not well," Windsor said. He lay flat on the couch, hands behind his head, trying to take in the last he would ever see of her.

"Did you expect it to?" She was a few feet above the chair, closer to the ceiling. Her image was dimmer, like an oil lamp being slowly turned down.

"I had hoped for better."

"But you learned the truth?"

"If I say yes, will you drift away forever?"

"I'm already gone."

All that was left of her was a faint outline of her body, but he could still see her face, her smile, then her last words: "I just wish I could have kissed you goodbye."

~*~

Other Books by Tom Towslee

Rich Man, Dead Man

The Drug Lord's Daughter

Graves Point

Chasing the Dead

Paradise Girls

Visit the author at:

https://www.facebook.com/ttowslee/

All books available on Amazon.com

and Barnesandnoble.com

Made in United States
Orlando, FL
28 January 2023